SUNMASTER

SUNMASTER

ISBN-13: 978-1-61317-188-2 (ebook)

ISBN 13: 978-1-61317-189-9 (print)

Editor: K.B Spangler

Cover Design: Fringe Element

Cover Art: Aleksandar Sotirovski

*for the clever boys, and the ruthless girls
and everyone who isn't either of those*

SUNMASTER

THE GUILDMASTER SAGA

BOOK IV

C.E. MURPHY

CHAPTER ONE

The river, Bayar said, was called 'The Crack in the Bowl.'

Rasim had imagined it as a *wide* crack. A crack that split the mountains which rose along the Shenryalan coast. A crack that allowed a river to pour into the Northern Sea. A crack that a tall-masted ship like the *Wafiya* could sail through.

"It's more like a hole in the bowl," Desimi said critically from where he leaned against the ship's rail. Half the ship's crew was pressed against the rail, jostling for position so they could see the river's mouth more clearly. Even Captain Nasira stood with them, grimly examining the soaring mountains and the narrow passage where the river cut through them.

"It's a crack elsewhere," Bayar replied with dignity.

"Well, that doesn't do us any good here, does it?" Desimi demanded. The river had bored a hole through the mountains, but hadn't made a canyon, at least not there. Rasim supposed there must have been a lot of very soft stone at the base of this particular mountain, making it easier for the river to dig its way through there, without ever having to cut away the height. It was a large tunnel—light could be seen on its far end, and the river didn't reach the top curve of the bore—but it wasn't nearly large enough for the *Wafiya*'s masts. They could row against the current with the shore-boats lashed to the *Wafiya*'s deck and go upstream that way, but that wasn't exactly the triumphant arrival in Shenryal that Rasim had expected.

"This can't be the way we've sent diplomats to Shen-ryal," he said uncertainly. The river's entrance was beautiful, water reflecting brilliantly off the top of the pale limestone tunnel it had carved, but it wasn't prac-tical for the great ships used by most of the sailing nations.

Bayar grinned up at him. Although he was a few years older than Rasim, the Shenryalan prince would never be as tall as even Rasim's modest height. He had shorter arms and legs than most, although no one knew why, except he'd been born that way. He was golden-skinned, with warm red in his cheeks whether he'd been out in the sun and wind or not, and black hair, straighter than even Nasira's. "There are harbors and wider rivers farther north, beyond the Jagged Tooth, but the Crack leads most quickly to where my people will be coming together for the Gathering."

"It won't be quickest if we can't get through!"

"You can go through," Bayar promised. "The small boats will fit, and you can paddle far inland before the Crack rises to be level with the steppes. There, Shenryalans will meet you with blade and bow. Or," he said cheerfully, pointing upward, "we can climb, and from a watchtower, proclaim our presence and my return."

The crew's gazes followed Bayar's gesture to what Rasim gradually realized was a path up a mountain with a remarkably flat top. Maybe. If he was generous about what defined a pathway. It looked like something a goat might consider but then reject as too difficult, for not enough reward. It went up a very long way, reminding Rasim of the Northern mountains to the east. Those rose straight out of the water and reached for the stars like they might find Tilarea, the sky goddess, bending to greet them.

Captain Nasira cursed under her breath, then cursed again more loudly. She was thin as a ship's rope, and stretched as taut. Her hair was very straight for an Ilyaran, and its short black length was tucked behind her ears, where bright gold earrings glimmered against it and her umber skin. It had been a narrow braid that swung between her shoulder blades a month or two ago, before an explosion had burned most of it away. Everywhere Rasim looked, there were signs of what they'd been through over the past few months. Bayar's wasn't the only new face on board, nor the only non-Ilyaran one. Lorens, the Northern prince, looked practically like a pale ghost among the dark-skinned Ilyarans, his yellow hair and blue eyes unlike anyone else's.

Some of their new crew carried scars from the chains they'd worn before being freed from the slave city of Moran. Others weren't scarred, but tattooed with necklaces of chain to indicate they had once been —and in Moranese eyes, would always be—slaves.

And that didn't take into consideration the faces that were no longer with them, people who had died in the explosion that burned away Nasira's hair, or had been lost months earlier in a sea serpent attack. The past year had been all chaos and upheaval, and nothing Rasim did seemed to move him any farther away from the center of it. They'd left Moran almost two weeks earlier, and although the daily tasks of keeping the ship sailing smoothly helped a little, every day they'd come closer to Shenryal, Rasim felt a little worse. Twitchy, uncertain, afraid of what was to come, and maybe more.

Nasira barked, "Fine! We'll go over your mountain, Bayar, but I don't like it."

Relief surged through Rasim. Maybe getting off the *Wafiya* for a little while would help settle his nerves, even if the flagship was his favorite place in the world. He turned hopefully toward the captain, who tried very hard not to glance his way, then did, and groaned. "All right, all of you journeymen, go on ahead. This ship is too full and there's not a soul on it who doesn't need some space. Hassin!"

The handsome first mate stepped forward, a grin flashing across his dark features. "Aye, Captain?"

"I suppose I'm going up a mountain," Nasira muttered. "You have the bridge."

Someone blasted a shrill whistle and seamasters burst into activity, dropping anchor and unlashing the shoreboats. The *Wafiya*'s regular crew didn't need them for a journey of a few hundred meters to the shore, but not everyone aboard was a sea witch, and some of them—the old beggar woman who had come with them from Moran, for example—absolutely refused to ride a funnel of water. Besides, it was easier to bring food back and forth in a boat.

Rasim looked hopefully at Bayar. "We could just swim over."

"Shenryalans," Bayar muttered, "don't *swim*."

"Don't worry." Kisia, a year older and visibly taller than Rasim, wormed her way up to Bayar's side. Her hair, cropped journeyman-short, stood out in short tight curls around her head, and the darkness of her brown skin made Bayar's golden tones look sunshine-bright next to her. She got a silly smile nearly every time she looked at him, and had one now, as she said, "I won't let you drown."

"Let's go," Rasim said eagerly. "The captain said we could."

"You just want to get off the ship because there's no chance for heroics here," Desimi said with a snort. The big journeyman's attitude toward Rasim had mellowed considerably, but he could never resist the chance to poke at him.

Rasim sighed. "Yes, Desimi. That's right. I'm itching for a chance to fight another horrible monster and carve my name in the Seamasters' lore. It sounds fun." Heroics, in his experience, were terrifying and miserable and no fun at all. He dove over the *Wafiya*'s railing without waiting for an answer, and after a moment felt the disturbances of other witches joining him in the water. They all came to shore a minute later, safely dry thanks to witchery. Even Bayar wasn't so much as damp, although his expression suggested he'd rather not do that again.

The healer's apprentice, Sesin, had joined them, and grinned when she saw Rasim's glance of surprise. "Captain said journeymen, and I'm not going to stay on board hauling ropes if I can be out here climbing a mountain!" Her enthusiasm faltered a little as they all looked up. "Although that's really high. Heights didn't used to bother me before I fell."

Rasim had fallen recently, too, and nodded sympathetically. "Just keep looking up."

"That doesn't do us any good getting back down!"

"Let's furl one sail at a time," Rasim said wryly. Bayar went ahead, climbing the narrow pathway easily. The steady upward climb gave Rasim something to concentrate on enough that his feeling of worry faded, although when they stopped to eat and drink, it got worse again almost immediately. He shook his head, trying to push it away, and heard Sesin murmuring to Kisia and Desimi about him. "I'm *fine*."

They fell guiltily silent until they were climbing again, when Sesin, maybe thinking she was too far back to be heard, murmured something about Rasim having been under pressure, and recently enslaved.

"For a few days, weeks ago!" Desimi said impatiently. "Bayar was enslaved longer than that and he's fine!"

"Bayar is not fine," the Shenryalan boy said with soft severity. He stopped, looking back down the mountain at the rest of them, and Rasim dared glance back to see discomfort and surprise lining Desimi's face. "I am not well at all," Bayar went on. "I am heartsick and afraid, and my dreams trouble me. It is my dearest hope that returning home will heal my soul. Rasim may well need the same, but I've drawn him off-course."

"No," Rasim protested. "I wanted to come to Shenryal. I really think we need to know if your people have been suffering from things like our Great Fire and the salt-poisoned lakes in the Northlands for the past decade. If we add in the unrest in the Islands, all the trouble seems to start looking like the points of a compass with Moran right there at the middle of it all. Shenryal is the western point, if I'm right. And someone did kidnap you. That's obviously a sign something is wrong. Even if trouble is only on its way, I want your people to be warned. It's hot," he added abruptly, wiping his arm across his forehead. "I didn't expect it to be so hot, this far north."

"It's not that hot," Desimi said. "You're just sweating from climbing a mountain. We all are."

"I don't know." Sesin frowned past Desimi at Rasim. "He's almost as red-cheeked as Bayar."

"Well, they're the only two who get red-faced, except Prince Lorens!"

That was true, and despite feeling woozy, it made Rasim smile. One of his parents had probably been Northern, because he had lighter brown skin than most Ilyarans, green eyes, and the loose curls of his hair, when bleached as they currently were, went yellow, not red. And he did blush sometimes, although not nearly as brightly as Lorens did. He smiled again at the thought.

Sesin, though, wasn't smiling. "You look like you're burning up, Rasi."

"It's not that bad. Desi's probably right. I'm not used to climbing mountains. I just need some air."

"We've been in the air for weeks! What do you call sailing? All it is, is air and water!" Desimi flapped his hands at them. "Go, can you go, I don't want to stand here on a mountainside all day."

Kisia muttered, "You're such a pain, Desimi. Why don't you just leave him alone?" and Rasim started climbing again, listening to them bicker and feeling better. They were his family, no matter how far they were from home. As long as they stayed together, things would be all right.

As long as he didn't look *down*, things would be all right. A sideways glimpse of the now-toy-sized *Wafiya* made his head swim, and he focused on Bayar's feet, taking the mountain path a step at a time. They were probably a thousand meters above the sea now, having been following the rough trail upward for hours. Bayar said, "We're almost there," over his shoulder, and a few minutes later climbed over the last lip to reach the mountain top. Rasim scrambled up after him and scurried forward, well away from the edge before he really dared look around.

It was as flat as it looked from the sea, and wide enough for them to all lie down feet to head without reaching both sides. Rasim relaxed a little, feeling more sure of himself, although he was much too hot and his stomach roiled if he didn't breathe carefully. It was worse than it had been on the *Wafiya*, but he didn't want to call attention to himself, so he made himself look around. The other journeymen did the same as they crested the flat peak, a brightness coming into all their eyes.

The Northern Sea stretched endlessly to one side, restless water breaking with faint whitecaps in the distance. Clouds skimmed the horizon, thickening in the middle distance and clearing again, with the ocean changing colors beneath them until it reached the shore. Above them, the sky stretched pale blue toward the other horizon as wind whipped by, Rasim saw the first hints of sunset as the light angled gently across plains that went on nearly as far as the ocean itself. Mountains shadowed the very farthest reaches of those steppes, and Rasim took a shallow breath as he suddenly understood why Bayar called the river the Crack in the Bowl. His homelands were the base of the bowl, and its sides were the mountains that surrounded Shenryal as far as Rasim could see. The river did make a crack, a canyon that was visible from this height, although it mended itself on the steppes side of the mountains, diving partially underground to reach that entrance the Wafiya couldn't sail through. "Bayar," Rasim said reverently. "It's beautiful."

The Shenryalan boy smiled brilliantly and put his hand over his heart as he bowed, as if taking credit for the stunning view. "The watchtower is dug into the westward face of the mountain, just below us. The journey down to it is easier than the one to here.

Come, if we set it quickly those who look east at sundown will see it, and know someone has come to Shenryal."

Moments later, all five of them scrambled over the side of the mountain into a hollow that hadn't been *dug*, Rasim thought. That did it no justice. It had been carved out of earth and stone into the shape of a giant's hands, in the middle of which sat a pile of well-dried wood that the mountain itself protected from the elements. Desimi muttered, "Why don't you just light it, Sunburn?" as he sat down with his back to the view, like there was too much of it for him to look at right now.

Rasim glared half-heartedly at him. Even if he thought he could work sun witchery—and he suspected he could, at this point, having learned to use three other magics—his stomach swam with sickness right now, and his head felt hot. It had been windy on the mountaintop, but the cave was still, and he missed the cooling breeze. "Why don't you?"

"I'm not the one with all the witchery!"

"Both of you be quiet and help me start a fire the way everybody who *isn't* a sun witch does," Sesin said irritably as she crouched beside Desimi and bent to the task. "Kisia, you too!"

"Just a minute. Bayar is showing me the rest of the cave." Kisia spoke from the back of the cave, and Rasim, squatting to help Sesin, glanced back.

It wasn't just the giant's hands that held the fire pit. The back of the hollow had been shaped into the lower part of a face, mouth pursed like it blew gently on the fire within its hands. Rasim shivered with awe, remembering the tremendous carvings that marked the entryways to Northern harbors. Stonemasters couldn't have done better work, in either case.

Red light glinted into the cave as the sun crashed behind the distant mountains. Rasim glanced forward, sweat beading on his forehead again as he squinted into the sunset. He felt like he might fall forward off the mountain face, even though he was nowhere near an edge. His stomach dipped and rose and dropped, though, like he was riding the swells of waves. The wind came up again in rhythmic sweeps, and he sat back, trying to catch his breath.

He was the only one looking out over the Bowl, so he was the only one who saw the cave mouth fill with a rising dragon.

CHAPTER TWO

It was red, gold, and utterly enormous, blocking the entrance to the hollow with its chest and belly alone. Massive wings spread wide, their thin crimson membranes dimming the setting sun behind it. Earth rained off its body, flying in a fine spray as the massive beast shook its huge sleek head. A mane of spikes around the back of its head flexed and expanded, giving it the look of a violent, living sunrise. Then it inhaled deeply, like it would suck all the wind and air into it and release it—Rasim was sure—as fire.

He threw himself past Desimi and Sesin with an incoherent shout, knocking them both aside. Desimi began a yell of outrage that died in his throat as he saw the dragon. Sesin cried out, and the dragon, to Rasim's relief, roared instead of spitting fire. Heat blasted over him anyway, breaking the feverish warmth that had been bothering him. Somewhere in the background, Kisia, high-pitched with fear, shrieked, "I thought you were going to start a *fire*, not—!"

She broke off, because 'summon a dragon' had obviously not been anybody's plan. The dragon inhaled again, and this time, for a heartbeat, Rasim saw fire coming to life at the back of its throat. They were trapped in the watchtower cavern, and would all die under the beast's breath. Flame rolled forward, brilliant orange and white, and Rasim screamed.

Witchery burst out of him, a wall of power he couldn't even name. Maybe it was skymastery, building a barrier of hard air between himself and the dragon's terrible breath. Maybe it was sun witchery, holding the rolling fire back. Rasim didn't know. He knew his throat hurt, and that his whole body trembled with strain, and that they weren't dead. He knew the dragon hung in the air just beyond the cave mouth, its great wings beating a slow pattern and a look of astonishment on its toothy face.

He knew Desimi, with a deliberately critical note, said, "Well, you could have let a *little* of it through, so we'd have the watch fire started!" and that he really wanted to punch the bigger journeyman in the face for being obnoxious. The next sound Desimi made was a shrill laugh, though, one of barely-contained fear, and Rasim's impulse to punch him faded somewhat.

"You need to get out of here." Rasim hardly knew his own voice, it was so tight and small. "Is there any way out of here besides the entrance, Bayar?"

"I'm afraid not." Unlike the rest of them, the Shenryalan boy sounded calm and controlled, although Rasim thought that might be because he had to think of words in Ilyaran, and the time to think helped him contain his own panic. Sesin was on her butt, staring wide-eyed at the dragon, cords standing out in her neck. She exhaled, a small sharp sound, and Rasim braced himself again as another fiery blast from the dragon scorched the cavern.

He couldn't tell. He couldn't *tell* what kind of witchery he was using. It felt—he thought—like skymastery, hardening the air against the dragon's breath. The air certainly heated up enough to make that seem likely. But he'd never used sunmastery, or at least, not on purpose, not knowing he'd done it, and maybe that was what stopping a wall of flame felt like. Maybe fire was hardly more than hot air, in the moment of shaping.

That seemed unlikely. The dragon gaped at him again, then rose higher into the sky, its shadow spilling across the mouth of the cave for a moment. Rasim whispered, "Run," and Sesin barked disbelief.

"So it can set us alight when we leave the cave? We have to stay behind you!"

Rasim cursed and edged forward. The sickness in his belly was gone, although he didn't know how he could tell the difference between the nausea of unde-termined dread and the gut-clenching certainty of terror. But he felt better, like the dragon was what had been making him ill, and now that it was here, the worst of it had passed. His heart hammered hard enough to break free of his chest as he tried to peek out of the watchtower's hollow without getting eaten.

Huge teeth snapped closed shockingly close to his hair and he screamed, falling backward into the cave again. The dragon was above them, perched on the flat mountaintop not so very far overhead, and had bent to bite at him. If it had been a hand's breadth longer of neck, it would have taken his head off. Furious with fear, Rasim snatched at sky witchery and smashed air upward like a tremendous fist.

It caught the dragon in the nose, hard enough to send the beast rearing backward and bellowing with anger as it swiped at its own face, trying to catch what had hit it. Rasim hissed, "Go, go, go, run, hurry!" but Bayar balked as the others ran to Rasim's side.

"The watchfire has to be lit. We must tell my people we're here, or your reception will be unpleasant." He knelt, focusing on the fire pit again as Kisia howled and grabbed his arm.

"Our reception is going to be a lot more unpleasant if we get roasted by a dragon, Bayar! We can come back and set a fire later!"

The dragon snarled and swept its head back down, spitting dangerous heat again. Rasim threw his arms upward, calling witchery, and the spattering flame sank around him in an arc that ignited bits of dried grass amidst the new growth. He was sure—almost sure—he was using skymastery to hold the fire back. It seemed like it would be much more efficient if he could use sun witchery and actually shape the flames, maybe even use them to attack the dragon in turn, rather than just avoid getting burned.

Although overall, *just* avoiding getting burned was certainly better than the alternative. "Desimi! Get some of the—"

The bigger boy was already doing it, gathering dried clumps of smoldering grass and blowing on them to get a real flame going as he rushed them back to the fire pit. Bayar, relieved that they were heeding his request even in the midst of chaos, rose as Kisia tugged at him again, while Sesin grabbed more of the sparking grass to try to light the signal fire. Above Rasim, the dragon cocked its head, staring down at him in clearly growing confusion.

Rasim couldn't help a nervous giggle. Dragons probably expected things they breathed fire on to scream and die. Well, they'd been screaming a lot, but nobody had died yet and the dragon obviously didn't know how to deal with that. It roared another fiery breath at them, and this time Rasim thought of the wind funnels he'd used in the Moranese war arena. He tried to grab a bit of the oncoming flame and spin it toward the fire pit, but it went out under the strength of air witchery.

The next blast of flame was so hot and fast that he fell to his knees, barely able to keep it from scorching him. "We have to go *now*!" He could hardly breathe the too-hot air, and tears scalded his face from fear and heat. But Bayar let out a shout of triumph, and the fire pit suddenly came alive with ordinary flame, warm and comforting compared to the blinding strength of the dragon's fire. The other four rushed to his side, but hesitated, unsure of where to go next.

For a heartbeat, Rasim didn't know either, but a terrible idea settled into his bones. A bad enough idea he couldn't even quite let himself think it, because if he thought it, he wouldn't do it. "I'm going to distract it," he said in a small voice. "You four go—wherever is safest. Back into the cave, if I can draw it away."

"Don't be stupid, Rasi." Kisia's own voice was small with fear.

He smiled weakly at her. "I don't think I have any choice. Run when I do the stupid thing."

He stepped out of the hollow's limited safety, which was stupid enough, and spun another blow of sky witchery upward to slam into the dragon. It inhaled and spat fire so fast that luck and instinct, not wisdom or quick thinking, was all that saved him. Skymastery formed a blade of air in front of him, splicing the dragonfire so it spilled around him at hair-sizzling temperatures. Rasim couldn't breathe. He couldn't even see. But he didn't burn, either, not quite, as the fire split in front of him and gouted in columns on either side of him. The mountainside around him went soft in places, heat pounding it until it melted, and when the flame finally subsided, the dragon fell to all fours again with an air of satisfaction as it tilted his head to examine the place where Rasim's dead body should be.

Rasim smiled feebly and waved, because he couldn't think of anything else to do. The dragon lifted a forepaw and pulled back half a step as if confused beyond comprehension, then sat on its back legs and tilted its head the other way, like it was checking to make sure it had seen him correctly. Rasim turned cold with fear despite the heat.

It was bigger than he could even understand. On its haunches it seemed as tall as the Seamasters' hall, and its wings spread so wide Rasim thought they might cover the whole flat top of the mountain. Its jaws looked big enough to swallow him whole, assuming he didn't get melted to a greasy spot on the mountainside by its fire, first. He, Rasim al Ilialio, who had slain a sea serpent and fought a stone snake and defeated an airy glasswing, was not going to *kill* that thing, not on his own. Not at all.

But, and this was the terrible idea, the one that he hardly dared put into words: *but it couldn't kill him, either.*

Not if he got on its back.

IT WOULD HAVE WORKED SO MUCH MORE easily if the dragon had been in the hollow and he, Rasim, had been up on the mountain's flat top. He thought he could lure it down, but he was less certain he could distract it from roasting his friends, so he had to go up. The dragon crashed back down to all fours, now watching him more like he was a baffling bit of prey than an enemy. Cats watched bugs and mice like that, and Rasim was about that size, to a dragon.

He wished desperately that his grasp of stone witchery was stronger. If he could at least raise a protective wall between himself and the dragon as he scrambled up the mountainside, he would feel better. Instead he had to watch and listen and hope that Tilarea had a little kindness to spare for a sea witch who had fumbled his way into skymastery.

Behind him, he heard Sesin wail, "Is this the stupid thing?" as he ran, and over the scrabble of stone and earth underfoot, he heard Desimi said, "If you have to ask, it's not it."

The dragon lowered itself further, getting on its belly and watching him with glinting eyes as he crested the mountain's flat top and raced toward its nearest paw. Just before he reached it, the beast smacked him aside like he *was* a mouse. For a few seconds Rasim didn't know which way was up, only that every part of him hurt as it hit the ground in horrible fast thumps. He staggered to his feet, ridiculously outraged, and brought his hands together like he was directing wind with the force of his clap. Air slammed forward, crashing into the dragon, and it sat up with a snarl, biting and clawing at an invisible enemy. Rasim rushed it again, and this time reached a hind foot.

Its overlapping scales gave him something to dig his fingers around, and he scrambled upward like the giant monster was the rigging on a ship. The dragon bent its head down, watching with glassy, bewildered eyes. Rasim thought he must weigh so little the dragon probably didn't even feel him, and hoped it wouldn't understand what he was doing until he reached its shoulder.

It kicked, and Rasim went flying, hitting the earth with more painful bounces. On his third try, it swatted at him and fire shot through the air. He was not going to successfully climb the dragon. Hopefully his friends were at least getting away, although since their only escape route was probably over the top of the mountain, he wasn't sure he was even doing them any good. He had to draw it away somehow, and his feet decided on a tactic without consulting his mind.

He ran for the farthest edge of the mountaintop, and launched himself off.

CHAPTER THREE

This was much, *much* stupider than riding the dragon.

Rasim's feet hadn't fully left the ground before he wondered what in the sea goddess's name he thought he was doing, but it was far too late by then. Maybe he thought the sky goddess would grant him the gift of flight, which no fully-trained Skymaster had ever achieved except in legend. Maybe he had such confidence in his quick thinking that he'd decided he would find a solution on his way to hitting the ground.

Maybe he just hadn't been thinking at all.

A shadow passed over him just before he smashed into the earth, and the dragon's massive claws curled around his fragile body, hauling him upward. Rasim screamed, then screamed again for good measure. As the dragon turned on a wingtip, he glimpsed his friends running frantically for the mountaintop.

Well, he'd told them to run when he did the stupid

thing. In all his life, he couldn't think of anything more stupid than what he'd just done.

It had gotten the dragon's attention, though.

The ground was getting very far away, very fast. Watching it recede made him realize he'd guessed he would probably hit an outcropping or a flat bit of mountainside before he'd fallen very far. After all, they'd been able to climb up one side of the mountain, and back down again to the now-glowing watch-cavern. Expecting there to be other places he could land hadn't been totally out of the question.

Except from above, flying away, it looked like he'd found a sheer cliff to throw himself off. There'd been nothing between himself and probable death except empty air and a dragon that thought its lunch was getting away.

If he concentrated very hard on how he wasn't dead, he could almost keep himself from being terrified out of his mind. Almost. The dragon's massive wings had taken them an impossibly far distance from the mountains already, striking out toward the sunset. Rasim had been too hot before, but the wind cut through him now, numbing his fingers. If he didn't get out of this soon, he would be too slow and thick to figure it out at all.

He glanced down through the gaps between the dragon's claws, down at a world a thousand feet below him, and wondered what made him think he could get out of it at all. At least when he'd fought the sea serpent, he could swim back to the surface. He was fairly certain he couldn't glide safely to the earth, far below.

But he was hooked in the dragon's front paws sort of like a fish wrapped in an eagle's claws. The dragon's feet were held closer together than an eagle's, and it hadn't dug its claws into him like a raptor would with a struggling fish, which was good, or he'd be dead. If he could get up to the front of the dragon's leg, he might be able to climb up to its shoulders. That seemed like it would be slightly better than his current situation. Eagles often dropped their prey before they landed. Rasim didn't want the dragon to drop him.

He moved a little, and the huge beast wrapped its feet around him more firmly. It felt much more secure and less frightening, like there was now no chance he might slip through its claws and fall. Just staying there seemed like it might be the very best idea, except for the part where Rasim assumed it would take him to a nest and eat him. A shiver rushed over him, and he couldn't tell if it was fear or cold.

The dragon had also drawn its legs closer to its chest when it tucked its feet around him more snugly. Through wind-wet eyes, Rasim could see that the tops of its feet made a nearly flat area above his head. It would be almost easy to climb up its leg from there, compared to how he'd been dangling low a moment earlier. He'd scaled much more difficult riggings in nearly as much wind, many times.

There hadn't been so far to fall, though. Not nearly so far to fall.

He scrambled forward before his wiser self froze

him in place. The dragon's paws tightened again, but without the claws actually digging into him, its feet didn't close tightly enough to hold him in place. Rasim stood on the side of its foot, clinging to its ankle, and swung his leg up so he was on top of the foot instead of inside it. The wind pushed him against the beast's leg, which helped considerably. He dug his cold fingers around the sharp edges of scales and pulled himself up and up and up, until he'd crawled over the dragon's shoulder and flattened himself along its spine.

It was hot, like the beast itself was warmed by the flame it spewed. Rasim released a small shrill laugh and almost melted with relief as feeling came back into his body. The dragon, finally realizing something was wrong, twisted its head toward him, snapping half-heartedly. It couldn't reach him between its shoulders, though. At least, not in flight. As if realizing that, it folded its wings and dove toward the earth. Rasim hung on for dear life, but as the dragon's dive picked up speed, a huge smile split across his face. Tears ran back from his eyes because of the wind, and even his teeth were cold, but he was *riding a dragon*. A shriek of joyous delight ripped from his lungs, disappearing instantly into the dimming sky.

The dragon banked as if startled, twisting to see where the noise had come from. It rolled in the air and Rasim's feet flew upward before he slammed back down against its spine, screaming in pure thrilled terror now. He was probably going to die, but it would be a really exciting minute or two before he did. The dragon spun in the air again, then roared with frustration and resumed its dive, careening toward the earth at an impossible speed. Its ears, and the flexible spikes around the back of its head, flattened back as it dove.

Rasim heard himself say, "Sure, why not," under the sound of whipping wind, and felt himself surge forward, climbing the dragon's neck to seize a couple of those spikes. Only after the fact did it occur to him that they might be sharp like the edges of its scales, but it was too late then. They were less rigid than he'd feared, more like cartilage than claw, but he had less than a heartbeat, less than a breath, to be relieved before he hauled back on the spikes he'd grabbed.

The dragon screamed with fury, but its head rose and climbed out of its dive, shaking with rage. Rasim clamped his legs around its neck as tightly as he could, trying to stay flat on his belly while he steered the dragon. He couldn't imagine how far they'd flown. Much farther than the *Wafiya* could ever sail in such a short time, for certain. All he could think was that getting safely to the ground before the sun fully set was his best chance at survival for the night, even if it meant being alone in a strange land with unknown predators.

Nothing could be more unknown or unexpected than a dragon. He'd stopped pulling on the beast's spiky mane and it had leveled out, still bellowing its frustration. It began to turn back toward the mountains, which was either very good or very bad. It would bring Rasim closer to his friends, but it might also bring him to the dragon's nest, and maybe *its* friends.

No one had ever mentioned dragons in Shenryal.

Not that he knew much about the steppelands at all, but surely someone would have mentioned them, if they were common. Surely Kif, the ancient Northerner who had been part of the Shenryalan tribes for a while, would have said something about dragons if he'd seen them. Maybe this one was solitary. Which wasn't as reassuring as Rasim might have hoped, because if it was solitary, there had to be a reason *he* had happened on it. That reason might just be bad luck, but it seemed like *extraordinarily* bad luck, if that was the case.

Rasim, flattened against a dragon's neck, flying hundreds of feet above an unfamiliar dusk-tinged grasslands, thought about the past year of his life and wondered what about it made him imagine his luck might suddenly turn out to be something other than extremely bad.

There was movement on the ground below, something running. A large number of somethings, rushing in the same direction, and until the dragon dove at them, Rasim didn't realize they were horses, spooked by the dragon's presence. It gouted flame and he hauled on its mane-spikes again, trying to pull it upward, but it screamed in fury and folded its wings, increasing the speed of its dive. Rasim yelled back and sat up so he could pull harder on the spikes, and the dragon leveled out again, bellowing its anger across the steppes. The herd below them scattered into several smaller groups and the dragon settled into a glide momentarily, its attention twitching from one herd to another like it was trying to make a decision.

So was Rasim. On one hand, he didn't really want to

be up close for a dragon kill. On the other, the dragon would have to get within a horse's height of the ground to catch one, and that was probably Rasim's only chance to jump free without killing himself.

On the third hand, jumping into a herd of panicked horses seemed…

…like only the third or fourth worst idea he'd had in the past hour, when he thought about it like that.

The herds swept back together again, as though the horses had decided one big target was better. The dragon squealed with delight and dove, but not nearly as steeply as before. Its wings snapped out into a glide as it came above the herd, which looked like a dark, roiling mass from Rasim's viewpoint. Jumping off the dragon was abruptly much harder than jumping off the mountainside had been. He hadn't known what he was doing, there. Now he could see the thundering animals and imagine their hooves crushing him, and he didn't like horses to begin with.

The dragon dropped so fast Rasim's stomach lurched. He could smell the horses now, and the sharp green scent of the new grass they crushed as they ran, and the dust from dry earth as it rose. Here and there, even in the growing darkness, some of the horses looked deformed, their backs too thick or their gait a little slower. The dragon dropped again, its neck stretched long and its attention focused sharply on some poor horse up ahead. One more drop and Rasim would be as close as he could get to the ground. His heart hammered and his hands were cold with fear, but his mind was strangely clear. That seemed to happen a lot when things were at their worst, maybe because he just couldn't afford to focus on anything but the moment as it happened.

The dragon dropped one more time, and a great many things happened at once.

He threw himself clear. That was the thing that seemed most important. It was harder than he thought, because the dragon was moving so fast that even when he jumped, its wing got to where he was aiming at about the same time he did. A great wing bone smashed into him, knocking him into a tumble instead of the semi-planned arc he'd hoped to fall in. Rasim called sky witchery, hoping to slow himself a little, but the ground came up very fast. Horses came up even faster, leaping over his balled-up form. Every single part of Rasim's body hurt from the impact with the earth, and he flinched with every hoof that just barely missed him as it sailed overhead.

Within a few seconds the herd split around him, and something reached down to snatch at him. It didn't quite catch him, but it got him halfway upright, which was not where he wanted to be. Rasim yelled, and something else—some*one* else—grabbed him and hauled him upward.

Riders. There were riders on a handful of the racing herd. That's what he'd seen. Not deformed horses, but horses bearing riders in the same colors as their pelts, hugging the animals' spines so closely they'd been unrecognizable as people. At least, not from above on dragonback.

The rider he was with slowed, letting the herd race

by. In the falling darkness, Rasim saw spears and arrows fly at the dragon as the herd split and closed together again and again, never giving the flying monster a predictable target. He didn't think any of the weapons were hurting the dragon, only harrying it. It bellowed with frustration and rose higher above the herd. More arrows flew at it, and after a minute it roared again, then took itself to the skies, leaving the grasslands behind.

A shout of satisfaction went up from the riders. They wheeled, taking themselves out of the larger herd, and joined the rider who had rescued Rasim. Words spoken far too quickly for Rasim's limited grasp of Shenryalan flowed around him before they obviously made a decision. A handful of riders fell back, apparently planning to stay where they were for the moment. Rasim guessed they might want to keep an eye out for the dragon, in case it came back.

The rest of them, though, including the one he rode with, urged their horses to speed again, and took off across the night without a word of explanation. Rasim briefly considered throwing himself off the horse, too, but he was already cold, tired, and in pain, and also quite certain they would come back for him and be really annoyed that he'd slowed them down.

Besides, Bayar had told him that his clan, the Horse clan, considered killing people to be one of its worst sins. Whatever lay ahead, it probably wasn't the almost-certain death the dragon had offered.

Probably.

CHAPTER FOUR

He had no real idea how long they rode for. Long enough for Rasim to become incredibly stiff and uncomfortable, but that would have happened even if he hadn't throw himself off both a mountain and a dragon today. Horse-riding was *awful*. He'd just about decided he needed to ask for a chance to walk when an encampment appeared in front of them, as if out of nowhere.

After a disbelieving stare, he realized it rested in an enormous hollow between hills so gradual and shallow that Rasim hadn't realized they actually existed. The steppe grasses were purple and white under the moon, and Rasim's impression of the whole prairie so far had been one of endless skies and bleached colors.

The encampment below was a riot of strong color in comparison, even in the moonlight. Wheels of brightly-dyed tents spiraled out from a single, enormous circular building. Wide paths lay between the spirals of tents, and the tents themselves got smaller as they moved away from the central one toward the tips of the spirals. Dogs lazed in front of the outermost tents, sprawled half in and out of them. As they approached, many of them sprang to their feet, not barking, but wary and prepared. Some of them were huge, nearly as big as the smaller ponies being ridden, and Rasim wondered if everything in the steppes came in unexpected sizes.

Between the smallest, personal tents and the enormous central one, there were cooking tents, and washing tents, forges and sewing circles, all with a strange air of prepared impermanence. Closer yet to the center were family living spaces, with a few older children still awake with their parents, sitting around fires and watching the returning riders curiously. Everything was filled with color: inset swatches of dark reds, rich blues, brighter tones layered over undyed hides, and softened with fur of every shade and length.

The Shenryalan people were nomadic, with no cities, just gatherings and gathering-places. This place had the feeling of a cozy village, but it had to be portable. Rasim could hardly believe it could be packed up and carried away on a moment's notice.

The central building was another a tremendous tent, capable of being put up and taken down swiftly and efficiently. Its walls were of thicker hide than many of the others, giving it a stiffer and more permanent look, but they *were* hide, and cloth, all held together with leather stitching and slender, sapling-width poles. A long, snapping flag flew from its peaked top, the colors of a white horse on a red background visible as it shifted and pulled in the wind. As they came closer, a wide soft door was thrown back and a small, ancient woman emerged. The door was closed behind her, and for a moment she stood framed against its brilliant orange-gold dye. She wore heavily embroidered purple silk robes, a color that reminded Rasim of the moon-touched new grass. Its sleeves were rolled back to expose her arms and the innumerable tattoos marked into her wrinkled skin. They were visible on her throat and face, too, faded with age but clearly a lifetime's work. The rider Rasim sat with unceremoniously dumped him off the horse, and when he staggered to a more or less upright position, booted him in the butt to send him forward to the tattooed woman. No one else moved.

He said, "Um," uncertainly, and a hiss erupted from the riders, and, he realized, from an awful lot of other people who had gathered around them with unfriendly expressions. He said, "But," and cringed as another silencing hiss drowned the word.

The old woman's expression didn't change at all. Her eyes were as black and sharp as Guildmaster Isidri's, and even in moonlight she had a warm redness in her cheeks that reminded Rasim of Bayar. She carried a staff in one hand, and Rasim thought it was carved with creatures that might match her tattoos, but firelight from somewhere nearby made the shadows shift and change, and he couldn't tell for sure. She pointed imperiously to the space right in front of her, and Rasim, wishing there was anyone else on his side here, stepped forward.

Without a word, she reached up—*up*, because even if Rasim wasn't tall, the old woman was considerably smaller—and seized the sides of his head. He froze, then tried not to resist as she pulled his head down to hers. She took a deep breath of his hair and held it as if she was tasting his scent. Rasim's heart started hammering hard, like he was afraid he wouldn't taste good enough. She released him, frowning, and he had the urge to ask her to sniff him again, to make sure he passed muster.

Instead she turned away, barking several commands to those around them. In the midst of them, Rasim heard a word he knew from Bayar, and blurted, "Sorcerer!" first in Ilyaran, then in Shenryalan. "I am a sorcerer, Bayar said—I know he said you don't trust witchery, but I know that word!"

He honestly thought they'd have been less surprised if one of the horses started talking. The old woman turned to him one muscle at a time, her black eyes very bright in the firelight. "Bayar?"

So much relief swept Rasim that he suddenly needed very badly to pee, and wondered how he could ask where a toilet was. From the old woman's expression, though, that was *not* what he should be talking about. "Bayar," he said again, then, struggling to pick out useful words from his limited Shenryalan, said something that he hoped they would understand as, "He's my friend. He's here, he's safe, he's—" He ended up pointing toward the mountains he'd left behind. "At the watchfire mountain with the flat top," he said in Ilyaran, because he didn't have anything like those words in their language, and then remembered he did, at least, know the river's name in their tongue. "Near the Crack in the Bowl!"

The old lady's expression didn't really change, but Rasim saw something new in it anyway. Satisfaction, maybe, or at least interest. She spoke again, and a handful of the riders he'd come in with, none of whom had dismounted, turned their horses and rode away. Then she poked Rasim in the chest with her staff and lifted iron-grey eyebrows expectantly before placing a hand on her own chest and saying, "Oyun."

"Oyun? Oh. You're O…I'm Rasim." He pushed the staff aside with a fingertip, not wanting to offend, and put his hand where it had been. "Rasim." Then he bowed just in case, because whatever Oyun was, it was clearly a role of importance.

She gave him a sharp smile of approval. "Rasim. Sorcerer-child."

Rasim mumbled, "Seamaster journeyman, not…" then sighed and agreed, "Sorcerer-child."

Oyun cackled and pointed her staff imperiously toward a second tent near the huge one. It was nearly as large, but dyed differently, with shadows and streaks that reminded Rasim of Oyun's tattoos and made him very strongly not want to go in it. Spirits belonged in that tent, not Ilyaran journeymen who were in over their heads. He shook his head, and the old lady smacked him with her staff. "Ow!"

She threatened him with the staff again and he glanced around, finding innumerable Shenryalan gazes staring at him with borderline offense. Clearly telling

Oyun 'no' was not an option. Rasim said, "I don't understand," but reluctantly went toward the second tent. Someone opened the soft hide door, letting him pass, and closed it again behind them.

It was *very* dark inside, although a small central fire glowed with embers. The fire sat in a bowl of its own, handles gleaming in the ember light, and the tent was surprisingly hot after the cool night air. Rasim could see very little beyond the fire bowl, but a smaller tent sat right next to the fire between two tall poles that held the ceiling up. Oyun thumped him in the back and pointed imperiously at the smaller tent. Rasim stood there a few seconds, trying to decide whether arguing was worth it or not, then just sighed and crawled inside.

It smelled appalling, like sweat and sweet sharp smoke. If the outer tent was hot, this one was roasting. Oyun crawled in behind him, then, with her stick, reached out to grab one of the fire's handles.

A whole sledge filled with embers came away. She pulled it into the little tent, closed the door behind her, and sat across from Rasim. The temperature soared and sweat broke out on his forehead as his mouth went dry. He looked for water, and Oyun opened a flask of it. He reached for it gratefully, but instead of giving him any, she squirted the water onto the embers. It filled the already-stinky little tent with steam and a terrible stench of sweet smoke. Rasim howled, "Siliaria's tits!" and lunged for the door, only to be stopped by the old woman's walking stick whacking him in the forehead.

He fell back with another howl, rubbing his fore-head, and she pushed him back into place with the stick, then poured more water on the coals. Steam billowed again, making him sick with the heat and scent. He clapped a hand over his mouth, trying not to vomit, and Oyun grinned gleefully and poured more water onto the embers. Rasim gave in and turned to the side, throwing up until his eyes dripped. More water went on the embers, sending the foul smoke smell and steam through the tiny space, and Rasim threw up again, and again, until he couldn't do anything but lie in a ball on the floor and whimper with tears sliding across his nose. Oyun was a blur on the other side of the still-glowing embers. A leering, grinning blur that picked up a drum and hit it hard with her walking stick.

The most horrifying reverberation wobbled through the tent, bounced against its thick hide walls, and sprang back again, rattling Rasim's bones both ways. He hadn't yet recovered from that when she hit the drum again, and then again, until she was keeping up a steady beat that wouldn't let him go, but shook him back and forth like a dog with a bone. He didn't think he had anything left to throw up, but he managed anyway, then put his head on his stinky arms and cried.

The tears took him by surprise, and wracked his body as hard as the drum beat did. He didn't know how long he cried, but he knew what he cried *for*, as memories and moments he thought he'd already mourned rose in him under the drum's incessant demand and the overwhelming heat in the little tent. He cried for

Agnet, and for the terrible destruction of Moran, and for all the friends who had died in Hongrunn and by the sea serpent and even, to his surprise, for the parents he had never known, and never truly missed. The sobs went on a long, long time, and the tears for even longer, but Oyun never missed a beat of her drumming.

Eventually, completely drained, Rasim sat up. He was so tired, tired from the past year, from the day's adventures, from not knowing what was happening. All he had left was waiting to see what happened next. The drumbeat couldn't dislodge any more emotion, or the smelly steam and smoke any more bile. If Oyun wanted him any more depleted, she would have to feed him something to empty his bowels, too. She didn't seem to feel that was necessary, and if he weren't so light-headed with exhaustion, he might have been grateful.

She had, somehow, built up the fire without stopping the drumbeat. It was only a tiny flame, enough to lick at the air and add a little more heat, but it danced there beautifully, almost solitary in the darkness. He watched it, because the only other thing to see was Oyun, and her intent gaze on him was too uncomfortable to meet. His thoughts, already slow, fell away gradually, until his eyes lidded heavily and the firelight seemed to take up a place behind his lashes. All at once he fell, a swift drop that left his body sitting in front of the fire, watching the flame, but his sense of *self* somewhere else entirely. There was no landscape, no movement, only gentle darkness and the endless thumping of the drum.

A sand snake wiggled up out of the darkness, slid around his leg, and disappeared again. It was speckled brown with a pale belly and reminded Rasim, a little, of the great stone snake he had fought at the edge of the Northern Sea. It came to him two or three times more in the darkness, then slithered off, leaving him feeling rather comforted. A spot of light—firelight—appeared in the black when it was gone, and, having nothing else to do, Rasim drifted toward it.

It sat there in the nothingness, burning nothing, simply *being*. Rasim had always thought of fire as destructive, even fearsome, as if a glimmer of memory about the Great Fire that had ravaged Ilyara in his infancy was stronger than his knowledge that fire was a useful tool when well-kept. Finding it alone, by itself, with nothing to even burn, made it seem less dangerous. Its light and warmth were the gifts it gave, and in this oddly quiet place of darkness, it took nothing in return. He sat down beside it, sighing, and compared the flame to water's surging strength, to stone's unmoving silence, to air's endless dance. Fire, he thought, *breathed*. It rose and fell, growing and shrinking, just as a breath did, like a living thing that could not live without air any more than a person could. He had the power now to take away its air, which took away the trace of fear, that hint of terror dissipating like smoke on the wind. The fire in the darkness went away, and Rasim opened his eyes.

He held a flame in his hand, cupped there like a

drinking cup with a round, warm base and a narrow neck. It didn't burn him, or go out in the moment he realized he held it; it only glowed there, softly lighting the too-hot tent. He closed his hand, and the flame faded; when he opened it again, the fire sprang back to life like a whisper at the back of his mind, crackling and satisfied and soft. That was what Sunmaster Endat had wanted him to feel, the life of the flame, and now that Rasim knew it, he would never lose it again. He let it die, so that only embers lit the room, and asked, "What did you do? Why did you do it?"

He didn't exactly expect her to answer, but he wasn't exactly surprised when she did, either. She shook her ancient head, grey braids beaded with bright colors falling over her shoulders as she did so. "Unbalanced, you. Sorcerer-child, but broken. Water, pah. Not by nature, not in you. Fire, yes, but fear quenches flame. Unbalanced, you," she repeated.

Rasim stared at her blearily, trying to work his way through that. "You mean I'm not a water witch?"

The old lady looked at him like he was thick in the head. "You are *now*. Touched by the sea herself, weren't you? But when the water god makes you hers, and the fire is long drowned, there is imbalance. So you find a stone god, and with him, maybe balance. But then you kill the water with *delzjha*—" She turned her head and spat, and Rasim thought of the fine grey dust that had taken his water witchery from master levels to something nearly god-like, but had almost killed him in the aftermath. No one he knew had given the drug a name, but he had no doubt it was what Oyun meant when she said *delzjha*.

He felt like he should have been shocked that she knew so much about his life, but he'd gone beyond that, somehow. No witchery *he* knew would tell someone his story, but Oyun's witchery was nothing at all like what he knew in Ilyara. She had learned what she needed to by sniffing his hair, and by casting him into the darkness with her drum and her sickly-sweet smoke and her steam in the sweltering tent.

Although he hadn't spoken, she nodded like he had, and finished what she had to say. "Delzjha is the wisdom-slayer. It makes the power rise, makes it flow, makes it all, before it takes all away. Delzjha kills the water, so the air god rises to balance the stone. Balance, balance, balance, all needs balancing in you. But the water is not *dead*, only retreated like the tide, and it comes back, back, back. The fear is there, though. The fire cannot burn, and without the fire, water has no balance. Without balance, *dragons*."

Rasim flinched at her vehemence, then tried to close his mouth again as what she meant hit him. "That was me? I called it?"

Oyun curled her lip. "Call, no, call means intent. Woke, annoy, bother, yes. Call, no." She scowled deeply, wrinkling some of her tattoos into invisibility, then curled her lip again and said, "Call, maybe," grudgingly. "It senses emptiness where fire should be in you. It seeks to fill the void. But no more. Spirit walk brings balance."

"So I won't accidentally call another dragon?"

Rasim's voice rose to a squeak and the old woman gave him a sharp grin.

"Accidentally, no."

Rasim groaned and put his face in his hands. "I don't want to call one on purpose, either! I mean, I guess that's better than accidentally, but..." He fell silent, then lifted his head with a sigh. "So I have all four witcheries now. Couldn't you have just told me all of this, instead of making me puke?"

Oyun jabbed at him with her walking stick. "Tell is no good. Must see, feel, be."

"Can we all do this? Not the throwing up part. Using all the different witcheries, or even two of them, for balance."

The old woman shook her head. "Some. Some might. Never all. Sorcery comes from the spiral, the King Horse, the starry gods. Some hear one god easily and need no more. There is balance with one, then."

Rasim closed his eyes, taking slow breaths and thinking through everything the old shaman had said. "So we do it wrong," he said after a while, softly. "We should wait to see what god orphans hear, before assigning them to a guild. Or for our first few years we should study all the magics."

Oyun spat again and Rasim's eyes flew open. "Wrong, right, pah! Maybe you teach child to hear a god, who could never hear it on their own. Maybe giving chance to listen to all gods means they will hear none. Do not doubt what has worked."

He stared at her a long time, wishing his thoughts were clearer, and then, with a touch of the wit he usually prided himself on, said, "How do you do it in the clans?"

The old woman cackled, revealing a few snaggly teeth. "Clever. Clever sorcerer-child. You ask for secrets. Secrets are not for you, boy. To learn secrets, return to old Oyun's tent when your duties to the spiral end, or make peace with never knowing."

"My duties?" Alarm shot through Rasim, distracting him from everything else. "Doesn't that mean I'll be dead?"

"Pah." Oyun made the sound gently, this time. "Spirals spin, gods touch, things happen, spirals turn, gods retreat, things calm. Death is *an* ending to a story, but not the only one."

Relief turned to cold bumps on Rasim's arms, despite the heat of the tent, but before he could speak, Oyun added, "And restless spirits can always return in another life, if death *is* the end." At Rasim's horrified stare, the old shaman let go a gleeful cackle, then thumped at him with her walking stick. "Out, out, out. Out of my tent. Rude boy, taking up old Oyun's time. Out!"

Rasim, offended, frightened, amused, and exhausted, scrambled out of the tent into the comparative coolness of the larger one, then stumbled wearily to the door, throwing it open to take a deep breath of fresh air.

The light that met him was morning-bright, and before he adjusted to its brilliance, hands grabbed his upper arms and dragged him away.

CHAPTER FIVE

His captors dragged him into another tent before Rasim even had a chance to get his feet under himself. They released him with enough violence that he stumbled, and turned to glare at them with righteous offense. "I wasn't doing anything! I would have come with you!"

Their impassive expressions told him they didn't understand him any more than he would have understood them if they'd tried explaining themselves. He inhaled deeply to sigh, caught a whiff of himself, and made an awful face as he caught his own sharp, sweaty stench. Whatever was happening, they should have let him bathe first, unless they were just planning to kill him.

The door behind him was deep orange, almost glowing with early morning sun. The largest tent had a door of that color. Rasim's stomach dropped as he turned back around again, overwhelmed and trying to get his bearings. Two thick central poles, braced in a wheel dug into the earth, supported the tent's top, where another wheel opened to the sky, allowing smoke and heat to drift out. There were beds and furs and chairs all pushed against the walls, making room for half a dozen large benches on either side of the room, all facing each other.

There were innumerable people in the tent, crowded around the walls or sitting on the benches, but two of them sat on magnificent wicker thrones. They were both exquisitely dressed, not so much matching as complementary, with the man in sky blue with white tufts of fur, and the woman in rich, earthy red and brown. The man's throne was piled with glorious soft-looking leathers and soft furs in the woman's colors, and the woman's framed hers in the beautiful blue the man wore. He was handsome and solemn, with a round face and black hair threaded with grey, and she had familiar high cheekbones and a full mouth that was, at the moment, trying not to smile. She was doing a good job of it, too, but Rasim had seen that expression, and the sparkle in similar black eyes, many times over the past several weeks.

"Oh," he said in a small voice. "You're Bayar's parents, aren't you? Hello."

The woman had not a trace of that smile in her voice as she spoke Ilyaran every bit as well as her son did. "I am Irlin, daughter of Sūyin, mother to Bayar, and Great Mare of the Shenryalan tribes. My chosen mate is Bikat, King Horse and father to Bayar."

Rasim whispered, "I thought the King Horse was a god," and Irlin's eyes widened at the interruption. Her gaze skittered to Bikat, then back to Rasim. "It is a title of honor, for no one who cannot carry the honor of the god is worthy of leading the tribes. We do not ask our chief to bear the weight of the god's presence. That is for the shamans."

The relief of understanding washed through Rasim, and he gave Irlin a nervous smile. "Oh. Thank you for explaining. I like to know things." There was someone practically behind the thrones, he realized, murmuring in Shenryalan. He thought maybe they were translating for the larger group in the tent, but he didn't quite dare look away from Bayar's parents to see how people were reacting.

The invisible smile returned to Irlin's dark eyes, but still came nowhere near her voice. "You are Rasim. Tell us more. Name your mothers and your purpose here."

"Uhm." Rasim's voice cracked on the sound. "I don't have a mother?"

A murmur of distress went around the tent, making Rasim certain there was a translator. Irlin's eyes widened in disbelief. "I have heard many stories about Golden Ilyara, but not that their children rise fully formed from the soil. How do you know your lineage and your destiny, if you have no mothers?"

Rasim hesitated with dismay, unsure of how to respond. "Our legends do say the first Ilyarans were born of the sun and the soil, but, um, no, it's just that I'm an orphan. Adopted by the Seamasters' Guild because the river, the Ilialio, brought me to them after the Great Fire. I don't know who my mother was. Isidri is my Guildmaster, though. She's like a mother, sort of."

A terrifying, ruthless, untouchable mother that he adored, kind of like the sea goddess herself made human. Rasim swallowed, noticed his hands had turned to nervous bunches, and tried to loosen them as another murmur went around the tent.

"Very well," Irlin said after a moment. "Rasim, heart-son to Isidri, grandson to the Ilialio, tell us of our son, whose name you know."

A breath of relief shivered from Rasim's chest. At least he knew the right thing to say, now. "He's alive. He's fine. He's my friend. We were captives together, and escaped together and my captain agreed to bring him home. They're at the flat-topped mountain at the edge of the Northern Sea, or they were yesterday."

"You claim to come to us as a friend, then." Bayar's father, Bikat, spoke for the first time, in a deep, soothing voice.

Rasim hunched his shoulders guiltily. "I do, yes, and I'm really sorry about the dragon. Are there a lot of those here? I never heard of them, but the old lady, Oyun, said it might have..." He sighed. "No, she said it was my fault, not that it might have been."

A little too late, he realized that possibly referring to Oyun as 'the old lady' might have been a mistake. A silence filled the tent, one that somehow sounded like everyone had collectively stopped to blink at him in astonished insult. One single blink from all of them at the same time, followed by an offended glare from everybody in the tent.

After a *very* long time, Irlin said, "It reflects well upon you that you admit your fault with the dragon. In normal times, you would have been brought to see us first, not given to the shamans for a spirit quest to quiet your troubled soul. An early rider came to us and spoke of the sorcerer-child who tamed and rode the dragon, though, and Oyun knew she must guide you before the rest of us could be exposed to your dangerous presence."

"I'm not—" Rasim swallowed. "I don't mean to be dangerous."

Bikat's heavy eyebrows rose. "So you admit that you are. Tell me, sorcerer-child, if you are the herald of your people, how can we believe you do not endanger *us*? That your people are not a danger to us?"

Rasim had a deep, desperate wish that Sunmaster Endat was there. Endat was a diplomat, accustomed to offering adept answers to complicated situations. People shouldn't even be asking someone like Rasim questions like this.

But he was the only one there, so he spread his hands helplessly and shook his head. "I don't think Ilyarans are dangerous to other people, generally. We can be, because we have so much magic, but we're also *not*, because we have so much magic. We don't need to expand and we're hard to conquer. The only reason we're here—well, one of the reasons we're here is to bring Bayar home. The other is to ask if you've been under any kind of siege or trouble, in case we can help." That, Rasim felt, glossed over the truth so much as to be almost a lie, but if he tried to explain in detail he'd be standing there until dinnertime.

His stomach rumbled astonishingly at the thought,

and he realized he had no real idea when he'd eaten last. Probably a snack on the mountainside the day before.

Bikat, however, wasn't interested in a small Ilyaran journeyman's noisy belly. "So you believe that no Ilyaran witch would attack our tribes? Kidnap a boy from his family?"

Rasim stared at Bayar's father a long moment, trying to work his way through the different things he was being asked. "I don't believe *Ilyara* would do that," he said finally. "I don't believe King Taishm would ever support something like that. But Ilyarans? Maybe. Somebody who'd left the city to make money from their witchery, or been enslaved so they didn't have a choice? A year ago I would have said none of us would ever do that, but I know more now."

Bikat leaned forward, elbows on his knees, like a master about to impart secrets to an eager apprentice. His black eyes were dark and serious in the firelight. "Tell me, sorcerer-child. If you were the leader of a great tribe, a tribe who did not trust outsider magic, and someone using magic took your child, what would you do with the next people who came to you proclaiming their power and wishing to speak with you?"

Dismay churned through Rasim's gut, wiping out his hunger. "I wouldn't trust them at all."

"Indeed. Let me tell you what has happened, Ilyaran sorcerer-child." Bikat straightened from his intimate pose and spread his arms wide, as if he told a story that encompassed all of his people. "Before the last cold season, sorcerers stole away my son. I would have cast off the ways of our people and made war, but Oyun counseled me to wait until the Great Gathering. The stars in the sky and the breath of the King Horse told her he would survive, and through my anger, I waited. The five tribes are gathering now, and Oyun warned us, too, that untrustworthy sorcery would come from afar before Bayar was returned to us."

"Oh no," Rasim blurted. "I'm trustworthy. I am. I don't know how to show you, but I am. I think—I think Bayar will tell you that."

"I do not speak of you, sorcerer-child." Bikat raised a hand and beckoned with two fingers. The broad door in the tent behind them opened again and a dozen grim-faced guards entered, their leather armor shadowed and threatening in the spill of sunlight. They marched straight toward Bikat and Irlin's thrones, forcing Rasim to the side as they came into the supplicant's circle in front of the them. Only then did they step aside to reveal the prisoner they escorted.

For a few seconds, Rasim didn't recognize the disheveled, dark-skinned man who stood there, and then with a shock, he realized it was Sunmaster Endat.

"SUNMASTER?" Rasim's voice broke on the single word. He surged forward to hug Endat, more out of relief at a familiar face than great affection, but came up short as guards crossed spears in front of him, blocking the way. His relief fell away into confusion, which was also written large over the Sunmaster's face. "What are you doing here?"

"I might ask you the same thing." Endat managed to sound almost droll. "*I* sailed for Shenryal weeks ago, remember? We parted ways in Hongrunn."

"Oh." Rasim actually shook himself, remembering. "Right. Wait." Panic spurted through him and he stepped forward, glaring at the guards when they moved to block him again. One of them lifted her eyebrows in obvious surprise, and Rasim supposed foreign near-prisoners weren't supposed to glower at people with weaponry. He shot a glance that he hoped was pleading toward Bayar's parents. Byy the flicker of Irlin's expression, thought maybe he'd accidentally glared at them, too, but she gestured and the guards let him cross to Sunmaster Endat's side. "Where are the others? Telun? Milu? Pynda? Lars?" He stopped himself before he'd listed everyone he could remember who had sailed west to the steppes, and the rumpled Sunmaster smiled briefly.

"Pynda and the journeymen are here, as is your friend Lars, and the Northman Kif." The master's eyebrows rose a little, as if asking whether Rasim remembered Kif, and at his impatient nod, continued. "Most of us have not been made precisely welcome in the weeks we've been here, but neither are we unwell. But you." Faint dismay creased the Sunmaster's round face. He looked tired, and thinner than Rasim remembered, but curiosity brightened his dark eyes, which was also as Rasim remembered.

He opened his mouth, hesitated, and, because

explaining was too much, summarized with a woefully inadequate, "We met Bikat and Irlin's son, and brought him home. Except I got kidnapped by a dragon and left the rest of them behind."

Slowly, line by line, Endat's expression fell into a studied neutrality. Embarrassed guilt rose in Rasim, making him squirm even though he didn't think he'd actually done anything wrong. When Endat finally spoke, his voice was as carefully bland as his face. "I look forward to hearing the details of your adventures. Where is the young prince now?"

"He didn't like us calling him that, but I think some of the riders who brought me here last night went back for him." Rasim cast a glance toward Bayar's parents to see if they showed any signs of agreement, but they were as scrupulously detached as Endat was trying to be.

Rasim thought that was completely unfair. He was in over his head and trying to do his best and nobody around him gave even a hint of whether he was messing everything up or not. Teeth gritted, he said, "I don't understand," to Bikat and Irlin. If they were going to leave him flapping like a loose rope, he would flap. "Sunmaster Endat is one of our king's diplomats, and the other Ilyarans are journeymen witches, like me."

"Sorcerers," Bikat said somewhat dangerously.

"Well, yes. But...friends. Of mine, at least."

"And you would have us trust you," Irlin said in her clear quiet voice. "Because you claim our son as your friend, and because you claim to be his saviour."

"What? No." Heat spilled through Rasim's face. "No,

if anybody was his saviour it was Agnet. Another slave in the arena we fought in," he explained. "A Northerner. She did a lot more to keep him safe than I did, for a lot longer. And…yes? I'd like you to trust us?" He wanted to kick Endat and make him do the talking, but if the Sunmaster had been there for weeks and Bayar's parents were asking *him* questions, Rasim thought there was probably a reason for it.

The reason, he thought, might be that they were setting a trap, because a moment later Irlin said, "Would you have us ignore the advice of our shamans, then, and release these sorcerers you call friends?"

For a moment Rasim had the sensation of falling into the abyss, of a blackness closing over him as he plummeted without control. All he had ever wanted in life was to earn a place on the *Wafiya*. He had never imagined having that wish granted would mean his life would become unending chaos, or that it might end up meaning the words he chose could doom not only himself, but possibly everyone he knew on this part of the continent. He closed his eyes for a few seconds, trying to steady himself against the feeling of being in over his head. Seamasters could always find their way to the surface. Then he took a deep breath, opened his eyes, and met Irlin's piercing gaze.

"I wouldn't tell anyone not to listen to their most trusted advisors. I *might* ask what those advisors had to gain from giving the advice they have—" A gasp went around the quiet, gathered crowd as that was translated — "but your shaman reminds me of my old guildmaster. She might be conniving and manipulative, but she doesn't hurt people. She just likes setting situations up so people can find the best in themselves."

Anything else he might have said was lost in a rush of noisy commentary from the tribe. Suggesting that their shaman was conniving and manipulative had obviously offended many, amused others, and shocked everyone. Sunmaster Endat put a hand over his face and drew it down, gazing incredulously at Rasim through his fingers. After several minutes the crowd settled down, although they had a less friendly air about them than they had before. Rasim sighed. "The point is I can't, or won't, tell you to ignore your advisors. I can tell you I trust these people, but I know you don't have any reason to trust *me*."

"Except you claim to have saved our son, and brought him from the horseless lands back to us."

Rasim said, "Well, they have horses," and winced as Endat gave him a truly appalled look. "Yes, except for that. But we didn't do that to earn your trust. We did it because it was the right thing to do and we were coming to visit you anyway. There's been trouble spread all over the continent and we were afraid Shen-ryal was suffering from it, too."

"Yes," Bikat replied. "Your Sunmaster has spoken of these things. The great fire in your home city, poisoned lakes in the Northlands, and so on."

"Right," Rasim said desperately. "Coups in the Islands. It's as if someone is trying to destabilize places all over the points of the compass, and the last point is here, in the steppes. And Bayar is your heir. The King Horse's son. Kidnapping him has brought you all to the brink of war, hasn't it? Even though war isn't the way of your people? So it might be a different approach than what they've done elsewhere, but they're still trying to drill holes in your hulls." At Bikat and Irlin's blank looks, Rasim searched for an idea that might translate. "Trying to loosen your saddle straps?"

"Girth," Bikat said with amusement, but nodded, clearly understanding now. "Go on. Your Sunmaster spoke of the Moranese as the, mmm, instigators."

"I think so, but I'm not sure. They're at the center of the compass point, anyway, and the slaves we rescued, some of them talked about how their masters had plans for beyond Moran itself. But that was before half the city got drowned."

Endat said, "*What?*" and Rasim gave him a defensive look.

"It's been a really busy month!"

"Rasim…" Endat's controlled calm visibly slipped. Rasim braced, surprising himself with a sudden ferocious willingness to argue with the Sunmaster, if necessary. He wasn't happy about what had happened in Moran, but he wasn't going to let someone who hadn't been there yell at him for it, either.

Before Endat got the chance, there was a commotion outside, and Bayar burst into the tent to rush into his parents' arms.

CHAPTER SIX

The guards hauled Rasim and Endat outside before either of them had a chance to catch their breaths, much less speak to Bayar. The ancient shaman, Oyun, hustled past them, going into the tent as they left it. Rasim was impressed the old lady could move that fast. Seconds later nearly everyone else poured out of the tent, many of them with tense, pinched expressions that landed on Rasim and tightened further. One girl, though, three or four years older than Rasim, gave him a brilliant smile of gratitude before another woman, tall, with grey-streaked hair and a grim set to her jaw, pulled the girl out of Rasim's sight. He stood on his toes, trying to see where they'd gone, but Kisia shouted "Rasim!" and he spun toward the sound of his name.

Kisia fell off a horse and tumbled toward him for a hug. Desimi followed with less grace, if possible, although Sesin dismounted like she knew what she was doing. All of the riders exchanged looks, but didn't stop them, and the guards who gathered around them eyed one another uncomfortably, as if they weren't sure what to do with the outsiders. Kisia hissed, "What happened to you? You flew away—you *flew away,* Rasim!"

"Where's Captain Nasira? They keep asking questions and I don't know what to tell them." Rasim returned her hug, unbelievably glad to see her, and almost as glad to see Desimi.

"She's on the way," the bigger boy said. "We were already down this side of the mountain and trying to track where the dragon had gone when the riders showed up. Bayar made some of them stay behind to bring Nasira and Lorens, but the rest of them insisted on escorting him home as fast as they could."

"Well, Endat and Telun and Milu and everybody are here but I think they're in some kind of trouble." Rasim faltered as even more Shenryalans began to gather around the great central tent, so hushed that speaking at all seemed rude. Rasim's hands went cold with worry and he didn't know why. Nor did he dare ask, with the weight of silence all around.

It went on for an unbearably long time. The sun shifted across the sky, but tension kept everyone on their feet, surrounding the tent. Rasim thought that somewhere in the camp, people must be going on with their day like everything was normal, but he could hear almost no sign of it, save a dog whining and a few babies crying, as if they, too, felt something important was happening and were worried about the outcome.

Kisia's hand stole into Rasim's and she glanced at him, wide-eyed, but he shrugged, unable to tell her what was going on. Desimi crowded closer, too, and Sesin joined them, the four of them huddled together and watching the central tent like everyone else. Rasim knew he was hungry and tired, and knew that neither of those things would matter to the people gathered around the tent.

Finally, a voice rose from within, crying out something joyous in the Shenryalan language.

The roar that answered reminded Rasim of the Moranese slave arena, only there was no blood lust in it, just gladness. Before its strength died, it shifted into song with high tonal ranges and a low, deep thrum that sounded instrumental but came, Rasim realized after a moment, from people casting their voices almost too low to be heard. Kisia's shoulders dropped in relief and she whispered, "Bayar is still one of his people. He was gone so long, he was afraid his soul might have been corrupted and they'd throw him out. He thought that maybe because he's the King Horse's son they might try what he called a three-moon cleansing, but he thought if they had to try that he was pretty much lost anyway."

Rasim and Desimi both blinked at her in astonishment, and Desimi whispered, "When'd he tell you all that?"

Kisia shrugged uncomfortably. "We've been talking a lot."

"I guess so!"

"Rasim, what's going on? What's—"

Any hope Kisia had of answers died as Oyun left the central tent, her hands lifted high as if in triumph. She had silk wrapped around her hands now, all sorts of colors that matched the dyed tents and the bright flags that flew above them, and the rich shades of clothing everyone wore. Rasim shifted from one foot to another, finally daring to look around a little at where he was, and the people around him, but Oyun drew everyone's attention as she spoke at length. Once in a while, Kisia whispered, "She's talking about us," or, "She's reassuring them," and every time she did, Desimi squinted at her.

"When did you learn so much Shenryalan?" he hissed in a momentary lull.

Kisia shrugged again, more stiffly than before. "I told you, Bayar and I have been talking a lot. I guess we were practicing."

"Uh-*huh*."

Before Desimi could say anything else, Oyun came forward. Rasim wasn't at all surprised when she grabbed his head again, hauling him down to sniff him thoroughly. This time she released him with an expression of satisfaction that ended in a sharp nod. Rasim smiled weakly in return. At least she hadn't hauled him off to her tent to make him throw up again.

Instead, she shouldered past him and grabbed Kisia's head. Kisia yelped with offense, her expression one of barely controlled outrage as she submitted to the shaman's sniff. The old woman let her go with a sharp, pleased-sounding laugh, and clapped Kisia on the shoulder so hard the girl staggered. She rubbed her shoulder and stared at the old lady, clearly bewildered.

Desimi, who had a neck like a bull even at thirteen, ducked his head on his own so he didn't get yanked around. Oyun grunted approval and lingered over her inhalation, then, eyebrows drawn deeply down, took another breath of the big Seamaster journeyman. A frown dug into the lines around her mouth and between her eyebrows, and she took a third, even deeper breath before finally stepping back to stare frankly at Desimi for several long seconds. Then, swiftly but with great deliberation, she shook the silk wrappings around her hands loose and re-wove them into bands of green, brown, blue, and gold before opening both palms to the young man in a flash of color. Desimi shot a look of confusion toward Kisia, whose knowledge of Shenryalan tradition obviously didn't cover this. She shrugged and Desimi, left to his own devices, looked back at the shaman and offered a slight, cautious bow.

Oyun gave another grunt of satisfaction, reached up to pat his cheek, and finally seized Sesin to sniff her, too. Interest creased her tattooed forehead, and she stepped back to survey all the Ilyaran journeymen before grunting a final time and turning on her heel to return to the enormous tent. Desimi hissed, "What was *that* about?" and the others shrugged.

"She's a shaman," Rasim whispered, using the Shenryalan word Bayar's parents had used. "I think we'd say spirit master, maybe? She knows things about people. She knew I was—"

Before he finished, the tent door opened again and Oyun marched out as imperiously as she'd entered. This time, though, Bikat and Irlin followed. Bayar walked between them, Irlin's hand on his shoulder. None of them made any effort to hide the tremendous emotion they felt. Bikat's face was bright with tears, and Bayar and Irlin's smiles made them look even more alike than Rasim had thought. All three of them came to a stop in front of the gathered Ilyarans, and Bayar's parents both lifted silk-wrapped palms to Desimi, Rasim supposed, because Oyun had done that. Desimi, still bewildered, shot Rasim a look, then bowed to them the same way he'd done to the shaman. They inclined their heads with evident satisfaction, then turned joyfully solemn gazes on Rasim. "Our son has told us a different story than yours, sorcerer-child," Irlin said. "Bayar has said that without you he would still be enslaved, or more likely dead and his soul lost to the spiral of stars."

"Maybe, but..." Rasim shrugged uncomfortably. "Agnet did a lot more."

Interest creased their faces and they conferred quietly, speaking far too quickly for Rasim's limited grasp of their language to understand. After what felt like a very long discussion, Bikat spoke in a deep, quiet voice. "What do you know of the customs of our people, sorcerer-child?"

"Um." Rasim cast the same sort of nervous glance at Desimi that Desimi had given him only moments earlier. "Not very much?"

"I thought not. It is considered the mark of an old

and generous spirit, one that has often ridden through the spiral, to praise the efforts of others when they are themselves praised. Of course, this is known among our people, and so to be, mmm. Modest?" He nodded as Rasim bobbled his head in agreement with the term. "To be modest becomes, in its way, a method of earning further praise. But you did not know this, and still spoke of this woman Agnet as the true hero."

"She was." Tears suddenly filled Rasim's eyes. "She was a fighter, and she wanted freedom, and if she couldn't have that, she wanted a good death. She ended up with both, and saved Bayar. And then really Desimi and Kisia—" He gestured to the two now beside him— "did most of the rest, along with our ship's crew. I was just…there."

Bikat said something loudly to the gathered tribe, and a laugh ran through them. Heat rushed up Rasim's cheeks even if he didn't know what had been said, and Bayar's mother gave him an amused look. "He speaks well of you, sorcerer-child. You are not what we expected, when we were warned of sorcery from afar. You say this one," she nodded at Endat, "and the others are like you, thinking only of helping, but someone took our son, and we must have a path forward, when we find the kidnappers."

Desimi said, "Well, I'd kill them," and a burst of unexpected, overwhelming frustration slammed through Rasim. He forgot to be on his best behavior and spun toward the bigger boy with an inarticulate roar.

"That's a stupid answer! That's just doing what your

anger tells you to do! If I did what my anger told me to I'd have punched your stupid face and lost any chance I ever had of getting a place on the *Wafiya*! You have to be smarter than that, Desimi! You have to think more! It would be awful to kill somebody who had nothing to do with Bayar being kidnapped, even if you were angry at everybody who used magic right then! You'd be taking your anger out on the wrong people! Maybe the people who kidnapped him deserve to be killed, I don't know, but Sunmaster Endat, and then *we*, were the next people who use witchery to come along, so do you think we should get killed because some slaver stole Bayar from his family?"

Desimi recoiled, as much from Rasim's approach as the onslaught of words. "What? No! We didn't do anything wrong! We brought him back!"

"That's what I'm saying," Rasim shouted. "That's why you have to use your big thick head to think with, Desi! You can't just go around punishing people for what other people did, even if you're mad at the whole world!"

Kisia touched Rasim's arm, trying to calm him. He turned away from Desimi, panting with effort, and she lifted her chin to meet Bikat's eyes. "Rasim isn't wrong, you know," she said to him. "He's shouty, but he's not wrong."

Bayar's father addressed her as directly as she'd spoken to him. "It is difficult to be one who clearly sees the long path, especially, perhaps, when one is still a child. In our culture," he said to Rasim, "you would be sent to study with Oyun, who would show you the shaman's road, and as you aged you would be called upon to speak with the spirits and guide our people toward their ever-changing destiny. There is no such path in your land?" When Rasim shook his head, Bikat smiled, almost sadly. "A shame. To learn from Oyun might ease your heart."

Rasim put his hand on his chest, trying to make himself breathe slowly. "I guess it might not seem like it right now, but I think she's helped me a lot already."

A glimmer of humor washed through Bikat's face. "Well, there are no dragons," he said. "Perhaps that is sign enough of what she has done for you."

Desimi elbowed him. "What'd she do?"

Rasim elbowed him back. "I'll tell you *later.*"

Kisia smacked both of them, and Bikat struggled not to laugh. "Bayar says your mothers come to join us. We will speak with them about how—"

Desimi said, "We don't have mothers," and this time Kisia elbowed him.

"He means Captain Nasira. Shenryalan priests are mostly women, and they guide their clans' spiritual lives and make the decisions as to where they ride and when they rest. 'Mother' covers a lot of territory in Bayar's language. And they pluralize it because they draw on their ancestors' knowledge and wisdom, and also because they make a lot of group decisions."

All the Ilyarans were blinking at her by the time she was done, and Desimi raised his hands in exasperation. "You're turning into Rasim, just having to know everything."

"I don't have to know everything!" Rasim protested. "And I said the same thing about not having mothers!"

Desimi looked mollified as Bikat and Irlin exchanged glances over Bayar's head, the King Horse clearly giving up on whatever he'd intended to say. Instead, Irlin offered, "Perhaps you might like to eat and bathe," in a gentle voice. "All of you have traveled a long way, and the sorcerer-child has certainly undergone a great trial in the little time he has been with us."

Rasim, who had remembered his hunger earlier, remembered it again, and the volume his stomach rumbled at made everyone around him grin. "Come," Bayar said. "Mother and Father say that your friends are in a nearby tent. I'll bring you to them. The rest we can determine later."

Kisia smiled uncertainly at him. "Are you sure? I wouldn't want to let my parents out of my sight."

Bayar crooked an uncertain smile back at her. "I fear if I do not leave their sides immediately, and prove to myself that I can return, I may never leave them at all." He offered Kisia his hand, and she loosened hers from Rasim's to take it. A lump formed in Rasim's chest as they walked a step or two ahead and he thumped his stomach, even though it didn't feel like hunger. Bayar led them around a half-spiral path to a large, but rather plain, tent not too far from the central one. There he bowed and left them again, with Kisia lingering at the tent door to watch him go before she joined them.

The group within were mostly Ilyarans, although Lars, the round-shouldered Northerner Rasim had befriended was also there, and looked up with a smile as Rasim yelped with delight to see everyone. Pynda, a broad-shouldered Sunmaster journeyman who had been sullen even before her friend's death in the North, didn't even look up, but Milu, a gangly Stonemaster journeyman in his twenties, lurched to his feet to offer hugs. His partner Telun, built like a slab of stone himself, rose to squish them all in greeting. "What are you *doing* here?"

"What are *you* doing here?" Rasim demanded.

"We're being not on a boat," Milu said happily. "Nothing else matters."

All three Seamaster journeymen said, "Ship," and Milu grinned as he and Telun sat again, with Milu leaning back into the broader man's embrace. "Are you all right?"

Rasim made a face. "We're here. What did we miss?"

"The Northerners sailed us to a cove at the foot of a mountain pass. We walked from there, three days into the steppes, before we saw a single soul. Then a whole —herd—of them arrived, out of nowhere. I think they would have killed us all, if Kif hadn't been with us."

Rasim's head came up in surprise. He'd thought of Kif a few times, but the old Northerner had slipped his mind. "Kif, right. Where is he?"

"He spoke to them for us. He told them who he was, and said he was an exile, and then he invoked…" Milu shook his head. "Something. And it made them stop in their tracks."

"The blood of his daughters." Pynda spoke in a low voice. Rasim, who hadn't heard her speak since Daka's death, felt a wave of relief that she was talking again.

Her gaze was hard when it met his, as if she was challenging him to say something. He didn't, and after a moment she went on. "The Shenryal trace their bloodlines through the women, so Kif calling on the blood of his daughters meant he was asking for the protection of their bloodline, which he had earned as the chosen husband of their mother. They had to respect that, or lose honor in the endless spiral."

"That worked even though he was an exile? Doesn't that mean he could have stayed when his wife died?"

Pynda shook her head. "No. It was his wife's sisters who cast him out when she died. They were adults, so they had a lot more power than his daughters, who were children, did. But his daughters are adults now and their aunts are mostly dead, so Kif calling on their bloodline was meaningful enough to at least get us to the encampment in one piece."

No wonder Kif had been so angry with the Shenryalans, Rasim thought. To lose his wife and then be sent away from his children must have been unbearable. He was an old, old man now. To return to the steppes so late in life was in itself a challenge against the unfairness that had cast him out so long ago. Rasim could hardly contemplate the courage it had taken the old man to even try.

Having said her piece, Pynda fell silent, waiting for Milu to pick up the story again. He did, using witchery to create a little map in the hard earth, with shapes and shadows coming to life as riders and tents while he spoke. Rasim watched, fascinated, and Telun squeezed the slender Stonemaster journeyman in his arms.

"You're showing off."

"A little," Milu murmured. "Anyway, they brought us hundreds of miles inland on those sturdy little ponies. I felt like my feet would drag on the ground, when I wasn't rattling my teeth together or rubbing the sores out of my back and bum." He met Rasim's eyes and said, "I don't travel well," rather drolly, and everyone, even Pynda, laughed quietly. "When we arrived they took Kif away and we haven't seen him since, but we're not dead, so he must have said something in our favor."

"Maybe," Rasim said, not helpfully. "It's against their beliefs to kill people. They consider it a corrupting act, a stain on their souls."

Telun's heavy eyebrows rose and he looked into the distance, not that they could see much more than legs and torsos from their vantage on the ground. "They look pretty war-like for pacifists. All that armor."

"I think their spirit master can grant them permission to kill, but there's a whole cleansing cycle that has to be done, and even then it's still a pretty awful thing to do. But they thought they were going to have to go to war to get Bayar back, so they were preparing for it. Their great gathering—we haven't missed it, have we?"

"Not yet. The gathering is in two days, but I think they were kind of planning to just stop for a few minutes on the day and agree that riding out to the continent to get Bayar back was what the King Horse wanted, and then cross the mountain border by the afternoon," Telun said. "You showing up changed everything. I think they're trying to figure out what to do now."

"Thank Siliaria," Rasim said with feeling. "Imagine an army this size sweeping out of the west and rushing across the continent with no warning. I don't think anything could stand against them."

"Except Ilyara," Kisia said proudly, but Pynda shook her head.

"You're wrong, though. It turns out the horse clans have magic."

CHAPTER SEVEN

"Hah!" Rasim brought his hands together with a sharp clap. "I knew it. Oyun said she wouldn't tell me, but I knew it! Well," he added in a mumble mostly to himself, "she said she wouldn't tell me how they chose people to study witchery, I guess. I guess that's not quite the same thing."

"They work earth and wood," Milu said almost dreamily. The shapes he'd built in the hard ground reformed into a witch creating a bowl before settling back down to just be dirt again. "That old woman sniffed my head and sent me to study with one of their witches. I don't know why, if they don't trust us, but I've learned so much. Earth-working is close to stone shaping, but...mellower. The stone is deep and hard and slow, and earth moves much more easily."

"But you could do that already," Rasim said. "You shaped the clay in the north."

"Oh, but that's..." Milu paused, somewhere between

dismissive and confused, but Telun grunted an affirmation.

"Milu keeps saying anybody can do it, but he's wrong. Most Stonemasters can't even come close, I told you that. These steppes people might be able to, but not Ilyarans."

"There isn't much wood out here, is there?" Kisia looked around like she could see through the tent walls into the far distance.

"There are few trees in sheltered areas. Wood-shaping witchery is rare and prized. They use it to make the frames for their tents, and to keep them supple long past when they might have otherwise dried out. They work fire and air, too, just like we do," Pynda said.

Rasim lifted his head slowly. "So, but, wait, if they have witchery, how do we even know that the shaman's vision was of *outside* sorcery? They said—" He got up, going to the tent door. There were guards outside, which didn't surprise him much. "Excuse me, but can I talk to King Bikat? King?" he added in more of a whisper, to his friends. "Is that right?"

They shrugged as the guards looked blankly at him. Rasim groaned and took a step outside, which earned him crossed spears in front of his path, although they were careful not to touch him. "I just need to talk to the King Horse and the Great Mare," he said, mostly in Shenryalan. "Please?"

The guards looked at each other, at him, and back at each other before one sighed enormously and left. Rasim smiled hopefully and the remaining guard pointed imperiously back into the tent. Rasim, shoulders hunched, scooted back in and waited impatiently, dancing from foot to foot and shaking his head when the others looked questioningly at him. He was afraid if he spoke he'd lose the idea, like it would fly away never to be heard again.

The tent flap opened once and Rasim's heart leaped with hope, but it was only someone bringing in a large bucket of water. They indicated it was for bathing with, and for the next little while everyone was occupied with scrubbing themselves as clean as they could without full immersion.

Rasim almost felt human again by the time the tent flap opened a second time. The guard ushered him out with another sigh; clearly if it had been up to her, Rasim would not be brought to the King Horse. Kisia and Desimi jumped up and followed him, sticking close. The guard hesitated, then rolled her eyes in an act of resignation that crossed language barriers. A moment later they were ushered into the central tent, where all the attention turned their way immediately. Many of them were people who had been there the night before, when he'd first been presented to the Shenryalan leaders, and not all of them looked friendly.

Rasim's stomach clenched with nervousness. Somehow he hadn't expected everybody to fall quiet and wait expectantly, but since he was there, he swallowed and said, "You said *sorcery from afar*, didn't you?" to Bayar's parents. "Untrustworthy sorcery from afar?"

"We did." Bikat drew the words out as if he was both curious and reluctant to learn Rasim's thoughts.

Those thoughts burst out of Rasim in a flood. "But Telun and Milu just said the horse clans have witchery! So how do you know it's not magic from somewhere on the steppes that threatens you? These grasslands go on for thousands of miles. That's pretty far. Ilyarans are the obvious answer, since Endat and everybody showed up here before Bayar came back, but if you have magic of your own, isn't it more likely that your sorcerous threats would be internal? We *could* be the threat," he admitted, "and I don't know, maybe we really are, but I think you should at least consider looking closer to home."

He had become accustomed, in the short while it had happened, to hearing the echo of a translator sharing Ilyaran words with the tribe. That echo had stopped early in his speech, as if the translator thought his words might be dangerous. It felt very, very quiet in the big tent all of a sudden.

In the silence, Irlin, the Great Mare, spoke. "Do you know the difference, sorcerer-child, in the argument that you have made, and the one that your elder here has made?" She nodded to Endat, and when Rasim, confounded, shrugged, Irlin said, "He argued as you have, that our enemy may lie closer to home, but never once did this elder sorcerer suggest that he and his companions *could* be the threat. What would you make of that?"

Rasim wished people would stop asking him questions like that, and avoided Master Endat's eyes as he answered. "If I were the suspicious type I'd think maybe he was just trying to make you look elsewhere so he could go about his wicked business. If I were the *very* suspicious type, I might say what *I've* said to make you think I'm trustworthy because I'm willing to consider myself as a potential problem."

To his surprise, Bikat laughed. "But you are not a suspicious type, are you, sorcerer-child?"

"No," Rasim said dismally. "I'm more a 'shout everything I'm thinking at everybody' type." Absolutely everyone who understood him laughed, and he slumped in embarrassment. "But really, I don't think Sunmaster Endat is the suspicious type either. I'm not sure it would occur to him that it could look like he was trying to misdirect you."

"Then he is not a good diplomat," Irlin said, "and you are more suspicious of soul than you imagine."

Rasim made a face. "I don't think I am."

Irlin's eyebrows rose slightly, and too late, it occurred to him that people probably didn't argue with her very often. She and Princess Inga of the Northlands would probably have a lot to say about him, if they got together. He sagged, then shrugged. "Either way, the captain and probably Prince Lorens are on their way here and maybe they'll be..." He trailed off, thinking about Captain Nasira, and mumbled, "Well, Lorens will probably be more diplomatic, anyway, and maybe you can all figure out who's really the enemy here."

Bayar, who had been listening quietly off to one side, seated in a chair built to suit his height, chuckled. "Are you sure you can bear not being part of that discovery, Rasim?"

Rasim made another face, this time more deliberately, at his friend. "I keep telling people I don't really want to be in the middle of all these messes. I just want people to think about what's going on, so they can make smart decisions."

By that time the translator was doing their job again, and Rasim sort of wished they weren't, when a muffled sound of outrage rushed around the tent. "I'm not saying you won't make smart decisions otherwise!" he howled in dismay. "It's just, a lot of the time people don't!"

He had the distinct impression Bayar's parents were once again struggling not to laugh at him. Others in the big tent were clearly not as amused. Rasim caught a dire look from the grey-streaked woman he'd noticed the evening before, as Irlin said, "But you, with all the wit and wisdom of your thirteen years, do?"

Rasim inhaled to answer and a big hand clapped itself over his mouth. Desimi pulled him backward, and Kisia whispered, "Maybe you should stop talking now, Rasi."

Unable to speak anyway, he nodded and made a muffled sound of agreement that caused Desimi to very cautiously loosen his grip over Rasim's mouth. Irlin, now definitely amused, said, "Perhaps not *all* Ilyarans are terrible diplomats," to her husband, who grinned and turned to Rasim.

"You wanted to speak of sorcerers from afar, and who they might be. Is there anything else of importance you wish to discuss now, sorcerer-child? Because I believe there should be hot food in your tent by now, and I know a hungry child's face when I see one. I cannot promise we will say nothing of relevance in your absence," he said, his now expression so sincere he was obviously laughing, "but perhaps with a full belly you will be more prepared to permit the adults to stumble along on their own."

Kisia's hand stole to Rasim's upper arm and squeezed like she was warning him not to say something wrong. He said, "Food would be good," in a low, mortified tone, and they were escorted once more to their tent, where an entire low table of unfamiliar, amazing-smelling food had been laid out. Telun and the others were already seated at it, cross-legged and reaching for the things they liked best. Rasim sat, and Desimi sat beside him on purpose so he could grab the things Rasim reached for first. After a minute, Pynda smacked Desimi's hand with a long-handled spoon, and he yelped, pulled back, and looked injured at her.

She snorted. Desimi grinned, but didn't try to steal any more of the food Rasim was trying to collect. There were meat-filled dumplings with a spice he'd never had before, one that filled his nose with its strength, and sweet barbecued meats that stuck to his teeth and fingers as he chewed happily. A sour cheese went well with the dumplings, and Milu warned, "That one's spicy," just as Rasim bit into a tightly-wrapped piece of meat with something fragrant in its interior. His vision went blurry as heat filled his mouth, and Milu, grinning, handed him a cup of unfamiliar milk that helped lessen the heat a little.

"It's the only one that's really spicy," Milu said

apologetically. "I've gotten used to it so I didn't think to warn you in time."

Rasim wiped his eyes with the back of his sleeve and sniffled as his sinuses melted. "It's good," he said after a second, more careful bite. "I just didn't expect the spice. What is it?"

"We don't know." Telun sounded complacent. "They won't really talk to us, except teaching Milu earth witchery. Sometimes the old lady looks at me like she wants something, but I don't think she knows any Ilyaran."

Rasim nearly said, "She does," then decided if Oyun wanted Telun to know she spoke Ilyaran, she would have told him. Instead he put another bite of cheese in his mouth, then discovered it went even better with the spicy meat than it had with the dumplings. He alternated bites and mumbled contentedly.

"I want to see you do that again," Desimi said to Milu. "When we're done eating."

"Mmhmm." When he'd finished, Milu rose and beckoned Desimi over to the side of the tent, where he cleared a space to practice earth witchery.

Kisia watched them, then leaned toward Rasim. "Think Desimi will pick it up?"

"Earthmastery? I don't know. Stone witchery, probably. He's such a strong natural sea witch, but Milu is like him with stone. I don't know if anybody who isn't, or at least, any Ilyaran who isn't, could learn to do earth witchery."

"What about you?"

"Me?" Rasim shook his head. "No. Not earth magic."

Kisia hesitated. "I saw what you did in Hongrunn. The sculptures."

"What?" Rasim's attention snapped from Desimi to her. "You what?"

"I followed you up the mountain," she said cautiously. "You knew that, because I met you up there. But when you went around the shore bend and didn't come back...I came to look. You were there with all that cold stone, concentrating, and then it started to shape itself, and I knew it was your way of..." Her mouth pinched and twisted as she tried to fight off sudden tears. "Of saying goodbye. Especially to Stone-master Lusa. You made that beautiful sculpture for her. Of her. For all of them." The tears spilled down her face and she wiped them away roughly. Rasim, his heart aching, put his arms around her and they both held on for a minute, overwhelmed by the losses and trauma of the past few months. Finally Kisia took a shuddering breath and straightened away from Rasim, wiping her nose and eyes again. "So I knew you could do it, even before you told anybody."

"I thought you might have suspected," Rasim said hoarsely. "From the way you looked all thoughtful. But you didn't say anything, and I wasn't going to say anything myself, so..."

"I thought it would make you snap closed like a clam if I did," Kisia confessed. "So I decided I'd better keep my own mouth shut until you were ready to talk about it. What's it like, using more than one magic?"

"I don't know. Sky witchery dances. It's light and bright and quick, like really clear water. I can't feel anything when I do stone witchery, though. I think if we hadn't spent all those days in the mine, with the mindkiller keeping me from using sea witchery...I think maybe I never would have learned to master stone witchery at all. It just feels empty to me, and I keep being surprised when it works. It'll be interesting to see what it feels like to you, when you learn."

"I don't know if I will. I'm already too old to be learning witchery at all, much less more than one kind."

"Do you *want* to?"

Kisia shrugged thoughtfully. "King Taishm wants me to, so I've been trying. I studied with Sunmaster Endat on the *Wafiya* on the way to the Northlands, and I've been listening to Sunmaster Arrat on the way here. But..." She cast him a quick look, as if afraid she would find him judging her, then smiled with a strange combination of defiance and apology. "According to Ilyaran tradition, I'm already doing something impossible. I started learning sea witchery at age fourteen. So I think I don't really want to learn another magic. I want to be..." She lifted her chin, more defiant now. "I want to be *good*," she said in a low, passionate voice. "I'll never be Isidri or Desimi or you, I know that. I don't have the same raw power. But I want to be *so* good that no one can ever doubt I made the right choice. That no one can even doubt that Ilyara made the *wrong* choice when it decided only orphans would learn witchery. I want them to wonder who else got left behind because of tradition, and I want them to have to change their ways going forward."

She clamped her mouth shut suddenly and hunched

in on herself, like she was afraid she'd said too much, but Rasim grinned hugely. "So you're like me, then. You don't want much."

She gave him a dirty look that dissolved into an embarrassed smile, and knocked her shoulder against his. "Not much," she agreed. "Just to change the way we do everything, forever."

"You, me, and..." Rasim glanced toward where Desimi was sitting with Milu, and fell silent to see Desi shaping an exaggerated female figure in the earth, not with magic, but just with his hands and the dirt.

Kisia followed Rasim's gaze and her mouth pursed in an amused line. "Siliaria help us if *Desimi* is going to change the world."

"Yeah, well, somebody's got to shorten our sails, right?" Rasim grinned. "Who better than Desimi?"

"Oh, I'm pretty sure he'd say nobody." Kisia yawned hugely, and Rasim realized he hadn't slept in at least a day and a half.

"Tomorrow," he said through an abrupt wave of tiredness. "Tomorrow the captain will be here and they'll get it all sorted out." Belly full, he crawled onto a pillow-heavy sleeping pad and didn't wake up again until somebody called his name in alarm.

CHAPTER EIGHT

It was hard to fall out of a bed on the ground, but Rasim managed anyway, groaning with surprise as he discovered most of him was sore. For a second he couldn't think why, and then he lay on his face, chortling tiredly into the earth. Maybe, just *maybe*, he was sore because he'd climbed a mountain, then jumped off it, then ridden a dragon and jumped off *it*, then ridden a horse for hours, then been thrown in a sweaty little tent where he threw up for half the night.

It had been a very long couple of days, and whatever was so alarming that people were shouting his name, he hoped it could wait until he'd had a very hot, full-body bath, and some more food.

Captain Nasira burst into the tent before he'd even managed to get off the floor. Her voice, pinched with aggravation, swept toward him, and he thought maybe he should just stay where he was. "How do you keep ending up in the thick of things, Journeyman, while those who should be where you are rush along behind you like a faltering tide?"

"I don't know." Rasim rolled onto his back to stare up at his captain, who looked very tall and narrow from that vantage. "If we ever get home to Ilyara, I promise I'll never do anything exciting again as long as I live."

To his surprise, Nasira chuckled. "Don't make promises you can't keep, Rasim. Ugh." The last sound came with a wrinkled nose. "I want to know what happened when you went up that mountain, journeyman, but Siliaria's fins, you need a bath first."

"When did you get here?" Rasim didn't even try to get off the ground. It wasn't comfortable, but he bet he could go back to sleep anyway.

"With the dawn. Long enough to greet Bayar's parents and eat roast lamb for breakfast." Nasira exhaled with satisfaction. "Not eating fish is one of my favorite things about coming back to land."

"I thought you liked fish." Rasim's stomach rumbled again at the idea of food and Nasira lifted her eyebrows.

"I do, but it wears on a body if it's every meal. Sounds like your own belly is telling you as much. I'll ask for bathing water to be sent. Do they bathe in tubs here? There's not much water on these steppes."

Rasim shrugged and the captain went to the door, where a translator apparently waited for her, because she spoke in Ilyaran before returning. "Buckets," she said, almost cheerfully. "We scrub with buckets. At least witchery will keep the water clean."

"They don't like casual use of witchery much," Rasim warned. "I know Bayar told us that, but I think he understated it. They've been keeping Endat and the rest of them under guard."

"Except Milu," Telun said sleepily, from their bed mat. "The old witch sniffed him and sent him to study with their own witches."

Nasira focused on the big sleepy Stonemaster journeyman. "And why is he special?"

Telun grinned sappily at her. "Born that way."

The captain tried, and failed, to contain a snort of amusement as the tent door was opened from the outside and buckets of water were brought in, along with food. Rasim couldn't decide if he wanted to scrub or eat more, but the captain went to wash, so Rasim joined Kisia and the others eating a breakfast of lamb and milk. The adults drew to one side to eat once they were clean, and the journeymen washed up afterward, all of them eyeing Nasira, Endat and Lorens as they spoke quietly with each other.

"Rasim." Nasira's voice cracked across the tent almost as soon as he finished eating. "Come tell me what happened yesterday."

He slunk over, and, under the gimlet stares of his elders, explained what had happened on the mountain and in the hours afterward, although he maybe wasn't *very* clear on the whole ritual he'd undergone in Oyun's tent. He was fairly certain the captain didn't come away with the impression he could work sun witchery, anyway. It seemed like he should let King Taishm know about that before any other adults. Partly because it had all been the king's idea to begin with, but mostly because if they didn't know, none of them could try to tell him to do things to further their own ends.

Not that he really thought Nasira had an agenda of her own, but he was less certain of Sunmaster Endat, and still couldn't help remembering how easily Prince Lorens had seemed to turn on them in Moran. But then, so had Nasira.

A year ago he'd believed adults were mostly trustworthy. Not with things like sneaking out early to the bakery for the best treats, but with the big things. He missed thinking that. It had been easier. But it wasn't just whether they could be trusted, anymore. So many of them either didn't seem to think very fast, or thought fast and then decided things were all right as they were. He didn't know how they could even live that way. There were so many things that could be better.

Nasira sighed explosively as he wrapped up his explanation. "Their—what did you call her? Spiritmaster? Sniffed all of us, too. I don't know what she learned from it."

"I don't know. She liked Kisia and I guess she recognized how strong Desimi is and she gave Sesin a *look*, but she—they—are afraid we're dangerous to their people. All of us, not just me and Kees and Desi."

"A look?"

Rasim nearly stomped his foot in aggravation. "A look. I don't know, Captain. You'd have to ask her what the look meant. Oyun, not Sesin."

"Bayar's mother called us harbingers of danger."

Nasira's eyebrows rose a little. "Harbingers is hardly a word I know in Ilyaran. I don't know how a horse clan matriarch learned it."

"Diplomatic language asks an unusual breadth of word choices of its practitioners," Endat murmured.

Nasira gave *him* a look. "This is why nobody likes Sunmasters."

Endat laughed and Prince Lorens grinned, but brought the topic back on point by saying, "Harbingers doesn't mean we're dangerous ourselves."

"From their point of view, that remains to be seen," Endat said.

Rasim, impatiently, said, "But you could say that about anybody or anything, couldn't you? Anything could be a sign of danger if you decided it was. This morning I fell out of a bed that's not even off the ground. You could say that was a warning sign of something."

"Yeah," Desimi said from where he wasn't supposed to be listening, "a sign of your clumsiness."

"Ugh." Rasim curled a lip, but mostly tried to ignore the bigger boy to appeal to Nasira. "But I'm right, aren't I? It kind of doesn't mean anything, because it *could* mean anything."

Endat regarded Rasim steadily. "Are you proposing we go tell our hosts, and I use the word advisedly because until your arrival I feel we were unquestionably captives—"

"And why is that?" Nasira demanded. "Because you rode on in a dragon?"

"Because I, we, brought Bayar back!" Rasim was

afraid the dragon might have had something to do with it, but he still didn't want to tell them about Oyun's guidance and his not-yet-retested ability to use sun witchery.

"Ah," Nasira said, like she'd forgotten, and Endat went on more or less as if she hadn't interrupted.

"Do you propose we tell our hosts that we've dismissed their concerns because a first-year journeyman has explained their portents are meaningless?"

Rasim stared at him, half a dozen increasingly rude things fighting to be said first. "Sure," he eventually said. "If that's the best you can do, go for it. But if that's the best you can do, you should probably let me talk to them, because at least I'm thirteen and being *stupid* is probably expected of me."

Lorens coughed and found somewhere else to look as Endat's eyebrows beetled down. Anger flushed through Rasim and he clenched his fists, suddenly prepared to have a real argument with the Sunmaster if he pushed it. Twice, Endat took a breath like he'd speak, then paused as if reconsidering, and ended up with his mouth as pinched as his eyebrows. "You are a remarkably arrogant child," he finally said, and Rasim flung his hands upward in expressive outrage.

"Yeah, but I'm *right*. If that's the best you can do, it's amazing Ilyara hasn't been invaded or crushed by people who've met our diplomats and think we're too stupid to drink water instead of drown in it! Sunmasters have been taking over the palace step by step for most of Guildmaster Isidri's life, but either the royal family is really dumb or you're a terrible example of your guild. For a while there I thought you were maybe actually dangerous, but right now I wonder if your whole stupid guild is just really lucky!"

Chest heaving and breath coming in short bursts, Rasim fell silent and realized nearly everyone, including the guards at their tent door, was staring at him in horrified astonishment. Desimi's eyes were so wide he looked almost impressed, and Sesin had a hand pressed over her mouth. Endat's expression was one of controlled anger, and Lorens still studiously looked the other way as Nasira waited with a thunderous gaze to be sure Rasim had nothing more to say.

Kisia, off to the side, behind Nasira, where the captain couldn't see her, grinned like a hyena.

"Are you quite finished, Journeyman?" Nasira's voice was as cool as Rasim had ever heard it, and he had heard her icy with rage, all directed at him, in the past.

For a heartbeat, for more than a heartbeat, he seriously considered *not* being finished. He was fairly certain Bayar's parents and the old shaman both rather liked him. He could go talk to them without yelling or telling them they were stupid, and try to figure out if Bayar's kidnapping came from the same place that the Ilyaran fire or the poisoned lake in the Northlands had. He could try to do all of that himself. Maybe he could even succeed.

He could almost hear the question like he was outside himself, though: And then what? Once he had gone off to have an opinion at the King Horse and Great Mare, then what? He was still a journeyman, unexpectedly powerful in a witchery sense but not at all powerful politically. He couldn't make binding treaties or make any promises on the part of his king. Solving the question of who'd taken Bayar might warm the Shenryalan people to him, but that wouldn't do him any good if Nasira decided to make him walk home, and judging from the set of her jaw, she might.

Rasim muttered, "Yes, Captain," and dropped his gaze to the tent floor, because at least there, he couldn't be accused of glaring at anyone.

"I believe we will continue this discussion later. Master Endat, my apologies, and the apologies of the Seamasters' Guild, for our ill-mannered journeyman. Steps," Nasira said furiously, "will be taken."

Every word dripped cold down Rasim's spine. Endat's response was cool and polite, all too clearly angry and careful not to direct that anger at Nasira. "Thank you, Captain. Now, I'm afraid we inept adults had best tend to our duties, and speak with the Shenryalan leaders." With a gesture of overstated courtesy, he offered Nasira his elbow, and Nasira, who was the last person in the world Rasim could imagine doing this, took it. They exited together in a show of distressing solidarity, with Prince Lorens in their wake.

Everyone else gathered in the tent waited until they were absolutely certain the masters were out of earshot. Then a cacophony arose, incredulous voices expressing—mostly—horror and dismay. Pynda actually shoved her way past the others to get in Rasim's face, her dark eyes snapping with anger. "Is that really what you think of Sunmasters, Rasim? Is that what you think of me? Of Daka, who *died* because of your schemes? You think we're stupid and greedy and dangerous to ourselves? I'll show you who's *dangerous*, you nasty little sea slug—" He thought she might have lit her very fists on fire if she could have, but almost every sun witch needed a spark to build their witchery around.

Even so, everyone else saw the threat clearly enough that before Rasim could respond, Telun let out a hoarse shout. Suddenly he and Milu were there, pulling the young woman away from Rasim. Sesin got between them, too, and a whole new bout of shouting started as Desimi and Kisia closed in on Rasim.

Desimi's eyes were still wide. "If that's what you're like when you get mad, no wonder you try not to, Sunburn. I've never heard you like that."

"Except when he yelled at you yesterday." Kisia hadn't lost her broad grin. "That was amazing, Rasi."

"That was stupid," Rasim whispered.

"Maybe, but it was amazing. Imagine if anybody had stood up to the Sunmasters like that any time in the last eighty years or so. Maybe Ilyara wouldn't be in this mess. Maybe Queen Annaken and her baby wouldn't have died in the fire, if the Sunmasters hadn't been in control when it happened. They're *Sunmasters.* They should have been able to stop it before it got out of control like that. Maybe King Laishn wouldn't have died of a broken heart a couple months later. Maybe—"

"Maybe Captain Nasira is going to make me swim home," Rasim said in a small voice. "Maybe they needed to hear it, but maybe I was right when I yelled at

Desimi yesterday about not making decisions when you're angry."

Desimi rolled his eyes. "You make smart decisions all the time. Maybe sometimes yelling is a smart decision, too, and you just can't see it yet. In the meantime..." He cast a glance at the tent door, then slid a wicked smile at Rasim and Kisia. "The guards are gone."

Rasim said, "The captain would kill me," instantly, but Kisia grabbed his elbow.

"First, she can't kill you if she can't find you, and second, if she's already mad enough to kill you, it's not like she can get any madder, right?"

"You know what? I think you're right." Rasim gave her a wild-eyed grin, and the three of them bolted from the tent.

CHAPTER NINE

A shout of protest went up as they raced outside. Rasim thought it was mostly Sesin, dismayed at being left behind, but a handful of Shenryalans saw them make their escape, and had differing reactions. A couple chased them like they'd send them back inside, and a few more grinned and cheered them on. Desimi ducked sideways, behind a smaller tent than the ones they'd been in so far. A minute later they were well lost in the spirals and gathered people.

Nearly all of them cast curious glances at the three Ilyaran journeymen, who looked nothing at all like the Shenryalans around them. Bayar's people were mostly paler and more golden of skin than Ilyarans. Even Rasim, who wasn't as dark as Kisia or Desimi, was distinctly browner than the people around them, and his hair, straight by Ilyaran standards, was full of curves and waves compared to the Shenryalans. Like Kisia and Desimi, though, everyone around them had brown or black eyes, and grins that were indistinguishable from anyone else's, all the world over.

A small horde of children rushed toward them, tripping and shouting with excitement to meet the strangers. Rasim laughed, crouched to greet them, and was bowled over by a couple of especially enthusiastic little ones who didn't have quite enough control to stop in time. They were dressed more warmly than the Ilyarans, in brightly-dyed coats with pale seams and dramatic shoulder swoops. Their red cheeks shone under fur-lined hats, although some of them were warm enough that when they pulled the hats off to try them on Rasim, their hair stuck to their foreheads in soft sweaty lines.

One of the bigger children, old enough to understand that hiding from adults was fun, grabbed Kisia's hand and started tugging. A few of them cast Desimi slightly nervous looks, because he was so much larger than they were, but within moments they'd pulled all three journeymen deep into the camp. Their clear intent was to show the strangers things they thought were important—dogs, a swing set up between two tents, someone's younger sibling—with a particular reverence for the sturdy little horses that were gathered loosely throughout the spirals.

Adults greeted them with amusement and sometimes offered drinks or a taste of something from over an open fire. One or two, studying them openly, said, "Sorcerer-child?" in expectation, leaving Rasim and the other journeymen to exchange glances.

"We all are," Rasim said uncertainly. "We all work water sorcery."

Interested faces crowded closer, mugs of water or milk or an alcoholic-smelling amber drink being offered. Rasim wasn't sure they should, but Desimi, cheerfully confident, spun water upward, making it dance between the mugs and cups. Awed cries rose around them, and more people came to see the magic on display. Rasim whispered, "I thought Shenryalans didn't trust witchery," to Kisia, who shrugged, smiling as she watched Desimi.

"Bayar says they don't, but they obviously know we're witches, and Shenryalans don't have water witchery. Maybe it's all right because it's foreign. Or maybe it's all right because Bayar has come home." She shrugged, then caught her breath as a woman placed a brightly-dyed hat into her hands. It had rows of alternating-color bead work and braids of dyed hair that Rasim thought might be horse hair, and looked like it had taken a very long time to make. It fit her snugly, and the woman who'd offered it beamed like she'd made it for Kisia herself.

The gift seemed to unlock a wave of similar impulses in others around them. A man even broader across the shoulder than Desimi sized him up, then produced one of the beautifully-made patchwork coats, full of color and rough seams, and insisted Desimi put it on.

It fit him well and its long dark red side patches somehow made him look taller and more slender than he was. The man wrapped a long, bright yellow sash around Desimi's waist, folded his arms in tremendous satisfaction, and spoke in rapid Shenryalan. Rasim understood almost none of it, but he understood the sentiment. Kisia clearly understood more, and whispered, "It's in thanks for saving Bayar." Out loud, she said, "But Rasim—" and Rasim kicked her ankle. She hissed, "But you *are* the one who rescued him!"

Rasim shook his head. "Doesn't matter. We were all part of it and the coat wouldn't fit me and Desimi's more impressive-looking than I am anyway."

Desimi, after several attempts at refusal that both seemed to please the man and make him increasingly adamant, finally said, "Thank you," in awkward Shenryalan, and an actual cheer rose around them. Someone dropped a fur-lined hat on Rasim's head, and he started sweating as much as the little ones were. He had hardly anything he could offer in exchange, but the giver seemed delighted when Rasim uncertainly loosened his tunic's belt and placed it in their hands.

They spent hours wandering the camp, trading what little they had with the Shenryalans, until the only things they had left of their Ilyaran garb were the pouches that they each carried a small carving of Siliaria in. Someone tried bargaining for Rasim's, and he grinned ruefully and shook his head. "This is our goddess. Like King Horse," he said as clearly as he could in their language. "We can't trade her away."

There was some surprise over their goddess being so small, but Rasim couldn't explain it any better, and Kisia, with her better command of the language, didn't improve things. Eventually she was fairly certain the

Shenryalans thought maybe the peculiar outsiders put all their little carvings together to make a big god, which Rasim had to admit seemed as likely as anything. They didn't try to trade for the carvings after that, though, so it appeared enough understanding had been reached.

All three of them were exhausted and giggling by the time they found their way back to the central tent. A grim-faced guard stepped inside, obviously informing them that their wayward journeymen had returned, because Nasira exited in a jaw-clenched towering fury that struck Rasim as so funny that he had to chew on his inner cheek to keep from laughing. Kisia clutched his elbow as the captain began yelling at them, and when he glanced at her, her entire face was contorted into an attempt at looking guilty, but mostly looked like she had to empty her bladder. Desimi, on Kisia's other side, studied the ground very hard, and when Nasira's tirade came around to demanding what they thought they'd been doing, the big journeyman looked at her without a trace of remorse.

"Improving Ilyaran relations with Shenryal, Captain."

Nasira came up short, stared first at Desimi, then at the other two, and visibly realized not one of them felt any regret at running away for most of the day. A single drop of cool dread started to form in Rasim's stomach as he started to wonder what kind of punishment they'd earned for themselves, but the Great Mare's pleasant voice rose from the tent, inviting not just Nasira, but the journeymen in as well. Nasira's nostrils flared, but she shortened the sails of her temper and gestured them in with a sharp motion.

The foreigners were grouped together near the door, and a path the width of Bikat and Irlin's thrones was cleared down the center. Rasim blinked, his eyes adjusting to the dimmer light, then blinked again as he realized that aside from his own people and their companions, the tent was segregated. Men sat on one side, women on the other, although Irlin's throne was on the male side, and Bikat's, on the women's. On both sides, the ages of those gathered ranged from close to Rasim's own, to the obviously-ancient Oyun, whose age and status earned her a chair heaped with furs and pillows. She sat at Bikat's side, and across from her, in the men's half of the tent, Bayar sat beside his mother in a chair built to suit his particular stature.

Rasim slowed as he entered, partly because of the great heat—a small, carefully tended fire sat in the center wheel, and managed to stifle the tent—and partly because no council he'd ever seen had been so divided between men and women. It made the Shenryalan's way of life seem suddenly and distinctly *different* in a way he hadn't expected, and he took a moment, trying to adjust to it.

It was also *very* formal and solemn. A trio of sweaty, giggling Ilyaran journeymen shouldn't be there under any circumstances. He and the other two exchanged nervous glances, their laughter falling away as they edged forward when Irlin beckoned.

Unlike their captain, the Shenryalan Great Mare appeared pleased with their state, examining their new clothes with amusement. "That is a very excellent coat, Journeyman Desimi. One of our finest makers has gifted that to you."

Desimi cast Rasim a panicked look, then mustered a smile for Irlin. "Thank you. I wish I had something better to give them in return than my tunic."

"I am sure they are quite pleased with the trade," Irlin replied with genuine serenity. "Outsiders are rarely seen in the tribes, and more rarely welcomed, but you...Waifians?" she enquired with a lifted eyebrow. "Those who sail on the *Wafiya?*"

A grin split Desimi's face. "We'd just call ourselves Ilyarans, ma'am, but Waifians is good."

"But you are not all Ilyarans," she pointed out, and Rasim had to sneak a glance at the group of non-Shenryalans who sat together near the door.

They were mostly Ilyaran, it was true, but Nikki, the old Moranese beggar woman who had cast her lot with theirs when the city fell, was among them. So was Prince Lorens, and Lars, although he and Endat hadn't actually sailed to Shenryal on the *Wafiya.* But Karluk, the Ilyaran Skymaster who had helped Rasim escape the Moranese arena and earned his own freedom by doing so, was there too, as was his wife, who had also been enslaved. Their children must be nearby, Rasim thought, although they were even younger than the journeymen, and probably didn't belong in the great tent right now.

There were several other former slaves, not all Ilyaran, who had escaped to the Wafiya when Moran had fallen, and a few of the Northerners who'd sailed with Endat were there, too. All in all, they were a more diverse crew than Rasim was used to seeing on the *Wafiya*, but he still liked the idea of them all being Waifians. Without meaning to, he said, "If being Waifians is what's made us welcome here, then it's worth it. Everyone was kind to us today, and they were interested in Desimi's witchery," then winced under the weight of Captain Nasira's glare.

Irlin, though, smiled again. "So we have heard. Rumor spreads quickly through this camp, sorcerer-child," she said to his surprise. "Rumor of sorcery being used spreads more quickly than most. But today, with Bayar's return, even the most conservative of our people do not look fearfully on Ilyaran water magic, or on outsiders. And now you have the look of our own people—"

She had more to say, but first the Ilyaran group, and then the larger gathering in the tent laughed as the translator's quick words caught up to them. Desimi patted his chest, then briefly curled his fingers around the necklace he hadn't taken off since King Taishm had given it to him months earlier. For an instant, Rasim had a flash of envy, or something close to it. The bigger boy looked so confident and certain of himself, like wearing another culture's clothes and bearing a mark of appreciation from the king suited him unexpectedly well.

The moment faded as quickly as it had come, an equally strange sense of relief sweeping over Rasim. Having someone else be the center of attention for a while was exactly what he wanted. Now all they needed to do was figure out who'd kidnapped Bayar, determine whether Shenryal was in danger as a whole, and go home to fight off the Moranese army that was probably bearing down on Ilyara.

He said, "Oh, well, if that's all," far enough under his breath to not distract Irlin, whose smile stayed in place as she said, "Very well, you have *something* of the look of our people," to the dark brown boy with his curly short hair and Shenryalan clothes. "We would like to make a gift of more of our garb to you. To all of you," she said, raising her eyes to the rest of their group. "Tonight is the beginning of our Great Gathering, where all five of our tribes come together to share the journeys we've taken through the Great Spiral over the past hand-span of years. We had not," she said solemnly, "expected to find joy in our gathering, this year. We had imagined we would gather to ask our shamans for forgiveness for what must be done, and that we would ride to the east to take back, or avenge, our lost son."

As she spoke, several people rose from around the tent, carrying bundles of folded clothes that they brought to the foreigners who sat together. Nasira was given hers first, and shook open a beautiful, loose-fitted tunic that would fall to her shins, and a contrasting sash like the one Desimi had been given. There was a plainer pair of trousers with them, but the long tunic was clearly the highlight of the gift. The captain stood with the richly dyed fabric in her hands, her expression stunned and awed, before she gathered the clothes against her chest and bowed toward first the woman who'd brought it to her, and then to the Shenryalan leaders.

"Now we have not only Bayar's return to celebrate," Bikat said, taking up where Irlin left off, "but a long-missing tribesman to welcome home. We would like you to be part of our celebrations, and to accept these clothes as a measure of our gratitude."

Nasira, tight-voiced in a very different way than she'd been while yelling at her errant journeymen, bowed again. "We would be honored, King Horse. We thank you, Great Mare. We thank all of you, whose craftsmanship has gone into these gifts. We could never repay you."

"You already have." Bikat made a dismissive motion that was also somehow polite, and the Waifians were escorted from the central tent before Rasim even realized that was what the gesture meant.

He hadn't thought they'd been in the tent all that long, but the sun was on the horizon now, and there were clearings where there hadn't been, before. People in gorgeous clothes, some as simple but beautiful as the tunic Nasira had been given, and others layered with those tunics beneath coats like Desimi's, were gathering around bonfires that Rasim swore hadn't been there before. The smell of roasting meat rose in the air, making Rasim's mouth water and his stomach growl, even though they'd been snacking all day.

Desimi eyed one of the bonfires and the meat-roasting spits nearby like he might make a run for it, but Nasira somehow knew. "Try it and you'll spend the rest of your life cleaning keels with your teeth."

The threat might have been over-the-top, but Nasira's tone brooked no arguments. Everyone—journeymen, former slaves, Northerners and all—went into their tent to change into the clothes they'd been given, and not very much later, Rasim emerged with Kisia and Desimi, feeling both self-conscious and pleased with his appearance. They'd given him green to wear, with a bold sky-colored sash and undyed trousers thick enough to keep the evening's chill away. Desimi had his coat and a new tunic beneath it in the same red as the side patches of the coat, but Kisia's clothes were extraordinary.

A Shenryalan woman had come into dress her, and now she wore robes of gold and white embroidered with red, with pictures of horses and stars running through the embroidery. Her short hair was oiled so it gleamed, and tiny tendrils of curls had been pulled down in front of her ears. Golden paint glittered along her cheekbones, and her eyes were painted with white and red and gold so they looked enormous in the setting sun's light. Rasim had never seen her in makeup before, although at home, girls and boys alike only a little older than they were began to wear it, especially at the festivals. It made her look older, and even prettier than usual. The robes had a high collar that brushed her jaw, and she had golden loops dangling from her ears.

He hardly understood why she was so magnificently dressed until they rounded the spiral leading to the central tent. Irlin and Bikat's thrones had been moved outside and now sat framed against the deep orange backdrop of the tent door. The Great Mare and King Horse were splendidly dressed and smiling, but Bayar, who was beautiful to begin with, wore robes that matched Kisia's, with the colors reversed. Where Kisia's were mostly gold, Bayar's were white, with the same red embroidery. His hair was loose and long and shining with braids that held spirals of gold and scarlet, and his face was painted with gold and black and cream that brought him beyond beauty into ethereal grace. It seemed like it had to be on purpose, and from the smile that lit Bayar's face when he saw Kisia, Rasim knew it was. His stomach lurched and he smiled uncertainly, wondering how he hadn't noticed how much time they'd spent together on the *Wafiya*, and then a commotion pulled his attention away.

The laughing, dancing crowd parted to make a pathway. Two old women in gold and red escorted an even older man, who wore grey and white embroidered with blue mountains. Five or six younger women walked behind them, and behind *them* came more than a dozen children, some older than Rasim, others barely toddling. One of the younger women carried a well-swaddled baby in her arms. The old man's cheeks glowed red with pride and joy beneath a warm white fur hat, and for all his obvious age, he walked strong and tall. It wasn't until the second look that Rasim realized the two oldest women favored him, their Northern father. His breath caught, and Kisia clapped a hand over her mouth.

Kif's daughters were not just adults in the prime of their own power, but grandmothers themselves, as proud and joyful to be reunited with their father as he was. That would be enough, Rasim thought. That would be enough for any father, but to find himself the grandfather of many, and the great-grandfather of so many more, had to fill a place in the old man's heart that had been hollowed out upon his exile, decades ago. Rasim, smiling so widely it hurt, wiped tears away, and felt Kisia's hand snake into his and squeeze.

The three oldest of them, Kif and his daughters, walked together, solemnly, to Irlin and Bikat's thrones, while the younger people stopped at the outer edges of the gathered group. Irlin gave them all a fond smile, then nodded. Kif turned to Rasim, and, seeing Rasim's tears, had to wipe at his own watery blue eyes.

"You found your family," Rasim whispered in Kif's own language. "By Siliaria's grace, you found them. I'm so glad, Kif."

The old man chuckled gruffly. "Must've been her grace, if that's what dumped you on our shores and started all this nonsense. I'd have never come back, without you," he said more quietly. "I'd have never known my daughters, or theirs. This old Northerner owes you, Ilyaran."

"No." Rasim shook his head, trying to speak around a tight throat. "No, you don't owe me anything, Kif. I'm happy you found your family. Does that mean—is your exile lifted?"

"Our mother's sisters are no more," said one of his daughters, carefully, in the Northern tongue. "The banishing ended with their deaths. Now Father is with us again, and the lost years melt away like snow in sunshine."

Bikat rose, speaking in the Northern tongue as well. "We learned, from the surprise of those who came with him, that this outlander who loved one of our own took our secrets with him when he left, and kept them as close to his heart as he kept the memories of his daughters. We do not boast of our sorcery, and to speak of it to outsiders is to betray the Shenryalan people. This outlander has known the truth all these long years and told no one, even, I think, when that knowledge would have been prized by his mothers. Tonight, as our Great Gathering begins, I ask all the tribes of Shenryal to speak his name to the King Horse, and make him one of us in the endless spiral. He is Kif to you, but to us he will be *Nedet Alū* , Grandfather Winter. Grandfather, let us welcome you home."

CHAPTER TEN

Someone pressed a brilliant orange drink that smelled of fruit and alcohol into Rasim's hands soon after that. He sipped it, coughed, and handed it to the celebrant next to him, who drank it with a gesture of thanks. Even without alcohol, the night spun into something like a story, with dancing and singing, all volume and joy with very little understanding on Rasim's part. He danced with Kisia, and then Sesin, and then with several Shenryalan girls, including the pretty one whose mother had glared at her for smiling at him the day before. Then somehow he was dancing with Captain Nasira, whose short black hair stuck to the sides of her face with the effort and heat of the evening.

That was how everyone, whether Ilyaran or Shenryalan or Northern or something else entirely, looked: bright-eyed and sweaty and joyful, as if they needed a moment of rest and laughter more than anything else. He bowed to his captain as they found new dance partners, and for a moment, thought she even forgot she'd been mad at them. Eventually, exhausted, Rasim moved to the side of the dancing, watching people move through firelight and a drumbeat that felt so strong it seemed like the air jumped with it. Bayar and Kisia were still dancing, flashes of gold and white and red in the night. Rasim's stomach hurt, even though he thought he'd eaten enough. Maybe he needed more, though.

He got up and made his way through the crowds, trying to be awake and suspicious of mind, as if someone would show themselves as a great evil while they danced. He found Sunmaster Endat sleeping peacefully under a fur somebody had thrown over him, and couldn't decide if he was more envious or astonished that the ambassador could sleep through all the noise.

More food didn't do much to settle his stomach, but cold water helped him stay awake as he wandered through the dances and conversations that he couldn't understand. Prince Lorens was deep in conversation with Bayar's mother, who looked faintly impatient, to Rasim's eyes. Maybe she wanted to be dancing. He took the next flask of orange drink that was offered to him and brought it to Lorens, shouting, "You look too serious, your highness! Drink this and go ask Kisia to dance!"

"Last I saw she was dancing with Bayar," Lorens said as he took the drink with a grin. Rasim thought that was exactly why Lorens should go dance with her.

He frowned at his feet. Wanting Lorens to go dance

with Kisia because she was dancing with Bayar didn't make any sense. Still, the Northern prince waved his newly-acquired drink and said, "Forgive me, Great Mare, I'm not celebrating well enough, and dragging you down with me. I shall amend the error of my ways." He left with a bow, and Irlin turned a curious look on Rasim.

"You did that on purpose, sorcerer-child."

"You looked like you were being too polite to tell him to go jump in the harbor," Rasim said, more honestly than diplomatically.

Irlin laughed. "And perhaps I was. But surely you are too serious. A young man at such a celebration should be enjoying himself, not looking out for his friend's mother."

"I am enjoying myself, but I thought you should be too." Rasim lifted his chin like he could point to Kif among the crowd. "This doesn't happen very often, does it? Welcoming an outsider to your tribes?"

"Very rarely indeed," Irlin agreed solemnly. "Not in my lifetime, and I do not myself recall Grandfather Winter's banishment. Oyun does, but Oyun, I think, is eternal."

Rasim smiled. "Our Guildmaster is like that. Well, former Guildmaster. She retired. But we still call her Guildmaster. Anyway, she's a hundred and four years old and I think the guild would crumble if anything happened to her."

"Your guilds sound very like our clans, I think," Irlin murmured. "All part of the same great curve of the spiral, but fiercely independent and proud of our differences. But you are not plagued with dragons, in your land."

"No! Is that something that happens a lot here?" Guilt swam over Rasim, but Irlin chuckled and shook her head reassuringly. That didn't help much, because it suggested the dragon really *did* have something to do with Rasim specifically, though.

"We have legends, as I think most peoples must. Ancient legend, from before Oyun's grandmothers' time. Have you no such myths?"

"That's what the oldest Northerners say about them having magic," Rasim said, looking for Kif again. "That they did, in their grandmothers' grandmothers' time. But you have magic."

"We do. Not as much as Golden Ilyara, and it is kept more closely to our hearts. The shamans search the hearts of every child in their fifth year. Some are set on the shaman's path, and some few others are given sorcerous training. Earth, air, and wood. Those are the domains of our sorcery."

"Why did you let Milu study with your earth witches when everybody else got locked up?"

"Oyun sensed imbalance in him," Irlin replied gravely. "As she did in you, sorcerer-child. Sorcerous imbalance is dangerous, distressing the very arms of the spiral itself, and so Milu's training is of great importance. In the large stone sorcerer, she sensed long-sleeping air magic, but no imbalance. The air god who might have guided him through the Great Spiral slumbers now, at peace as he works his little stone sorcery."

Rasim's eyebrows shot upward. "Telun? Telun might have been a skymaster? I wonder if he can learn it now, even though he's really old!"

Laughter creased Irlin's eyes. "Telun is certainly young enough to be my son. I wonder how ancient you must think me."

Heat coursed through Rasim's face. "Old to learn new witchery, I mean. Everyone in Ilyara thinks only little kids can learn it. Kisia capsized *that* ship by joining the Seamasters' Guild of her own choice at fourteen and starting to learn magic, but Telun's probably ten years older than I am. I'll have to tell Skymaster Arrat about his sleeping sky witchery, though. Maybe he can wake it up." He started looking around as if he'd see the master sky witch, although Arrat had remained on board the *Wafiya* with most of its crew.

"Speak to Oyun first," Irlin said so sternly that a chill wrapped around Rasim's lungs. "Learn whether a new sorcery will unbalance him, and do not try without her assistance if she believes it will."

"Has she been helping Milu? Did he have to do that awful sweat tent thing?"

He could tell some of Irlin's sternness faded from the softening in her eyes, but her voice still sounded quite forbidding. "That is for Milu or Oyun alone to tell you. It is shaman's business, not mine." Then she tipped her head, and more gently, said, "I believe he was less imbalanced than you, Rasim. Earth and stone sorcery both rose in him naturally, but only one was nurtured. The other only needed tending to, to balance his spirit."

Rasim nodded. "That makes sense, I think. From what Oyun said about my witchery, that makes sense." A vague thought crossed his mind and he tried to put it in words, not sure he was succeeding as he asked, "Does anyone here ever want to be taught sorcery and not get to learn it?"

"Does anyone in Ilyara?"

"Well..." He blinked up at the Great Mare, taken aback by the thought. "Kisia and I were kind of talking about that. It's only orphans who study witchery at home, and I don't know if there are any, or many, people with families who might want to. Kisia's like a flagship, leading the fleet where it needs to go. She wants to be able to lead others to the guilds, if that's what they want. But you do it differently here."

"We are a herd people," Irlin said after a moment, with a brief, thoughtful smile. "We see our duties as to our families, our tribes, and our clans. Very few are chosen for the shaman's or sorcerer's paths, and most of them, I think, are chosen too young to have thought of much beyond being riders. It is, I think, more likely to dream of being the Great Mare or the King Horse, than to dream of being a sorcerer, in Shenryal. The Mare is a political posi-tion, and the Horse, her worthy consort. Those can be maneuvered toward in a way a shaman's role cannot be."

"In other words, you don't think so."

Irlin inclined her head, then lifted it to watch the dancers and the fires they danced around, their light and shadows ever-changing on her face. "I don't think so. But." She took a deep breath. "I believe I see where your thoughts ride, sorcerer-child. Perhaps there are those who covet sorcerous power, and have found a way to learn. Perhaps the danger from afar is, as you suggested, closer than we think." She pursed her lips and glanced down at him. "Your mother-captain says you cause trouble wherever you go. This is how. By making people think of questions they may prefer not to learn the answers to."

It was *not* a question. Rasim shrugged and fixed his gaze on the ground. "I don't mean to."

"You would have been a shaman, in Shenryal." To his utter surprise, Irlin leaned over and kissed Rasim's forehead. "Go enjoy the night, sorcerer-child. I will speak with my husband, and we will think on what to do with these thoughts."

"Thinking on thoughts sounds like something I would do." Rasim smiled and went back into the weaving, laughing, dancing crowd. The numbers of people had thinned out somewhat, but there were still a lot of them, often dancing so close to the bonfires Rasim didn't know how their clothes didn't catch on fire. If Lorens had gone to dance with Kisia, there was no evidence of it: she was with Bayar, the two of them sitting near a smaller fire and resting, their heads ducked close together as they talked. He caught a glimpse of the pretty girl he'd danced with earlier watching them, and had a funny feeling his own expression looked a lot like hers. Not sad or angry, exactly, but still a little dismayed somehow.

She looked away from the quietly chatting couple and met Rasim's eyes. A smile ran across her face and she waved, but turned and went into a nearby tent rather than coming over. Her mother, whose stern face didn't seem to be able to crack a smile, followed her. So did two or three other women with similarly stern faces. Rasim wondered if the smiling girl would grow up to look as strict as the rest of her family.

Prince Lorens reappeared without the orange drink in his hand anymore, and looking rather worse for the wear. He bounced off a couple of Shenryalans whose patient glances were underlined with a warning that he'd better be more careful, and Rasim could briefly hear his apology, shouted even over the sound of the celebration. The crowd parted to let Lorens through, and Rasim saw Desimi with his arm around a girl he thought might be one of Kif's grand-daughters.

Rasim couldn't help grinning. That would be a good thing to tease Desi about later. People swirled around him, cutting off his view, but he was still grinning as he worked his way toward Kisia and Bayar. There were so many faces around him, people he thought he almost recognized from the meeting in the big tent earlier, some who smiled at him and others who scowled, and more who didn't seem to notice him at all. None of them looked particularly like hidden sorcerers, but then, Rasim couldn't imagine what that would look like. *He* didn't look like he could use four different kinds of witchery. Desimi looked like he could, maybe, but Rasim was still small and unobtrusive, and would go forever unnoticed if he would just stop making trouble.

But maybe that's what a good secret sorcerer would be, too. Nobody. Someone easy to overlook. Rasim gradually stopped trying to make his way through the crush of people and just watched them, feeling a little distant from the chaos around him. There was no way to *tell* who could use magic, just by looking at them.

Not unless you gave them the mindkiller drug, and ordered them to use their power.

Except that was stupid, because even if they had whole mountains of the stuff, they could hardly make every single person in Shenryal take it. Those who volunteered to would probably be the least likely suspects, and those who refused, well, Rasim couldn't imagine how he would even try to round them up.

He would have to think of a better solution. Brows furrowed in thought, he edged through the crowd again, until he got to Kisia and Bayar, who looked up with bright eyes. Bayar said, "Something troubles you, Rasim?" but Kisia gave a huge raspberry of exasperation and stood up to smack him.

"It's a *party*, Rasi. Stop thinking so much! Ow." She winced, rubbing at her side like her robes had cut into her ribs. "I'm all wrapped up under this robe. I don't know why, it's not like anybody can even see it. Ow." She pulled a bit of pin out of the robes and cast it away with another wince. "They forgot some of the fasteners, I guess. Why aren't you having fun?"

"I am having fun! I'm just thinking a lot."

"That's not *fun*." Kisia pulled Bayar to his feet, and

he winced too, then made a show of wiggling like he was shaking out sore muscles.

"We've sat too long after dancing," he said solemnly. "Any Shenryalan child knows not to make such a mistake after a long ride. I embarrass my people."

"Probably not," Rasim said with a little smile. "You two look beautiful, you know."

Bayar bowed and Kisia dimpled, then frowned. "I don't feel so well." Her voice had gone strangely thin and distant, like it was being carried a long way on the wind. "Rasi, I don't feel so well."

"Kees?" Rasim reached for her, just in time to watch her eyes roll back and for her to fall in a rush of gold and crimson robes.

CHAPTER ELEVEN

R asim surged to catch Kisia and realized Bayar was falling, too. He tried to catch them both and failed, although he mostly managed to get under Kisia, whose weight knocked him down, as well. His head bounced off the hard earth, but hers bounced off his chest, which seemed better. He rolled over, pushing her off him, and put his head to her chest, trying to hear a heartbeat.

He couldn't hear one, but he felt her shallow breath on his hair. "Sesin!" He put sky witchery into his voice and roared, silencing the entire celebration. "*Sesin!* Where's Sesin? I need a healer!"

Someone barked an answer, and suddenly old Oyun was there. She seized Bayar's head, sniffed his hair, and spat, her hands searching his torso until she came up with a dart. "*Hinzjha.*"

Very nearby, Irlin made a terrible sound, like a scream that couldn't be voiced. It tore at her throat and shook through her, as if a lifetime of being the Great

Mare couldn't allow her to also be a frightened mother. Rasim's thoughts flew at the word Oyun had used, taking it apart for meaning. She'd called Missio's power-boosting drug *delzjha,* wisdom-slayer, and *hin* meant many things. It was part of the word that meant the great spiral, part of the word that meant *life,* part of the word that meant *horse.*

His stomach twisted. Any of those were enough to tell him what the drug did. Spiral-slayer, life-slayer, horse-slayer; in the clans, they were all among the worst evils that could be committed. Kisia and Bayar had been poisoned, and he'd stood there and watched it happened without even realizing it.

Oyun had forgotten him already. She gathered Bayar in her own arms, a nearly impossible task, and snarled and bit at those who tried to help. They fell back, giving her space, and the ancient, gnarled shaman somehow *ran* to her tent, Bayar in her arms. Rasim knew she would bring him to the little spirit-walking tent within her own larger space, and also knew that whatever magic she had, if she could spend it on a life, it would be spent on the King Horse's son, and not on the Ilyaran girl who had only just come to Shenryal.

"*Sesin?*" He shouted with sky witchery again, watching people flinch and stare in awe at the vast sound. "Sesin, please, Kisia's been poisoned, I need your help, I need—"

A rush of skymastery reached for him in turn, as Karluk, the formerly enslaved sky witch, spoke to him. "She's on her way, Rasim. We went to watch horse races at the edge of the camp. I'll give you her voice."

Sesin spoke in Rasim's ear almost instantly, sharp with worry. "What kind of poison, Rasim? If I talk you through it can you purge her system?"

"I don't know! They call it life-slayer and Bayar's sick with it too and his mother thinks he's going to die."

Sesin swore. "Can you find someone who speaks Ilyaran and knows how it acts? What can I do from here?"

Rasim looked up frantically, searching the suddenly-quiet gathering. Irlin was gone, probably with Oyun and Bayar. Bikat stood between Rasim and Oyun's tent, holding himself as if only the need to remain calm for his people kept him from being at his son's side. "Bikat? Bikat, please, can you tell me how the poison works?"

The King Horse focused on him, his gaze almost relieved. Maybe having something to do, however little, was of some help to him. "It sets the guts against each other, twisting like a nest of poison snakes. Then it crawls to the heart, setting it afire, and finally to the mind, where it takes memory and speech from those few who survive it. They are forever bent in body and spirit, those who live." Bikat's deep voice sounded hollow, as if it had been dropped into a terrible bleak space from which it could never return.

"Did she drink it?" Sesin demanded.

"No. No, it was a dart. A needle."

"Ask if it matters whether it's eaten or injected."

Rasim did, and Bikat shook his head. "It is always the same, the belly, the heart, the mind."

Sesin cursed again when Rasim told her. "I don't

know, Rasim. I don't know what to do. How long does it take to kill someone?"

He asked Bikat, and echoed his answer of, "A few hours."

"All right." Sesin's voice became determined. "Make her purge, Rasim. Force the water out of her belly so she throws up. Out of her bowels, too, if you can. Make her drink more water, if you can. And…" She made a helpless noise. "And clean her blood."

"I don't know how! I can't do that, Sesin! I don't feel the body the way you do! The way Kisia does!"

"Try." The healer's voice went even flatter. "Try, Rasim. We'll be there soon."

Rasim whispered, "Please hurry," and turned his attention to Kisia. "I'm sorry." He rolled her on her belly and sent water witchery to churn the bile in her stomach, forcing it upward. Stinking liquid splashed out of her mouth all over the ground, and she woke up for a few seconds, hacking and spitting.

"Sesin's coming," Rasim said. "Hang on. *Desimi!*" He threw the name into the air, asking witchery to carry it to the other journeyman's ears, and started to strip Kisia's magnificent robes off her. Someone yelled an objection and he snarled, "Unless you want dung all over this stuff, you should help." He twisted magic through Kisia's belly again, pushing more bile out, and threw the robes to the side as soon as he could.

She hadn't been kidding about being all wrapped up beneath them. Deep orange silk bound her from her armpits all the way to her hips, so snugly he didn't know how she'd sat in it. A flowing skirt fell from the wrappings' lower edge, and Rasim was about to rip the whole thing off when the pretty young woman who had watched Bayar put her hand on top of his. He froze. She reached, did *something* that seemed magical at the top of the wrappings, and the whole thing loosened instantly.

Rasim whispered, "Thank you," and she nodded, then pulled her own under-tunic off—Rasim didn't know how she did that, either—and slid it over Kisia's shoulders, tugging it down her body before taking the flame-orange undergown off the semi-conscious Ilyaran girl. Rasim whispered, "Thank you," again, and slid himself under Kisia's arm, surging to his feet.

The girl helped again, putting herself under Kisia's other arm and helped Rasim get her to a standing position. He said, "Toilet," in Shenryalan, and a flash of understanding rushed through the girl's eyes. She tugged toward a pot—not one meant for eliminating in, but it didn't matter just then—and hitched Kisia's tunic up around her hips as Rasim sat her over the pot. He whispered, "I'm really sorry," to her while the girl held her in place, and sent witchery coursing through her again, turning her bowels to liquid.

A roar of disgust and dismay filled the area, which emptied as thoroughly as Kisia's bowels did. Given the smell, Rasim couldn't blame them, but he was terribly glad it had worked, and hoped the sweat breaking on Kisia's brow lwas a good sign.

Almost as importantly, it cleared space for Desimi to crash at Rasim's side, his breathing rough, like he'd been fighting his way through the gathered crowd. His brown face was ashy with fear, and pale as it could be.

"Oh, thank Siliaria. Desi, can you purge blood? I—I can't."

"I've never tried." Desimi sounded as grim, as desperate, as Rasim felt. Rasim nodded, sending magic coursing through Kisia again and watching her color go from bad to worse.

"I don't think I can wring any more out of her without making her bleed," Rasim whispered. "Sesin says to purge her blood, but I don't…"

"I don't either. Lie her down." Desimi knelt beside Kisia as Rasim and the Shenryalan girl lay her down in a shivering ball. The girl made a questioning gesture at the chamberpot and Rasim shrugged uncertainly. She nodded and—very nobly, Rasim thought—sat and held the smelly thing to the side, in case they needed it again. Rasim said, "*Thank* you," and she nodded.

Rasim knelt on Kisia's other side, across from Desimi. The other boy had already called witchery, the same profoundly deep magic that had once pulled water up from below the Ilyaran palace and splashed it through the wide, bright halls. "It's not like clearing salt water," he said tensely. "There's so much more in it. I don't know what—I can't *feel* what—" Then he fell silent, his head bowed and his face tight with concentration, until he finally grated, "I've slowed her blood down. It's hard—I have to concentrate—but I can't—I can't feel it. I can't feel what I'm supposed to take away, to clean it. I don't know—" He looked up, his eyes brilliant with fear. "I don't know if what I can do is enough."

"It'll be enough," Rasim whispered. "It'll be enough. You're doing more than I could. I can't make..." He reached for Kisia, too, sending witchery toward her, and shivered at the care Desimi held her in, the way he slowed her heartbeat and the flow of her blood. "She doesn't feel worse," he whispered. "Let me see if I can get her to drink."

He looked around frantically for a flask, and the Shenryalan girl gave him hers without him having to ask. She was murmuring something, almost singing, a tune and words he didn't know, but he thanked her and dripped water onto Kisia's lips, soothing it down her throat with witchery so that she wouldn't choke. For what felt like horrible hours upon horrible hours, although it probably wasn't really very long at all, they kept doing that. Rasim fed Kisia dribbles of water, Desimi held her heart rate down, and the girl kept up her song. Eventually Rasim realized it was a prayer, and a sob choked him so hard that Desimi looked up in alarm. He shook his head, trying to swallow the tears, but Desimi gave him a short, nod of understanding, and looked back down at Kisia.

"We can see you." Karluk's voice sounded in Rasim's ear, making him gasp with disbelief and relief. He lifted his gaze, looking out, and saw a herd of Shenryalan riders curving toward them at a full gallop.

Riding *directly* toward them, charging along in a straight line, even though the temporary city was built with curving paths. Rasim stared around them in bewilderment for a moment, and saw that everywhere around them, everywhere in front of them, had been cleared. Tents ahead of them were still falling, in fact, whisking out of the way just before the riders thundered through. Behind them, the tents were being returned to their former state as if nothing unusual had happened.

Another sob choked him as the riders wheeled to a stop, so close he could touch a horse's heaving flanks if he wanted to. Sesin tumbled down from behind one of the Shenryalans and threw herself toward Kisia, knocking Rasim aside. He moved back, getting out of the way, and knelt with his hands knotted in his lap. Sesin spread her hands over Kisia's trembling body, snapped, "Don't stop," at Desimi, and bent her head to work.

The witchery she called felt nothing like the magic Desimi was using. His ran deep, like a connection to the heart of the sea. Sesin's was so light, so delicate, that it felt almost like light dancing on the waves, instead of the waves themselves. Rasim had seen her stop terrible bleeding before, or soften the lumps of deep bruises so broken bones within them could be set, and had felt the power of her purging magic on himself. It had been different from what he'd done, emptying Kisia's belly and bowels. That was comparatively simple witchery, just pushing water around. But Sesin had stripped a drug from his very *blood* and given it a place to exit—he'd vomited so hard he'd gotten dizzy—and if she could do that for him...but a drug wasn't poison, and Sesin was only a journeyman healer, not a master. Rasim's hands clenched again as he lost hope.

The Shenryalan riders brought fire pots and set them up close enough to warm the Ilyarans. Rasim shivered gratefully, but couldn't take his eyes from the work that Sesin and Desimi did. Sesin bit her lower lip in concentration, her eyes closed, and once in a while her hands would move like she was throwing something away.

All at once, without warning, Kisia rolled over and threw up all over Desimi, who let go a roaring laugh of relief and collapsed beside her. Kisia fumbled blindly, then croaked, "Toilet," and suddenly the Shenryalan girl was there again, helping her. Terrible shudders wracked Kisia's body, but Rasim grabbed hold of her, crying with uncontrollable relief as she clung to him.

Sesin, eyes glassy, smiled blindingly at Desimi. "You saved her. Slowing her heartbeat down. You saved her. I would have been too late." Desimi rolled over on his belly, face buried in the crook of his elbow, his whole body shaking with sobs. Sesin went to lie down beside him, to curl up with him, but the Shenryalan girl put her hand on the healer's shoulder.

"Bayar?"

"What?" Sesin froze, staring from the girl to Rasim. "Bayar too?"

"They were poisoned at the same time," Rasim whispered hoarsely. "Their shaman took him, but she couldn't help both of them. I don't know if she can even help him."

Sesin lurched to her feet, small jaw set with fear and

determination. She nodded at the Shenryalan girl, repeating, "Bayar. I'll help Bayar, if I can. Where is he?"

A huge smile split the girl's face and she pointed toward Oyun's tent. Sesin bolted that direction and someone shouted a protest, then fell back as Bikat roared, "Let her through!" and followed her into the tent, as if he couldn't bear to stand alone any longer. Rasim turned back to Kisia to find her staring at him with wet, confused eyes.

"Rasim?" Her voice was a shaking wreck after throwing up so much. "Rasi, why am I in somebody else's underwear?"

CHAPTER TWELVE

Even Rasim couldn't tell if his answer was laughter or sobs. He curled Kisia, smelly and sweaty and shaky as she was, into his arms, and held her as fiercely as he dared. She felt fragile, like she had lost substance in the past hours. "Only you would wonder about your underwear."

"My other underwear was very fancy," Kisia protested weakly. "And tight. This isn't either. And I don't own anything like it. And…what happened?"

He wasn't certain she wanted an answer to that, because she turned her face against his shoulder and began to cry again. "I don't feel good, Rasi."

"You were poisoned," he said hoarsely. "Desimi and Sesin saved you. She's gone to see if she can help Bayar now. Their shaman is helping him but she couldn't help both of you. So now Sesi's going to help her, if she can. You're all right. You're all right, Kees." His heart lurched. "Are you all right?"

Kisia whispered, "I must be. Sesi wouldn't have left me if I wasn't. Desi? Desimi?"

The bigger boy had gotten to his knees, his presence a bulky shadow just behind Rasim, but he shook his head as Kisia fell toward him with a hug. "No, don't, I stink—"

"Not as bad as me," she promised, and Desimi choked on a laugh as he hugged her hard. After a second he pulled Rasim into the embrace and the three of them leaned on each other until Kisia let out a croaking giggle. "Am I on a chamberpot?"

"Um. Yes."

Kisia giggled again, although it sounded more panicked than amused. "I would like to not be."

Desimi scooted to get himself under one of Kisia's arms, and Rasim put himself under the other so they could help Kisia stand. She felt much lighter than she'd been when Rasim had half-caught her falling off the throne. "Do you think," she said dizzily before her chin dropped to her chest and her weight went limp between them. Desimi grunted, then grunted again, this time at Rasim.

"Let me take her." At Rasim's reluctant nod, Desimi scooped Kisia into his arms effortlessly, then exhaled. "A bucket bath isn't going to do it this time, Rasi. Do you think they'd let us call up water from the deep earth?"

Rasim cast him a startled, approving glance, then struggled to find the words to ask the people surrounding them whether that would be all right. One of them spoke in rapid Shenryalan, then made a face indicating she knew she wasn't being understood. More slowly, carefully, she said, "Go to your tent. We'll bring a," and while the last word was totally unfamiliar, the broad roundish gesture she made along with it suggested it meant 'tub.'

Rasim said, "*Thank* you," and they went to their tent, Desimi carrying Kisia carefully the whole way. Someone brought a waxed leather tub in moments after they arrived.

Desimi, without ever putting Kisia down, bent his head in concentration. The water was very deep, and for once, he didn't try to brute force it upward. The earth itself would crack under the power of rising water, if the big journeyman wanted it to—he'd done it before—but this time water rose in slow droplets, gathering together just above the ground until he directed them into the tub.

Journeyman Pynda studied the slowly-filling tub, then went outside to get a burning stick from one of the fires and began to weave flame around the tub, not quite close enough to melt the wax or burn the leather. "This would be easier if I could put the tub in the fire," she muttered. "But I can take the chill off, anyway."

This time Desimi said, "Thank you," and Pynda nodded with her jaw set. Rasim wasn't sure if she'd worked any sun witchery at all since Daka had died in the Northlands, but he was grateful she chose to now. After a few minutes, she said, "Well, it's not ground temperature anymore, anyway," and nodded at Desimi, who put Kisia in it, clothes and all.

She came awake with a shocked gasp of outrage,

flailed a little, then, with a cry, began to scrub herself and strip away the wrecked clothing she wore. Rasim gathered them and took them outside to clean, which drew the attention of those who weren't too focused on the shaman's tent. Water and witchery went a long way toward cleaning things easily, although he wished he had a bucket of his own to use.

Just as he wished that, and wondered if he had enough Shenryalan to ask, the girl who'd helped them before came over with not just a bucket, but a small washboard that fit inside it. She smiled crookedly and made a scrubbing motion, like she was showing him how to use the washboard. Rasim grinned back and said, "I know," as he scrubbed the clothes. Even witchery-washed stains needed extra help.

Wringing the clothes out was easier, and by that time the gathered Shenryalans were watching with open fascination. Some were visibly disturbed at such casual use of magic, and others obviously impressed with the apparent ease Rasim manipulated the water. They were not, Rasim thought, like the people earlier that day—yesterday now, he supposed—who had encouraged them to show off their abilities. This group had an altogether less friendly feel to it, but then, they were also waiting to see if Bayar lived or died. Rasim gathered Kisia's things and retreated into their tent, which felt, if not safer, at least less exposed.

Kisia was dressed in her Ilyaran clothes again, and sitting next to Desimi, who had his arm around her. Rasim stared blankly at the little tub, half full of stinking water, and wondered what the best way to get rid of it was. He could probably send it soaring through the air, but he didn't know how far away the edge of camp was and certainly didn't want to accidentally drop it on anybody if his power didn't reach far enough. He went back outside to ask, and the rider who had gotten the tub for them in the first place gestured to a couple of others, who followed Rasim in and took the tub away. He said, "Thank you," again, feeling like it was inadequate, and sat with Kisia and Desimi, all of them quietly, fearfully waiting.

It was almost dawn before a rough, relieved roar of joy rose around their tent. A few seconds later, Sesin staggered in. "Bayar's alive. He'll be all right. Their shaman got the poison out, but he had seizures. I was able to help with that. He's all right. He's sleeping now."

Rasim bent double, jagged sobs of relief ripping through him. Desimi put his arm over Rasim, too, and pulled him and Kisia closer, all three of them shaking with emotion until they simply fell asleep where they were.

EITHER THE FEAR of missing something or the mouth-watering scent of a heavily-spiced stew awakened him late in the afternoon. Someone had opened the tent door, letting deep gold sunlight spill through. Rasim sat up slowly, rubbing a hand over his face. His mouth tasted like something had died in it, and he couldn't remember the last time he'd even had a drink of water.

The tent was mostly empty, although Kisia slept in a

bed near its back, and Sesin was outlined in the sun's golden brilliance as she checked the other girl over. She noticed Rasim moving and smiled, then crept to his side to murmur, "She's doing well. She woke up a while ago and took some water, but went back to sleep before she ate. Here. You look ashy." She handed him a waterskin, and Rasim drained it gratefully.

"Bayar?" Even after the water, his voice croaked, but Sesin smiled again.

"Exhausted, like Kisia, but getting stronger." Her smile faltered. "The old woman, Oyun, says lucky doesn't even begin to cover it. If she hadn't been a few steps away when they were poisoned, if you and Desimi hadn't been right there, neither of them would have survived. She said that particular poison is only used when you *mean* it. As if you don't mean it when you poison somebody otherwise."

"Did they find who did it yet?" Part of Rasim wanted the answer to be yes. Another part of him wanted to find the culprit himself, and—

His hands clenched uselessly. *Kill them.* That's what his gut said. That's what Desimi would say. But killing them wouldn't solve anything and it wouldn't tell anybody *why* they'd been poisoned.

Sesin was shaking her head, though. "Nobody thought to wonder in the moment, and even if they had, there were hundreds, thousands, of people filing through all night. It could have been anyone. Maybe not at any time, because Oyun says the poison works fast once it touches the skin, but..."

"But there's not even any way to know whether they

were darted right then or if the needles worked their way through their clothes." Rasim shook his head heavily, then made himself get up. "Is there more water?"

"And stew." Sesin rose to go outside and returned with a bowl of bright yellow stew filled with root vegetables and lentils while Rasim got another waterskin and drained it.

"Oh, Siliaria's soul, thank you. This smells amazing." He ate hungrily with a shallow-bowled spoon, and mopped up the remains with a piece of tangy flat bread that had been tucked beneath the bowl. "Where is everyone?"

"They're pretty much all in the big tent. Desimi woke up a little while ago and ate and went to see Bayar, and I've been keeping an eye on him and Kisia. Bayar and Kisia, not Desimi."

"Is he all right?" Kisia, on the other side of the tent, pushed up on one elbow and addressed Sesin. "Bayar, is he all right?" At Sesin's nod, she dropped back into the furs like she'd used up all her strength. Rasim got up to go to her side, curling one of her hands in his as he sat. She still felt thin and fragile, a little like Missio had when the delzjha had run through her. She squeezed his fingers, though, and after a moment, said, "Do you know who did it, yet?"

"Not yet." Rasim went back to the line of thought he'd had before Sesin brought him food. "But it must have been someone who was there for a while, paying attention to you. Long enough to see you and Bayar had gone to sit down. Because they didn't dare miss, right? If someone else had been hit, everybody would have gotten wary, and if they missed entirely..." He hesitated. "I don't know how common it is. It might have been their only dose."

Sesin left the tent, and came back in with more food and water as he finished speaking. "Oyun says it's made from snake venom, but that even making it is very dangerous and takes a long time. Do you think you can eat, Kisia?"

Kisia waved her free hand uncertainly, then mumbled, "Help me sit up," to Rasim, who did. Sesin sat with a bowl of the bright yellow stew, and Kisia said, "Nope. I can't eat anything that color today," with absolute conviction.

Sesin laughed and stood again with the stew bowl. "I'll see if I can find something in a different color. Drink some water, at least."

Instead, Kisia sank down in the furs, resting until Sesin came back in again with a plate of bread and melted butter to dip it in. "Here you go. Not yellow. Small bites, though. Your system has been through a lot. I'm going to go check on Bayar again, if you're all right here with Rasim?"

"We're fine," Rasim promised, and Kisia, who had sat up to sink her teeth into the flat bread, nodded. Then she un-sank her teeth and tried a much smaller bite, obviously overwhelmed by even the idea of a big bite like she'd started with. Around nibbles, she said, "But Bayar only came home a couple of days ago. If it takes a long time to make that poison, how can they have made it in since he got home?"

Rasim, speaking from experience, said, "Maybe they

made it ages ago, before he was kidnapped, in case the kidnapping didn't work. Maybe it was a backup plan, and they just needed a chance. A party with a lot of people moving around is a chance. I don't understand why they poisoned you, though."

"They probably didn't." Kisia nibbled at the bread some more, but also giggled weakly at Rasim's expression. "Probably not on purpose. If you were trying to kill the king's heir, would you leave it to one chance, or would you shoot a couple of poison darts? I probably got in the way."

"You think you almost died accidentally?"

Kisia shrugged tiredly. "It makes a lot more sense than someone wanting to kill me. And if that's what's happened, Bayar is probably lucky, because if two doses had hit him I'm sure he would have died."

"That's a pretty terrible kind of luck, Kees."

"Not for Bayar." She closed her eyes and tilted over, still nibbling on the bread. "I'm so tired."

"I know. You should rest." Rasim smoothed her hair, and she gave him a tiny smile without opening her eyes. "You rest," he repeated. "I'll go try to learn everything and come back and tell you."

She laughed, much more quietly than he was used to from her. "I don't know about *everything*, Rasim. I think that would take even you a while."

He grinned, relieved she could tease him. "All right, *enough*, then, if not everything. I'll probably have solved everything by the time you wake up again."

"You'll probably have caused another international incident by the time I wake up again." Kisia smiled, yawned, and was asleep before Rasim even got up. He tucked the covers around her, then left the tent, squinting at bright, early-afternoon sunlight. Today no one was guarding their door, or guiding him where he needed to go.

It wasn't like he would get lost between the Ilyaran tent and the central one, and for a few steps, that's where Rasim thought he was going. But a thought trickled into the back of his mind, and he stepped out of the spiral pathway, holding himself still in the shadow of a smaller tent. There were so many pieces to the idea tickling his thoughts, and he was afraid if he moved, they wouldn't all come together.

The Shenryalans had this poison, made from a venom. That was part of it. It fluttered at the edge of Rasim's mind, trying to find the information it wanted to attach itself to, and after a long, long moment, it did.

Oyun had known what the power-enhancing drug was. She'd called it *delzjha*, and the poison, *hinzjha*. Wisdom-slayer, life-slayer. Rasim wondered briefly if they were derived from the same thing, but what mattered was that no one else he'd met, anywhere, had had a name for the stuff, or a name to assign to it from a description of what it did. So delzjha almost certainly *came* from the steppes.

Which meant *someone* here had provided it to the Seamaster journeyman who had died using it in the Northlands.

Rasim whispered, "Sorcery from afar," and bolted toward the central tent.

CHAPTER THIRTEEN

He burst through the tent's golden-orange door a few seconds later, yelling, "You were right!" loudly enough that it put a stop to whatever was happening in the tent. Behind him, an embarrassed guard cursed and grabbed his shoulder, trying to pull him back, but Bayar's mother lifted one eyebrow and beckoned, indicating Rasim should be let in. He straightened his tunic and his shoulders, and, a little more moderately, said, "You were right," to the gathering at large, but especially to old Oyun.

She sniffed, which said 'of course' as clearly as any words could do. Irlin, expression bright with the contained amusement he was becoming accustomed to, said, "Right about what, sorcerer-child?" so dryly that Rasim was certain he was being laughed at.

Just to one side of him, Captain Nasira, who was seated cross-legged on pillows along with Sunmaster Endat, Prince Lorens, and a few of their other vagabonds, lowered her face into one hand and sighed almost inaudibly. It still cut through Rasim like a knife, and, a little too late, it occurred to him that maybe he should have brought this up to her privately before crashing into a political gathering and shouting his thoughts to the represented world.

But it was much too late now, so he shuffled forward a few steps, apologetically, to say, "About sorcery from afar. I don't know if there are foreign witches here, but...you know how to make delzjha, don't you, Spiritmaster?"

The translator spoke, their words rolling softly through the tent as Nasira, *just* loud enough for Rasim to hear, demanded, "*What* is delzjha, Rasim?"

He whispered, "The power-enhancing drug," to her as Oyun gave him a calculating look, then nodded once. Nasira hissed and sat back, and on either side of her, Endat and Lorens exchanged startled glances.

"I used delzjha in the Northlands," Rasim said to the whole gathering. "We took it off the body of a dead witch, an Ilyaran, who said someone had given it to her. We didn't learn who, though. She died in Prince Lorens's arms, first."

A thread snapped tight through his mind, like a fishing line gone taut with a heavy catch. Roscord, the lord with ambitions of uniting the Islands and conquering the continent had all but died in Lorens's arms. Then Missio had literally died in Lorens's arms, in the Northlands. That had bothered Rasim even at the time, but he hadn't known what to do with it.

Now, though, he could see a clear path all the way through. Lorens had been the last person to speak to—

to even touch—Cindu, the awesomely powerful stone witch who had brought down the Moranese city walls in a fit of enraged vengeance. Lorens had given Cindu the last of his heartbreak drug, the stuff that made witchery inaccessible to Ilyaran witches, before they'd turned him over to the Moranese. And then, minutes later, impossibly, Cindu had renewed his attack on Moran, destroying even more of the city than he had the first time.

Heartbreak didn't work properly on Rasim, because he had multiple magics. In the rush of the moment, they had thought something similar might have happened with Cindu, or that, knowing he was going to die anyway, Cindu had somehow fought through the drug to bring down the city.

It made much, *much* more sense if Lorens had given Cindu delzjha instead, told him not to use his power until he was in the heart of Moran, and let him go to his death.

All of that fell through Rasim's mind so quickly he barely had time to take a breath, and in its wake, stiffened all his muscles so he wouldn't look at Prince Lorens. It took effort to keep talking, and he hoped his voice hadn't changed, although it sounded squeaky with nerves to his own ears. "But if delzjha comes from the steppes, then Oyun has to be right. There's some kind of sorcery, or sorcerers, from afar who are mixed up in—in I don't know what," he admitted. "Maybe Bayar's kidnapping and the attempt on his life, or maybe just trying to use Shenryalan drugs to change other parts of the world. But it all has to be tied together somehow. I'm sure of it."

In the silence that followed, Oyun said something in such a sarcastic tone that Rasim wilted. A ripple of laughter went around the tent, and the translator didn't bother to interpret, but Rasim was sure it was something along the lines of 'gee, thanks, kid.'

He drooped farther. He absolutely should have discussed this with Captain Nasira before coming in to yell at everyone about it. A quick look at the Shenryalans, who still sat separated by gender, told him that some of them thought he was amusing, but far more of them thought he was rude, at best. Tiresome, obnoxious, ill-mannered, and inconsiderate were more likely words for how they saw him.

Well, they might be right about all of that, but he was sure he was right about this, so he set his jaw and tried not to clench his fists as he met Irlin and Bikat's eyes. "Someone needs to look into it."

After a moment, Bikat said, "Someone will," with the gentle tone of an adult placating a child.

Embarrassed anger flushed through Rasim, but he didn't think it would help to tell the Shenryalan leader not to be condescending to him. Instead he muttered, "Thank you, King Horse," and backed up a few steps, not sure whether he should flee or join Captain Nasira and the others. Nasira glared at him when he glanced her way, and jerked a thumb toward the door.

Rasim fled.

He fled out the door, down the spiraling path toward

their tent, and straight into Desimi, at a high enough speed that he actually bounced off the bigger boy, who staggered back a step. "What's your rush, Sunburn?"

"Nothing!" All the anger that came with his embarrassment burst out in that one word, and Desimi, startled, took another step back before scowling hugely.

"Well, whatever your problem is, it isn't my fault, so don't take it out on me."

"Yeah, like you're so good at taking that advice yourself." Rasim regretted the snarl as soon as it passed his lips, and deflated. "I'm sorry. You're right."

A complex combination of irritation and resignation slid across Desimi's face. "What's wrong? Bayar and Kisia are all right, aren't they? I know Bayar is. I just saw him."

"Kees is sleeping. It's not them, it's..." Rasim took a few steps off the path and sank into a crouch, folding his hands behind his head.

Desimi hesitated, then came to crouch beside him, arms dangling over his knees. "All right, well, what is it, Sunburn?"

"I just did it again," Rasim said miserably. "Stomped in and yelled at a bunch of adults about what they should be doing." He explained about the delzjha, and Bikat's bland promise that it would be looked into. "It's not that I think he's lying. I just..."

"Don't think he's taking it very seriously, either." Desimi sucked in his cheeks, glancing toward their tent, then back the direction he'd come from, where Bayar's tent lay. "Kisia's going to be laid up a while. We could look into it." He shrugged stiffly as Rasim raised his head in astonishment. "It's better than sitting on our thumbs while the masters and royalty talk it all out, right?"

"We don't speak much Shenryalan," Rasim protested half-heartedly. "How are we going to learn anything if we can't talk to anybody?"

A slow grin crawled over Desimi's face. "I think I have an idea."

KIF'S GRANDDAUGHTERS all spoke the Northern tongue, even—especially—the one who had danced with Desimi again and again the night before. She came out of their tent with a curious look when they came to call "Daará?" which was the equivalent of knocking on the door, when the doors were too soft to knock on.

She looked more like her grandfather than most of his grandchildren did, with a narrow sharpness to her jaw and a pale Northern grey to her gaze. She considered them with that pale grey gaze before smiling broadly. "I am Ūrrin, daughter of Valūd, granddaughter of Mankah. You are sorcerer-Rasim," she said to him, and, with a much more flirtatious look to the bigger journeyman, "and sorcerer-Desimi."

Desimi wrinkled his face. "Just Desimi. And Rasim. Ūrrin...I don't speak enough Northern," he said to Rasim, visibly frustrated. "Can you tell her, ask her, if she can help us with some questions and do some translating? Why don't we all learn Northern in the guild? We sail all over the continent! We should speak more languages!"

"That's what I said!" Rasim grinned, feeling oddly justified, and spoke to Ūrrin in his limited Northern. Hers was much, much better than his, which had to have taken some very deliberate effort on the part of her mother, keeping her father's memory alive after his banishment. She listened to his proposal, then nodded, but made it clear she would be talking to Desimi, not Rasim, who ended up grinning again. "You're going to have to ask the questions, Desi. She wouldn't have a rotten fish gut to spare for me."

"But you're the one who has to do the talking!"

"And you're the one she wants to talk to." It was very strange, being the translator for someone who wasn't interested in his presence at all. Ūrrin barely glanced at him, walking alongside Desimi as she led them around the camp, touching his hand or tucking her arm through his to point him in the direction she wanted him to look. Rasim didn't necessarily understand all of the words she said, but at one point he said, helpfully, "She's flirting with you, Desi."

Desimi, sounding as if he would blush if he could, hissed, "I can see that, Sunburn!" and Rasim laughed.

Ūrrin got more out of their conversation than Rasim did, he thought in the end. She knew very little about the delzjha or the poison that had been used on Kisia and Bayar, except that the knowledge of how to make them was shamanic, and therefore not wide-spread. But that narrowed it down far less than Rasim might have hoped, because Ūrrin was able to tell him although Oyun was perhaps the oldest and most respected shaman in the tribes, she was far from the only one. Each of the five tribes had their own shaman whose position was nearly as important and well-regarded as Oyun's.

Even that would have been few enough to work with, but there were dozens of clans within the tribes, and even some individual families within those clans large enough to have a shaman of their own. Delzjha's secrets may have been known only to a comparative few, but those few still numbered a hundred or more, without even taking into account the apprentices and journeymen who had not yet reached spiritmaster status. At a mere two apprentices per shaman, there had to be easily over three hundred people who knew, or were learning, the secrets of the drugs and poisons of the steppes.

If Rasim had learned anything over the past months of high adventure and political turmoil, it was that while it was *possible* every soul out of three hundred was trustworthy, it was far, far more likely that at least one of them could be bought. He thanked Ūrrin and abandoned Desimi to her, figuring they could manage to communicate anything they felt was important enough.

Oyun seemed to like him. She might answer his questions in more detail, although Rasim wasn't quite sure what to ask. Shamanic and sorcerous apprentices were chosen by being sniffed, as far as Rasim could tell. Presumably anybody who had undergone Oyun's sniffing had been found suitable.

But people changed. The thoughts came slowly as Rasim wound his way down spiral pathways, trying not to get lost among the brightly-dyed tents while also trying to avoid going back to the little part of the temporary city that he knew reasonably well. Surely people changed. Rasim couldn't imagine that sniffing a child's hair could tell a shaman how that child might react to every heartbreaking twist or uplifting turn that their lives took. He could believe that spiritmastery might show whether someone was inclined to abuse power, and momentarily wandered down a path of wondering what, exactly, the Ilyaran guilds did with people of that nature. A small and nasty part of his own mind said the answer was 'made them Sunmasters,' but as with every guild, most orphans came to the Sunmasters too young to know whether they were power-hungry or not.

The Sunmasters, though, might encourage it in a way that some of the other guilds didn't, particularly in terms of political power. Like the Great Mare had said, a person had as much magical potential as they had, and no more, but political power could be gained or lost. Rasim shook himself and tried to put that idea away for a while, but it lingered. The problem with walking around alone was it gave him too much time to think, and his thoughts sank back to the cascade of coincidences he'd realized about Prince Lorens.

He'd known that Roscord and Missio had died—conveniently, for lack of a better term. And Lorens had understood it too, to the point of mentioning it to Rasim. But there was no way at all to know for certain that Lorens had given Cindu delzjha instead of heart-break. It wasn't like the Northern prince would admit to it if Rasim accused him, and the last thing he needed to do was make the Northerners mad at Ilyara, too. He closed his eyes, drifting to a stop in the middle of a spiral path as he tried to remember *exactly* what had happened on the *Wafiya* that chaotic day when Moran had fallen.

Someone bumped into him and grunted a scolding Shenryalan word. Rasim squeaked an apology and found a quiet spot between the backs of three tents, where he squatted and closed his eyes again to think. Lorens had poured a drug into Cindu's mouth from a pouch. The stone witch had fought back, turning on his belly, and Lorens had struggled with him a few seconds before pouring more of the drug into his palm and clapping his hand over Cindu's face until the witch had been forced to inhale.

Rasim tried to replay that moment in his mind, wondering if he'd missed something. What kept coming to mind was the unhappiness, the weary resignation in Lorens's pale eyes when Rasim had insisted the heartbreak be checked. Kisia had taken a dose, and it had worked on her. She'd been unable to feel her witchery. It seemed to clear Lorens of Rasim's suspicions.

The struggle with Cindu spun out in his mind again, an imperfect recollection. Lorens, pouring the drug directly from the pouch into Cindu's mouth. Cindu struggling. Lorens pouring more drug into his hand, forcing Cindu to swallow it. Lorens standing, brushing the dust from his hands, handing the pouch to Kisia so she could take a dose herself.

Lorens pouring the dust directly into Cindu's mouth, then struggling with the stone witch, then pouring a second dose into his hand to clap against Cindu's face.

Had it been the same pouch?

There had been time, during that brief struggle. There'd been time to switch one pouch for another, if Lorens was deft enough, and the Northern prince was. He was quick with his feet, his tongue, his hands, his blade. He was quick with his fists, too, because he'd punched Cindu hard enough to render the stone witch unconscious, after he'd administered the drug.

Rasim opened his eyes. At some point he'd plunked onto his butt, no longer crouching, like it was too hard to squat and think at the same time. Wind shifted the walls of the tents around him, a steady breeze and small motion that he barely saw or felt because of the size of his thoughts.

If *he* had given an already-powerful witch a drug that would allow them to pull a city apart, he would have wanted to make sure they didn't start doing that until after he was safe. If he'd done that in front of a lot of other people and didn't have the opportunity to explain, then hitting that witch so hard they lost consciousness for a few minutes was as good a way as any to keep their mouth shut.

"It makes more sense," Rasim whispered aloud. He could overcome heartbreak, but only because he had so many different kinds of witchery to command. There had been no reason at all to suspect Cindu was anything other than a stonemaster. It made more sense that Lorens had snuck Cindu a dose of delzjha, knocked him out, and sent him away to wreak havoc than that Cindu had somehow broken through the hold of a drug so consistent in its efficacy that the Ilyaran guilds used it to mute the powers of those who left the guilds.

It made more sense, but there was no way at all to prove it. Rasim held on to the thought, though. Held onto it with a light, fragile touch, like it would escape if he examined it too carefully.

There had to be those among the Shenryalan people who had wanted, at some point in their lives, to become shamans or sorcerers. People who hadn't been chosen by Oyun or her disciples. People who would seek out other sources of shamanic or sorcerous power.

People who might, for example, have known that once upon a time, Kif's people, the Northerners, had borne magics of their own.

The tribes and clans and families of Shenryal rode all over their tremendous plains, and there *was* a land bridge between Shenryal and the Northlands. It was not impossible, Rasim thought, so gingerly that he barely dared breathe around the idea of it, that somewhere, sometime, there had been a meeting of minds and magics between the outcasts and enslaved Northern students of witchery, and the rejected and resentful sorcery-seeking riders of Shenryal. And somewhere between those two groups there almost certainly had to be at least one shaman or sorcerer whose self-interests and desire for power outweighed their duties to the tribes.

It was a tenuous conviction, so very thin that Rasim knew convincing anyone would be nearly impossible. Kisia would believe him. Desimi would join them because he hated being left out. But it would take proof before Captain Nasira or Bayar's parents would even consider the possibility that Rasim was right.

With a fierce-feeling grin, Rasim got to his feet so he could go find his friends and find a way to prove his theory to the adults around him.

He got about two and a half steps before somebody clobbered him on the back of the head and he dropped to the ground, unconscious.

CHAPTER FOURTEEN

Rasim woke up to a blindfold, a gag, and a throbbing headache. It took a few seconds longer to realize his hands were also tied behind his back, but that was practically comfortable compared to the knot of cloth in his mouth. It tasted like horse hair. He was lying on his side on the ground, and there was a familiar scent in the air, almost strong enough to drown out the horsey taste. It might have been something like the golden-colored stew he'd eaten earlier, maybe, but that wasn't enough to tell him anything about where he was. From what he'd seen and smelled, people all over the temporary city ate food like that all the time. Rasim muffled a groan, then tried swallowing around the gag, which didn't work very well.

There were distant sounds that he recognized: people and horses. More horses than people, maybe. He was probably still somewhere in the Shenryalan gathering's enormous camp, unless he'd been unconscious a very long time. He thought his head hurt too much for that to be true, though, and after a slow contemplation of the rest of himself, decided he was neither hungry enough, nor had to pee badly enough, to have been out for much more than an hour or two.

He did wonder, for a moment, whether his captors thought he needed his eyes, mouth, or hands to work witchery. He needed none of those things, although he *did* need for his head to hurt less. Probably they'd tied him up more to keep him quiet and from knowing who they were. But maybe Shenryalan witches did need one, or all, of those abilities to work their own magic. He would have to ask Oyun, or maybe Milu.

Either his head hurt too much for him to be scared, or he'd gotten so accustomed to being in dangerous, out-of-control situations to panic. Rasim felt like it was maybe more the former than the latter, because if he started thinking about it like that, his heart began lurching and his stomach soured as his hands went sweaty.

Maybe it was better to just believe he'd find a way out of this, because he had every other time so far. He took a shaky breath through his nose. He didn't want his captors to know he was awake, but he wanted to throw up less, and he was afraid he might if he didn't get some fresh air into himself.

The deep breath tasted too much like horse hair to make him feel better. Rasim pressed his face against the ground for a moment, trying to steady himself through the nausea and the throbbing head, and then nodded a little. He could do this. He would be fine.

He had to be. Because somebody had presumably

overheard him with Desimi and Ūrrin, asking about delzjha, and had taken steps to remove his questions from the conversation. If he could stay alive and captive long enough, he might learn who, and then, at least, he would have something solid to go to Captain Nasira with.

Rasim actually laughed at himself, hardly a sound at all. It made his head hurt, and a tear leaked from the corner of his eye into his blindfold, but even he saw that his approach was a little bit funny. Stay captive to learn secrets. No one in their right mind would decide that was a good idea.

Well, he'd been hit on the head really hard. Maybe he wasn't in his right mind at all.

The ground vibrated with footsteps. There were hoofbeats farther away, too, but the footsteps were coming closer, and ended in a booted foot nudging him in the ribs. Nudging, not kicking. That was something. Maybe they didn't want to kill him or even beat him up, at least not right away.

Something seemed wrong with that, but he couldn't think clearly enough to understand why. He did groan, not entirely on purpose, when the boot nudged him again. A Shenryalan man said, "He's awake," which was simple enough for Rasim to understand. Then big hands folded themselves into his tunic and sat him upright. Rasim whimpered and swayed. He wasn't generally happy about being blindfolded, but just then he thought the world swimming by would have made him throw up, so not being able to open his eyes was something of a blessing.

The person holding him never let go, but somebody loosened his gag and brought liquid to his lips. Rasim was too thirsty to think of purifying the—milk, as it turned out—with witchery, and felt a rush of dismay as his tongue went numb, like he'd been drugged. He croaked, "What was that?" in passable-enough Shenryalan, and heard a woman's unpleasant chuckle.

"Zjhala. Shaman's milk."

Rasim crushed his eyes closed even tighter behind the blindfold. Zjhala sounded like it was related to the poison that had been used on Bayar. He tried to remember what exactly Oyun had given him to drink in her tent. Maybe it had tasted like that. Maybe she had poisoned him. His head hurt too much to think clearly. Then his mind *separated* from his body, leaving him staring down at himself from a few feet above his own head. His hair had dark brown roots growing out from the lemon-and-honey blond he'd bleached it when he was trying to escape slavery in Moran. The man holding him had straight black hair that fell over his shoulders from a center part, and, from above, a handsome nose.

Rasim had seen people from this angle most of his life. This is what they looked like if he climbed a mast and looked down, or even just looked down from a high hammock in the guildhall. But he had never been *detached* from himself when he'd looked down at them, before. He tried to cry out with alarm, and managed to, but slowly, as if he wasn't quite connected to himself anymore. The woman chuckled again. "Zjhala works fast."

He heard the words in two places: through his ears, but with that slow pace, like everything was traveling toward him through water. He also heard it in the air, thin ripples of sound that seemed to bounce at him at a normal speed, then speed away again at a much greater one. With effort, he raised his head—his spirit head, not his real one—to look toward the woman who was speaking.

A thump of dismay went through him, starting in his body down there on the floor and rising with no particular urgency to where he drifted above himself. He'd imagined he would know his captor, for some reason. That she would be a familiar face from the central tent, maybe. But if he'd ever seen her before, it had been in passing, at best. She was Shenryalan and much older than he was without being *old*, not grey-haired or wrinkled, just regular-old, like the *Wafiya*'s first mate, Hassin, or like Prince Lorens. She wasn't dressed in the furs or colors that seemed to mark people of particular importance in the tribe, nor did she have the tattoos that both Oyun and, to a lesser degree, the Great Mare Irlin bore. She was ordinary.

Rasim, drifting there out of his own body, had another peculiar twinge of his heart, this time of an aching recognition. *Ordinary*. He'd spent most of his life being ordinary, overlooked, wishing for great things and knowing he lacked the witchery talent that the guild required for those great things. There had been many paths open to him: shipwright, teacher to the apprentices, fisherman, cook. There were many jobs that the guild required, that didn't necessarily take much witchery skill. He could have done any of them.

But he'd dreamed of something bigger. He'd dreamed of captaining the *Wafiya*, and no matter how clever he was, having almost no witchery barred him from that path. The fleet captains needed to command enough magic to keep their ships upright in a storm, if necessary. They needed to be the ones who could keep their ships from foundering, alone if need be. Ilyaran fleet captains, *especially* the flagship captains, were extraordinary witches. Ordinary would never be enough.

Rasim understood ordinary, and the hopes that might make a person reach for more. If the sea serpents hadn't attacked the fleet months ago, he didn't think he would have ever even imagined *how* to reach for more. Not as an apprentice, anyway. Not for many years as a journeyman, either. The Guilds were too structured, and he'd never really thought of anything beyond them.

But if someone had come to him and suggested there was another way, that perhaps he could learn to command the things he'd been denied, or lacked? He wished he could say he would never do such a thing, but he thought he knew himself better. The opportunity might well have been too much to resist.

And maybe that's what this perfectly ordinary woman had encountered. A chance. An opportunity. One Rasim could understand, even if he almost would have preferred not to.

He dropped back down into his body with what

should have been a thud, except he had been all spirit outside of it, and spirits didn't thud. He still felt distant from himself: when he tried to swallow, it took a strangely long time, like returning to his body had only been a courtesy, not melding flesh and soul together again.

He'd felt *something* like that in Oyun's tent, but not nearly as strongly. His tongue hadn't gone numb when he'd drunk what she gave him then, though. Maybe these people had given him a much stronger dose. But he'd gotten a look at his captors now, so breaking free seemed like a better idea than it had before. That, and the drug they'd given him made his head hurt less, so that had been a bad idea on their part.

Stonemastery would take too long and he couldn't see to know if he was succeeding with it, and sea witchery meant dragging water up from deep beneath the plains. Sky magic would do. He could probably pull the whole tent up, exposing his captors and himself to whomever was around. He took a rough breath and reached for the light, dancing witchery of the air.

Nothing happened.

It was *there*. Rasim could feel it, just out of reach, but the detachment that made physical motion distant and awkward affected the ability to reach his witchery, too. He tried again, and the power swirled away like trying to hold sand in his hands, or water. On one level he understood it was the drug, but he still wheezed, "What's *wrong*?" in frightened confusion.

The woman cackled and came closer yet, crouching near enough that he could feel her body heat, and almost, if he didn't try too hard, *see* her, but not with his physical eyes. Just the spirit-eyes that weren't quite properly settled into place, because of the zjhala. "It's a spirit-walking drug," she said, obviously choosing her words carefully and speaking slowly so he had a hope of understanding. "Our shamans use it to teach their..."

Rasim didn't know the next word, but it still clearly meant something like 'apprentice.' The woman felt like she was watching him, making sure he understood before she carried on. "Sometimes, to heal the sick. It takes away pain. Mmm."

The last sound suggested she wasn't happy with her word choice, but Rasim understood anyway. It didn't take pain away, exactly. His head, for example, still hurt horribly. But the drug made everything distant, though, which made pain harder to care about. He cared very strongly that he couldn't get to his witchery, but it didn't matter. Regardless of which kind of magic he reached for, it slithered out of his grasp, leaving him helpless in the hands of his captors.

Panic finally set in. Blood rushed through his ears, drowning out something the woman said, and his hands went cold while his belly twisted with sickness. He said, "I'm—" and threw up before he could get any more of a warning out. Not that he knew how to say 'vomit' in Shenryalan anyway.

The man holding him let out a shout of disgust and dropped him. Rasim collapsed sideways, hitting his head again and sobbing with the impact. Stars exploded, then drifted against the back of his eyelids, and he had a few seconds where he thought that this would be the time to yell for help.

His body wouldn't respond to the impulse to yell. Or not fast enough, anyway. The woman, more irritated than disgusted, put her hand over his mouth, brought her own mouth to his ear, and said, "If you shout," and the rest of the threat was lost on him.

He understood the sentiment clearly enough, though. If he shouted, something awful would happen. Miserable with the peculiar distant pain and the chills of panic wracking his body, he nodded. The woman uncovered his mouth, and he didn't cry out, even though he wanted to. He wasn't even sure if he stayed quiet because of her warning, or because he just couldn't make himself shout. He heard the man cleaning up, and felt the earth he'd spattered bile on being brushed away and tidied, and through all of it, all he could do was lie there with tears leaking into his blindfold.

Eventually the woman spoke again, from nearby. "You haven't asked, sorcerer-child."

He laughed, a tiny hoarse sound. "You heard me asking about delzjha. You don't want me to find *you*. So you stole me. That seems dumb." His Shenryalan wasn't really that good, but the woman chuckled again, so he thought she got the point.

"Yes," she said. "That's some of it. But you have many kinds of sorcery. We want to know how, and to take them from you."

For a moment, Rasim's head felt so thick and stupid that he thought she actually meant *take* his witchery, like it could be lifted out of him and put in someone else. Then he said, "Teach," in Ilyaran. "You want me to teach you." Almost as an afterthought, he said, "No," in her own language.

"Then we have no reason to keep you alive."

Rasim whimpered, although from the inside it felt more like tiredness than fear. The woman, though, made a satisfied sound, like she thought the threat was getting her somewhere. And if it weren't for the fact that Rasim still felt completely detached from his witchery, he might even have agreed. He'd taught Islanders magic in exchange for his freedom. There wasn't any arguable difference in teaching Shenryalans.

Except the Islanders had at least dragged him out of the ocean, saving his life before enslaving him. This woman or her people had hit him over the head and dragged him off. Somehow that seemed important.

Of course, nothing was going to be very important if he was dead. Still, somehow he managed a rough little sound that might have been a chuckle of his own. "Can't. That drug...zjhala...can't get to my witchery." He used the Ilyaran word, then added, "Sorcery," in case the woman hadn't understood. "Besides, you're too old."

She smacked him alongside the head for that, which sent another spill of sparks across the backs of his eyelids. Rasim decided maybe he should be quiet for a while. Maybe take a nap. Master Usia would tell him not to nap after a head injury. Rasim wondered what had happened to the master healer. He hadn't seen him since the fight in Hongrunn when so many Seamasters had been captured and enslaved and, he was afraid, killed.

His captor, incredulously, said, "Are you *crying?*" although Rasim didn't think it was an unreasonable thing to do, under the circumstances. He didn't answer, only shuddered with tears for a long time, before he did drop off to sleep, no matter what Master Usia would have said.

There was a moment, when he woke, where he hoped his power would be back and he'd be able to escape. But the detachment was there instead, the feeling like his body and spirit weren't quite attached, and the magic was on the wrong side of that. It felt quieter outside, and he thought it must be night now. Then, slowly, he realized his hands weren't tied anymore, which seemed spectacularly stupid on his captors' parts. He pulled his blindfold off, wincing at glimpses of firelight, at the still-present throbbing in his skull, at the air on his eyes, strangely cold after having had them covered for hours.

The tent was empty, although there were signs of occupancy. The central fire, beneath the clever double-layered hole in the ceiling so smoke could escape, had burned low, but not out. There were sleeping pillows and pads, and utensils for cooking and eating. He hadn't been abandoned, just given more freedom than made any sense.

Getting to his feet was much harder than he expected it to be. The signals from his mind to his body traveled slowly, and he was clumsy and prone to waves of dizziness. It took him a minute or two to stagger to the tent door. He drew a deep breath, preparing to yell for help as soon as he stepped outside, then pushed the door open.

The cry for help died on his lips, astonishment sharp and clear enough to be painful.

There *were* no other tents around, no Great Gathering surrounding him, no roving bands of children or groups of gossiping adults. There were horses a little distance away, and a great, vast darkness that stretched in grassy waves to a horizon cut by stars. Rasim staggered a step, searching for something to hold on to so he wouldn't fall.

He was absolutely, entirely on his own.

CHAPTER FIFTEEN

Alaugh sounded off to one side, almost behind him, and Rasim knew he was worse than alone. He was alone except for the people who had taken him. He turned, head pounding, to discover there *were* a few other tents, after all, but the steppes behind them were as empty and endless as those in front of him. "There's no one here, sorcerer. Just you and your—"

Rasim didn't know the word the woman used, but thought 'enemy' or 'fear' would probably be a close enough translation. He nodded, the motion still feeling thick and slow, and cast his gaze upward for a moment.

He could navigate by the stars, but navigating was only useful if he had a destination. Rasim had no sense of where the gathering was, nor any way to escape except by foot over unfamiliar terrain, which the horse-riding nomads could cover at far greater speed.

For a brief, desperate moment he thought maybe his friends would rescue him. They'd look, but there were tens of thousands of Shenryalans gathered on the plains. Smaller groups almost certainly left on a daily basis, maybe to hunt, maybe just for some privacy from the vast congregation. Figuring out which of them he was with would be like—

Rasim giggled, a thin, high sound that made his head throb in that distant, disassociated way. It would be like finding a particular stalk of grass on an endless steppe. It was possible, but not very likely, especially quickly.

He really didn't want to teach these people any kind of witchery at all, and he wasn't sure he would have any choice. "Fine. All right. But I need to know what you know, already. Who taught you. How they taught you." Every word felt like it fought its way through thick mud, his concentration forced. "And I need my own witchery."

The woman strode up to him, got close enough to make him dizzy, and said, "Hah!" right in his face. In the faint firelight from inside the tent behind him, her eyes were almost gold, lighter in color than most Shenryalan's, or maybe just reflecting the flames. "Nice try, sorcerer. You'll drink the zjhala again before you rest tonight, and every day. Not every teacher can do."

Rasim, still dizzy and not always wise at the best of times, snapped, "Not every student can, either, and you're *old*."

At least he tried to snap it, but the words were still coming slowly, and he was pretty sure he'd spoken Ilyaran. She understood his tone well enough, though, and put her hand on his face to shove him backward. Rasim fell over, completely unable to catch himself, and smacked his skull against the ground again. The last thing he really remembered until morning was gagging down another zjhala-laced drink, and no longer caring that his head hurt.

They hadn't bothered tying him up again. There was nowhere to run, or maybe there was everywhere to run, but it wouldn't do him any good. Rasim got up carefully, wishing his body and spirit felt like they belonged together, and lurched out of the tent to find somewhere to relieve himself. That made his head hurt, too, which didn't seem particularly fair.

The camp had three tents, at least forty horses, and eight or ten people that Rasim could see. Mostly women, ranging from a girl not much older than he was to a set-jawed grey-haired woman who reminded Rasim of the mother of the helpful girl who liked Bayar, but it wasn't her. The man he'd thrown up on the day before was nowhere to be seen. That didn't mean he wasn't there, though. Rasim hadn't even looked around the tent he'd been in to see if he was alone before he'd gone out to empty his bladder. There could have been a dozen other people in there, for all he knew.

His gaze traveled to the horses, and some part of his mind that could work through the zjhala discounted the idea that there were dozens of people in any of the tents. The Shenryalans had a lot of horses per person. Never fewer than two, and often three or four. He counted the horses very slowly, wishing they would hold still, although they weren't really moving that much. It was just that concentrating was hard. Usually by now he would have come up with a stupid plan, but his mind felt miles away.

There were at *least* forty horses. That could mean as many as twenty or twenty-five people in the camp, or as few as the ten he could see. Rasim sat down, finding it too hard to think and stand at the same time. Maybe that was how Desimi felt all the time.

He was immediately ashamed of himself, and also thought he was very funny. Giggles started to rise in his chest and he clamped his mouth shut, trying to muffle them, which meant his shoulders shook with suppressed laughter, which made his head rattle and hurt even more. Master Usia and Sesin would be worried about him, with all the blows he'd taken to the head, but he couldn't do anything about that right now.

Split the difference. Call it fifteen or seventeen people in the camp. That meant there were at least that many people studying sorcery without their leaders' knowledge. The girl he'd noticed was practicing witchery right now, in fact. Shaping the earth, making sculptures. Horses and riders, tents and fires, pictures of the world she knew. Rasim, with effort, stopped giggling and got to his feet, weaving his way over to her side.

She had a square face and a set jaw like the older woman, although that might have just been concentration. She edged back as he approached, wary, and Rasim shook his head, which hurt. "I just wanted to see what you were doing. I can't do that." He gestured at the shapes she'd made with earth witchery, then shook his head again. "Who taught you?"

The girl's glance skittered toward the older woman, who watched them both with an eagle's intentness. Rasim followed her look, winced, and sat down gingerly. "Your grandmother?"

"My mother!"

Rasim had obviously offended her without meaning to, and tried not to think that was funny, too. Head injuries made strange things amusing. "Sorry. Your mother taught you? I'm Rasim. Sorcerer-child," he added, because that seemed to be what everybody wanted to call him, and he wanted her to understand he was introducing himself.

After a suspicious moment, the girl said, "Darracha, daughter of Alsari, granddaughter of Nirjeran," and stared at him expectantly.

"Darracha." Rasim thought she wanted him to give her his lineage, too, and after a moment, tried, "Rasim, son of the Ilialio, grandson of Ilyara," which seemed to satisfy her. He would have to tell the others that, when he got back.

If he got back.

He put that thought away, or tried to, and nodded at her earth-working. "Your mother taught you?"

Darracha hesitated, glancing toward the stern-jawed woman who must be Alsari. The older woman nodded once, and a thrum of distant relief ran through Rasim. She must think he intended to teach Darracha his witchery. Well, the girl was probably the only one young enough to learn, although through the fuzziness in his head Rasim suddenly wondered if Alsari had started learning magic as an adult. He'd have to try to ask.

"Sorcerers," Darracha said carefully, slowly. "From afar."

"Like me?" Rasim asked. "Brown, with dark hair?" It took quite a lot of pantomime and naming of colors before either of them understood each other's answers, but then Darracha reached out to capture the end of one of Rasim's bleached curls in her fingertips.

"Yellow. Orange. Brown, like earth, not like..." Her hand fell to one of her own braids and she said a word that Rasim thought meant 'night,' which he decided made sense. Night was black, most of the time.

Yellow or orange hair almost certainly meant not-Ilyaran, though. There weren't many redheads in Ilyara, and even fewer blonds. "Brown-skinned?" he asked, then turned his hand over, showing the lighter color of his palm. "Or more like this?"

She tapped his palm, and Rasim sagged. He wasn't surprised. Northerners had magic, historically, and he'd seen their recent command of ice witchery in Ilyara itself. They'd worked wood and metal, too, back in the day. He wondered, for the first time, whether some seed of Northern magic had been kept alive all along, taught in secret, or whether they'd rediscovered their power more recently. He thought it might matter, but his head felt too thick to figure out why. Instead he said, "Who made the zjhala?"

Darracha had been wary, before. She shrank in on herself now, shaking her head in a small, violent motion. Rasim lifted his hands, trying to take the question back. He hadn't meant to scare her. "Never mind. Show me your sorcery?"

She reached for the earth she'd shaped, rebuilding a falling-apart horse sculpture. Rasim tried, with everything he had, to feel her use of witchery, the way he almost always could with Ilyaran magic. But even though he watched the magic work in front of him, he felt absolutely nothing from it, and had no idea if it was his lack of sensitivity to stone witchery, or the drug thickening his skull. Or maybe just the pounding headache and tiredness, which seemed like they would be enough on their own. "I can't do that," he said again. "It's good."

Surprised pleasure darted across Darracha's face, before she gestured. "You do something."

"I can't."

Impatience replaced the delight in her expression. "Do *your* sorcery."

"I can't," Rasim repeated. "The zjhala. I can't even find my own nose." He tried, and if he went slowly enough, he could connect his finger to the end of it, but if he used any speed, finding his face was a triumph. Darracha laughed, and Rasim winced but chuckled too. "I honestly don't know how to teach you if I can't show you with my witchery. I can tell you what it feels like." Somewhere in there confusion filled Darracha's eyes and he realized he was speaking Ilyaran.

Rasim groaned and with some effort, turned toward the closest adults and yelled, "Does anybody speak Ilyaran? Or at least Northern? Honestly," he said under his breath, "we *really* need proper language lessons in the guild."

The woman he thought of as their ringleader exited the tent he'd been kept in, her mouth pinched with irritation. "Even if I could *get* to my witchery I don't know what I could show you," Rasim yelled in her direction, still speaking Ilyaran and not caring. "There's hardly any water around here, except deep! I can't feel stone well enough to do anything but hope with it anyway, and I haven't even practiced with sun witchery so there's no way I'm trying to teach somebody that! I might set the whole steppe on fire!"

Possibility itched at him, with that idea. A big enough fire would make enough smoke for his friends to guess that's where he was, because Rasim caused disaster wherever he went. Nasira, for certain, would assume an unexpected wildfire on the steppes was his fault.

Of course, if he brought up a lot of water at once, the Seamasters might notice that, and Milu might even notice the disturbance of the earth when the water rose, if they weren't *too* far away. So really all he needed was his witchery. Which the ringleader here knew, and wasn't going to let him have access to. He put the thoughts aside, but didn't let them go entirely. Something like them might be the chance he needed. He turned back to Darracha. "Who made the poison? Bayar lived, you know."

He assumed she *did* know, but her eyebrows flickered downward. "Bayar? Bayar is—" Her gaze twitched toward the older women, then locked on the ground. "Bayar is no problem of mine."

Even through the thick stupidity in his head, Rasim felt like he'd hit on something that mattered to this young woman, and dropped his voice. "How long have you been out here? Bayar returned to the tribes. I brought him home."

Darracha's shoulders tensed, the muscles in her neck going tight, although she tried to hide it. Rasim lowered his voice even more, wishing he spoke her language more fluently. "Someone using a shaman's poison tried to kill him the night after he came home. He lived because of Ilyaran sorcery." He felt like he was stretching the truth, but enough of it was true.

The girl's hand reached out and seized his wrist, squeezing the bones together with painful strength. "Teach me that," she whispered. "Teach me to make people live."

"I can't." Rasim emphasized the words. "Even if I wanted to. I don't have the skill. If you brought me back to the Gathering, though, our healers would teach you."

For an instant, hope light Darracha's eyes, so she clearly understood enough of what he'd said, even if he felt like he'd butchered it. But it faded as quickly as it had come. She shook her head sharply, and with obvious effort, didn't look toward her mother or the ringleader.

She was afraid of them, Rasim thought. Maybe she had always wanted sorcery of her own, or maybe they'd told her she would study it whether she wanted to or not. Either way, she was afraid, and he knew she wouldn't risk herself to help him. He couldn't even blame her, not really, but a trickle of curiosity made its way through the drug-induced distance in his mind. "Have you even been to the Great Gathering, or have you been out here on the plains?"

A trace of wistfulness, as brief and thoroughly denied as the hope, crossed Darracha's face. "If you can't teach me, leave me alone." She turned her back on him deliberately, and after a moment, Rasim rose, still feeling thick and clumsy.

The man emerged from a tent, carrying a mug to Rasim. He looked gloomily into it, said, "Zjhala?" to the man, and got a nod in response. He took the mug, because they were going to make him drink it one way or another and he preferred not to have his nose pinched and the liquid poured down his throat, but he did say, "I can't teach you if I drink this," as if it might make a difference to this captor, when it hadn't before.

"Then you'll die." The man didn't sound particularly concerned, and Rasim, staring up at him—not very far up; neither of them were very tall—realized something that he should have understood before. He'd seen nearly a dozen people in this camp. He could identify them. Odds were poor that he could find them if they rejoined the larger gathering, but if he saw them, he would be able to identify them.

They had never intended to let him go. They hoped he could, and would, teach them, but as far as they were concerned, his fate had always been to be left cold and lifeless on the endless plains.

Dimly, through the fog of the drug and his distantly aching head and the various dull fears he faced, Rasim finally clawed his way through to the idea that might get him out of there in one piece. Just a few days ago, he had accidentally summoned a dragon.

He wondered if he could call one on purpose, this time.

CHAPTER SIXTEEN

Rasim lifted the drug-laced drink to his lips, making a show of sipping reluctantly while trying to make his thick mind race through a plan. He'd been unbalanced. That was why the dragon had found him. It had been drawn to the untapped sun witchery within him. But now everything about him was unbalanced, his spirit barely attached to his body, and his magic entirely out of reach.

Even he didn't think that sounded like something that a dragon would respond to.

His captor, not fooled in the slightest, tilted the bottom of the mug upward, spilling the drink into Rasim's mouth and down his chin. He choked and swallowed, coughed, and knocked the mug away, tears streaking down his cheeks as he wheezed through liquid in his chest. His captor raised a threatening fist and Rasim glared at him, wet-eyed. "I was drinking. You didn't have to do that."

"You were—"

Once more, Rasim didn't understand the actual word, but he'd heard that tone and similar accusations often enough that the word itself hardly mattered. Indignation exploded through him. "Of course I was scheming! You're going to kill me! I'm drugged out of my head, not stupid! You'd be scheming too!"

As fast as the clarity of anger came, it was gone. For a moment there, though, Rasim had felt whole again, like his spirit and body were actually connected. Maybe if he could lose his temper again, he could use that connection to call a dragon or work witchery or anything that would get him out of there alive. But although he was still angry, it didn't connect the way it had in those few seconds of outrage. He wiped his eyes and staggered away, wondering if Darracha would talk to him again.

Instead he found himself face to face with her mother, whose stern face was as threatening as a storm at sea. "Keep away from my daughter."

Rasim threw his hands in the air clumsily, narrowly missing hitting the older woman. "I can't teach anybody if I stay away! I can't teach anybody if I'm drugged! I can't teach anybody if you're all going to be stupid!" As he fought his way through shouting the last words, he realized he was outraged again, almost connected, and yelled, "*Help!*" with all his heart and soul.

The sound barely even seemed to reach his own ears, never mind rolling out across the plains like it might have done if he could have put sky witchery behind it. It seemed muffled, like shouting into a particularly hot Ilyaran afternoon sometimes could. It felt like the air itself suppressed the cry, muting him. Rasim dropped to his knees, too wrung out to keep his feet anymore, and saw a terrible, smug smile crawl across Darracha's mother's face. He said, "Oh," stupidly. "You're a sky witch."

His voice hadn't just *seemed* muffled. It had been. Shenryalans had sky witchery of their own, but he couldn't imagine Oyun or any other shaman offering this hard-smiling woman the chance to learn it. "Who taught you?"

A little to his surprise, she crouched, bringing her face close to his again. "No one. I *stole* the sorcery." She went on for another few sentences with a glint of satisfaction in her eyes, apparently aware that her explanation far outstripped his ability to understand. Then she rose, leaving Rasim alone in a boneless puddle on the grassy steppes floor. The earth trembled, reminding Rasim of the thundering hoofbeats across the plains, but he couldn't even bring himself to lift his head and look for rescue. He felt like the pieces were all right there in front of him, scattered but providing an answer, if he could only put them together correctly.

Instead he detached from his body altogether once more, floating upward and looking with sympathy down at the poor lump of himself on the ground. He hadn't drunk quite enough zjhala to make the spirit journey happen instantaneously this time, but he'd apparently had enough for it to happen. Darracha stood, looking toward his unconscious form with concern, but someone called her name and she flinched and returned to her duties. Rasim felt a pull back toward his body and resisted it for a moment, trying to get a good look at everything around him.

He just wasn't high enough to get a feel for the landscape, but he at least tried to memorize the faces and clothes of the people in the camp. If he did get away, the more details he could remember, the easier it would be to identify them. A few more men had come out of the tents, but Darracha was the youngest person there besides himself. This group didn't have the feeling of a family, but the tension-ridden air of people who were together out of necessity, and aware that being noticed could spell their doom.

Several of them, including the woman who'd spoken to him first and seemed to be their leader, were arguing. About him, clearly: they gestured and pointed in his direction with increasing unhappiness, until the earth shook hard enough for them to scowl at it. The woman crouched, putting her hands against the ground, then frowned and shook her head. Rasim couldn't hear what she said, and doubted he'd under-stand it if he did.

The tug back to his body strengthened, and he thumped back down into himself again, waking grog-gily. His head still hurt with that drug-induced distance, and he hated it. Pushing up to his feet seemed too hard, so he lay there, cheek in the dirt, feeling the earth's vibrations. He hoped they meant there were whole herds of Shenryalan riders out looking for him, although that didn't seem very likely. He was going to have to rescue himself. He said,

"Help," again, thickly, but there wasn't any kind of power behind it at all.

The earth rumbled again, and the horses started moving away in a nervous group. Then one leaped into a gallop and the others followed like they had only needed a prompt to do so.

In their wake, the ground heaved, breaking apart in huge dark chunks. People and horses alike screamed, although the horses were at least out of the breaking earth's path. The ringleader woman fell backward, then scrambled to her feet, trying to escape as a massive, stone-sided snake rose from the broken earth.

It reared up and up and up, torn dirt and grass roots rolling from its slate-colored skin as it powered itself high into the air, then slammed down with a plains-rattling crash that completely flattened a tent. It slithered forward, great jaws gaping, and swallowed a screaming man effortlessly.

Rasim didn't know if it was astonishment, fear, or the drug that kept him lying on the ground just gaping at the vast beast. It was clearly *like* the stone snake he'd encountered in the Northern mountains, but it was unlike that other terrible creature, too. The Northern snake's skin had been boulder-like, rubbing against each other and dropping grit and stones, like the mountain itself shedding rocks. This monster had overlapping scales, but they were deep stony grey, edged in places with iron red. Somewhere far below them, Rasim thought, the bedrock must be made of stone like that, layers and layers of dark rock and traces of iron.

It destroyed the camp almost entirely in seconds. Rasim caught glimpses of some of his captors running. No one spared a thought for him. The great snake rose up again, lashing toward the escapees, then spat a spray of bad air after them before diving back into the earth. Huge piles of torn-up ground surged around it as it dove, and its tail wriggled in the air a moment before the rumbling of the plains faded. Rasim sat up, staring wide-eyed at the hills and holes around him, and at the ugly evidence that not everyone had survived the snake's attack.

He'd yelled 'help.' He hadn't asked specifically for anything in *particular* to help him. Maybe imbalance was imbalance, and beasts of magic responded to it.

Pure ice slid through him, freezing his thoughts with a horrible crystal clarity.

The sea serpents had attacked the very first time he'd sailed with the whole of the Ilyaran fleet. The Northern stone snake had come after them in the aftermath of him discovering his limited stone witchery. And the glasswing, that beautiful, tragic creature of air, had come to him from the windstorm he'd created upon learning skymastery.

He had been out of balance all that time. It suddenly seemed very real and possible that all of that destruction, all of those deaths, were because these magic-born creatures were drawn to the witchery struggling within him.

Rasim's heart unfroze, thudding wildly above a stomach sick with nerves before he twisted to one side and threw up. It felt and tasted terrible, but it was almost a relief. It might help get the zjhala out of his system. Wiping his mouth, he looked back at the wreckage, and then clumsily, unsure of himself, Rasim got to his feet and started walking. The mountains they'd crossed to get onto the Shenryalan plains were to the east. If he walked that way long enough, he would eventually find them. If he climbed one and went down the other side and headed south, sooner or later he would come to the *Wafiya*. It wasn't a good plan, but it was better than wandering the endless steppes hoping he might discover the gathering.

And his witchery would come back, sooner or later. He could try to call for less extraordinary help, then. But in the meantime, staying where the stone snake and his captors had been just seemed like a chance to get caught again. As it was, he'd be lucky if they didn't come back to their destroyed camp, because he was sure they would catch him quickly if they returned.

Even just an hour of walking gave him some hope that they were still running the other direction. If they'd turned around and come back in the wake of the stone snake's departure, he was confident they'd have caught him already, because it felt like he was walking only slightly faster than a snail. It was hard to keep all his parts going the same direction at the same time, and he had no idea how long it would take the zjhala to wear off. They'd made him take a dose every several hours, so he would probably be fine by morning, if he stayed free that long.

A glance at the sky made him laugh, in a rough uncertain way. It was *still* morning. He'd woken up fairly early, and it hadn't really been very long before the snake had smashed its way through the camp. So he might be fine by evening, which would make building a shelter of some kind easier.

Long before that became an issue, though, there were hoofbeats on the plains, and Bikat himself, flanked by the Stonemaster journeymen Milu and Telun, came to his rescue.

MOST OF WHAT Rasim could recall of the return to camp was that Milu seemed extremely good at riding a horse. He was so tall his feet nearly touched the ground when he sat astride, but the sturdy animal he rode seemed to find that acceptable, and Milu, who hated to travel, looked comfortable on its back. Telun was less good at it, but where Milu went, Telun did, so of course he was there.

And they were both there because the stone snake's emergence from deep in the plains bedrock had sent so many waves of disturbance through the earth that Milu had been able to lead them, unerringly, to where it had appeared. "We knew it was you," Telun said quite cheerfully. "Who else would create earthquakes all on his own?"

"I didn't mean to. I'm sorry," Rasim said, mostly to Bikat, with whom he was riding. Several of his escort had been shocked that the King Horse himself shared a saddle with the sorcerer-child, but Bikat had sworn to Nasira that he would take no chances with Rasim's safety. Rasim had apologized to him at least four times, and each time Bikat had passed it off, as he did this time, too.

"Your transgression is less than our own, which allowed you to be taken. If you apologize again I will take insult."

Rasim kept his mouth shut for the rest of the ride, and fell tiredly off the horse when they arrived back in camp. Kisia and Desimi crowded around him, and he hugged them gratefully. "Are you all right, Kees?"

"Am *I* all right?" Her eyes were very large and bright and her voice cracked on the question. "I'm fine. Are *you*?" She did look better than she had the last time Rasim had seen her, although her skin still looked a little drawn, like the poisoning had left some effects she hadn't yet thrown off. Rasim studied her, making sure she was really all right before he nodded carefully.

"I'm mostly all right, but I think I need to see Sesin. I got hit on the head and I haven't been right since. But they kept drugging me, too, so I don't know which it is that making me feel bad."

"We would hear your story, when you are well," Bikat said with great formality, and Rasim blinked at him, then nodded carefully.

"Of course, King Horse. I hope it'll be tonight, but..." Rasim cast a glance toward the now-setting sun. "But is another night really going to matter?"

A faint smile pulled at Bikat's mouth. "By morning our fugitives may well be in custody, and many questions will be answered. Rest and heal. We can wait."

"Thank you." Rasim, leaning more on Desimi than

he wanted to admit, went to their tent to find Sesin waiting with concern and Nasira with exasperation. He said, "I didn't *mean* to," to the captain, who sighed.

"You rarely do. See the healer, Journeyman. I'll save the shouting for later."

"Thanks. I think." Rasim sat at Sesin's order, feeling the soft weight of her witchery as she examined him. "Oh! The drug's wearing off. I can feel your power again."

"Mmm." She examined his eyes and sighed. "You're probably coming out of a concussion, but there's not much I can do now. You should have spent the past couple of days resting, not resisting being kidnapped, but none of this would have happened if you hadn't been kidnapped, so. I'd like you to get some sleep instead of going to talk to Irlin and Bikat."

Rasim closed his eyes, trying to see if the detachment of the zjhala had left him yet. All the same pieces of what he'd observed were still there, lingering around the edges of his mind, but none of them wanted to connect with each other and make sense yet. "Maybe that's a good idea."

"Really?" Sesin's voice rose sharply enough with surprise that she laughed. "I thought you'd argue with me."

"I think I'd rather sleep than argue."

"Well, that's a first," Captain Nasira said dryly. Rasim gave her a wounded look and she chuckled. "Get some rest, Journeyman. I expect you'll have a lot of explaining to do tomorrow."

"Yes, Captain." Despite his best efforts, though,

Rasim struggled to sleep. People were in and out of the tent, some of them surreptitiously checking on him, others just because they had things to do. Bayar came in to talk to Kisia for a while, and they both sat where they could see Rasim, like he might disappear again without supervision. Prince Lorens brought food in that almost everyone shared, but Rasim couldn't convince himself to sit up and eat.

Desimi noticed he was awake, though, and came to sit by him for a minute, mumbling, "I shouldn't have gone off with Ūrrin. This wouldn't have happened if you hadn't been alone."

"Or maybe they'd have clobbered both of us," Rasim whispered. "It wasn't your fault. But thanks."

"Yeah. Get some sleep, Sunburn." Desimi left him alone, and strangely enough, after that, Rasim slept.

CHAPTER SEVENTEEN

The pieces came together as Rasim woke up. Fragile, barely connected, but finally there. He lay very still and quiet in bed for a few minutes, making sure he wouldn't lose the pattern of how they fit with one another, and then rose, feeling like himself for the first time in days. His head no longer hurt, either distantly or urgently, and it was so nice to *not* hurt he thought he might cry from relief.

He was also actually hungry for the first time in days, and someone outside the tent was roasting lamb for breakfast. Rasim staggered out, his mouth watering, and found Bayar crouched at a nearby fire, watching the lamb cook on a spit. In daylight, it was clear that he was, like Kisia, more fragile than usual. The red warmth in his face burned too close to the surface, like his skin had become almost transparent, and his movements were a little careful. But he was clearly better enough to be waiting at a fire, and he stood to hug

Rasim hard as he approached. "We were afraid for you, 'sorcerer-child.'"

Rasim groaned, but returned the embrace gladly. "I'd rather be called Sunburn."

Bayar grinned. "Perhaps I'll simply call you Rasim. You're well?"

"Well enough." Rasim sat beside Bayar on the dirt, both of them watching the lamb cook, now. "Starving, but otherwise all right. But I had some ideas, Bayar. I thought of some things."

The handsome Shenryalan boy smiled. "Of course you did. Have you solved every mystery that's bothered us?"

"Some of them, maybe."

Bayar's eyebrows rose and he lifted a hand to stop Rasim's further explanations. "Best wait until you can speak with my parents, so you don't have to repeat everything."

"After breakfast," Rasim said hopefully, and Bayar's beautiful grin shone again.

"After breakfast. I have one question, though. Our earth-workers said there was a great disturbance, and your friend Milu ran from camp alone. I think he would have run all the way to you, if the riders hadn't caught up to him. What did you *do*?"

"I called for help," Rasim said slowly. "I was trying to call that dragon, but a stone snake came instead. I'd seen one like it before, in the Northern mountains. I think it came up from the bedrock, so Milu would have felt it even if no one else did, but it shoved so much earth aside when it came up that I'm not surprised your earth witches felt it, too. It wasn't what I meant to do at all."

"So it isn't just the dragon," Bayar said thoughtfully. "Or the glasswing, in the Moranese windstorm. You command all the monsters that legend has ever dreamed."

"Siliaria's teeth, I hope not. No. I don't think I was commanding anything, for one thing. I think it responded to me because…" Rasim sighed. "This might be better to just explain all at once to your parents and Captain Nasira and everyone, too, but Oyun said I'm unbalanced, or I was until she helped me, and I think maybe that's why they've responded to me. And one of the people who took me was a sky witch. She buried the sound of my voice, when I called for help. I think maybe the only thing that could hear me at all was the stone snake." He took a breath, about to add more, but ended up shaking his head and going in another direction. "Bayar, does anyone ever begin to study with the shamans but…fail, I guess? Decide it's not their path, or turn out to be not well-suited for it?"

Bayar blinked at him with interest. "Does that happen in Ilyara?"

Rasim sighed. "Not in the guilds, no. There are people like me who aren't very good at witchery, but they stay in the guild, at least until they're pretty grown-up. I'm just trying to figure out where along the line the secrets of making these drugs could slip out to people who aren't shamans."

"Ah." Bayar fell silent a moment, his gaze so entirely focused on the cooking lamb that it seemed to be his entire world for a few minutes. Finally, though, he said, "The venom is key. Concentrated, it becomes hinzjha, the life-slayer. Diluted, it is zjhala, the spirit-walker. Dried, ground up with a rare plant, it is delzjha, the wisdom-slayer that boosts magic and drives a sorcerer to use their power until they die of it."

Rasim's heart lurched. "It's all the same stuff?"

"Could you not guess, from the names?"

"I don't speak Shenryalan that well, Bayar!"

Bayar laughed. "Forgive me, then. Perhaps it would have been easier on you if you'd realized they were made of the same thing."

"Maybe! Does everybody know that? I should have saved myself the trouble of getting kidnapped and just asked you."

"Not everyone," Bayar replied thoughtfully. "The Great Mare, and those who are close to the shamans. Enough people, Rasim. Enough for the secret to slip out, although administering them correctly, that *is* a secret. If too much zjhala is given and the spirit leaves the body too quickly, for example, it may never find its way back."

"Siliaria's fins! I left my body really fast twice. At least twice."

Bayar's eyebrows drew down and he bowed his head toward Rasim. "You should meet with Oyun again, so that she may be certain that they are still properly bound to one another."

"I will!"

"Breakfast first." Bayar cut off a hunk of seared meat with a knife and offered it to Rasim, who ate greedily, and, for a little while, let everything else go. Desimi and Kisia came out to join them, and slowly, so did everyone else, until Rasim felt the weight of them not asking what had happened in the past few days.

He finally sat back with a groan and raised his hands like he was fending off a barrage of questions. "Bayar, when are your parents going to be ready to talk to me? I don't think I can stand everybody *looking* at me for much longer."

Bayar, with so much formality he was clearly teasing, said, "The King Horse and Great Mare await your pleasure, Sorcerer-Child," and laughed when Rasim threw a bit of lamb bone at him. "They should be ready. I think they hoped they would have captured your captors, and could end this with a show of strength, but thus far they have evaded us."

Rasim wrinkled his face. "Leaving them relying on a first-year journeyman to know what's going on. I'm sure they must really like that. All right." He stood, brushing his hands against his trousers, then wishing he hadn't put grease stains on them right before going to see royalty.

Bayar went ahead of him, leading quite an odd band into the largest Shenryalan tent. Kisia and Desimi flanked Rasim, which was normal enough, but Captain Nasira and Sunmaster Endat followed them, and then most of the rest of the Ilyaran contingent, including the old Moranese woman, and even Lars, the former Northern slave. The other journeymen had stayed behind, as Pynda still had almost nothing to say, and neither Milu nor Telun wanted to leave her entirely alone.

Angled sunlight spilled through raised sections of the tent's roof, brightening the interior. The Shenryalans within were seated more or less as he expected them to be, women on one side and men on another. To Rasim's surprise, Kif sat with the men, his back straight and an expression of grave pride on his old face. Across from him was the woman that Darracha's mother reminded Rasim of. He couldn't tell, studying her, whether they really looked alike, or if they just had similar scowls. Her daughter was beside her, hands clenched together in her lap and gaze downcast so Rasim couldn't see her face clearly. He didn't think she looked like Darracha either, but he wasn't sure about anything anymore. Especially since at the moment, men and women alike had similar foreboding expressions, as if they were trying to prepare for the worst.

Bayar's parents sat on their usual thrones, with Oyun and Bayar's chairs to either side. Neither of them looked as though they'd slept much, and, like those around them, both seemed to be braced for news they didn't really want to hear. But Irlin nodded graciously, then smiled when Rasim, unsure of what else to do, bowed briefly to both of them. "We thank you for the honor you offer, sorcerer-child."

"And we offer our apologies for the dishonor done to you." Bikat's usually-gentle voice held deep threads of anger. "I'm sorry that we must interrogate you on what has happened, Rasim. We have far fewer answers than we hoped to by now."

"It's all right. I hope I might have some for you." Rasim cast one apologetic look at Nasira, but she only rolled her eyes and waved a hand, as if recognizing that Rasim was the only person who could tell the Shenryalan royal family anything useful right now. "I don't even know if there was anybody left for you to catch, honestly. The stone snake smashed a lot of people. I know some ran away, but it might have gotten them before it went back underground."

A rather loud silence followed that, and every adult in the room seemed to take the time to exchange looks with every *other* adult in the room. Rasim, hands cold with sudden nerves, turned toward Kisia and Desimi, who both bugged their eyes and hissed for him to face forward again. Finally Irlin said, "I very much want an explanation about that, but perhaps you should start at the beginning, Rasim."

Rasim didn't think the story itself was very complicated. It was what he'd put together in the aftermath that seemed important, but he explained about being hit over the head and drugged, and about the small encampment of sorcerers and students. Somewhere in the middle explaining what had happened, Rasim realized he was avoiding saying Darracha's name. He didn't know if she was even still alive, and he thought that she'd been pretty nice, all things considered. He didn't want to get her in trouble. It seemed silly, but also important, somehow. "I never saw the woman I was calling the ringleader use any witchery. Neither did the man who gave me the zjhala. There was a girl who was an earth witch, and her mother, who was a sky witch, and—" Rasim took a deep breath. "And I don't know if it was *her*, but now that I know for sure there are rogue Shenryalan skymasters, I think one of them probably kidnapped Bayar."

A stir of interest ran through the room as the translator echoed his words in the Shenryalan language, but Irlin, who understood him directly, leaned forward intently. "Speak to me of why."

"Because Bayar said nobody ever said anything, the whole time they were taking him to the continent. And when I shouted for help, Alsari muted it with her witchery. It made me realize that a skymaster could have just kept Bayar's ears blocked, so he neve..." He trailed off into bewildered silence as a stir, and then an uproar swept through the tent. People surged to their feet, shouting questions. On the women's side of the tent, a space opened up around the stern-jawed woman with the grey-streaked hair. She sat unmoving, her eyes wide and mouth open, staring at Rasim with shock. The girl beside her lifted her eyes, dismay written in her face.

Bikat snapped, "Speak that name again!" to Rasim, who flinched toward the King Horse in confusion.

"Did I say a name? I..." He closed his eyes, trying to hear what he'd said, and then, all at once, remembering how Darracha had introduced herself. Darracha, daughter of Alsari, granddaughter of Nirjeran. Rasim had completely forgotten that on a conscious level, with the uncomfortable distance between his body and spirit, and the ache in his head. "Alsari, daughter of Nirjeran. She didn't give me her name, but her daughter Darracha did." Guilt swam through him at bringing Darracha's name into it, and he added, "She wanted to be a healer," very softly, as if that might somehow make a difference.

Cacophony filled the tent again, and the group around the grey-streaked woman closed in, anger and fear in their voices. She jolted to her feet, expression rich with loathing, and then earth witchery tore the ground to pieces.

The great tent's floor simply fell in. Rasim, at the very center of the rift, fell twice his height straight down, the ground just no longer there beneath him. He yowled with shock and fear, then threw an arm over his head, trying to protect himself as others followed him into the growing chasm. The grey-streaked woman's daughter landed on top of him as her mother dove past them. The earth opened farther for her, sorcery creating an escape route. Her daughter jolted to her feet, but stood frozen, staring after where her mother had gone.

Other people cascaded down, nearly landing on top of Rasim as he tried to crawl out of the way. Thrones and chairs toppled sideways and downward, sending Bayar and Oyun toward the earthy rift. Desimi threw himself toward Oyun, catching her with his shoulder in her belly. With a bullish roar, he scrambled out of the sudden chasm as if the earth itself shaped steps beneath his feet. Rasim lurched after them, but the ground turned to soft crumbling loam beneath his hands, unclimbable. Bayar hit the bottom of the crevasse beside him, and they both staggered back, looking for a way out.

Kisia crashed down, clawing at the tearing earth as she fell. Her shriek was more angry than afraid, but Rasim and Bayar both turned toward her, as if they could rescue her while they were all in the bottom of the pit. She snarled, pushing past them as a crash sounded almost above their heads. Rasim twisted, looking upward to see that Bikat and Irlin's thrones had slammed into each other, which kept them from falling into the pit. There were people on their bellies all around the hole's lip, reaching for those who had fallen. A hopeful Shenryalan man grabbed a fist full of deep grass root that had been torn apart as the pit opened, and tried to use it to climb upward. It almost worked, but the torn ground crumbled under his feet and he fell back down.

Kisia shrieked with rage and Rasim spun around again. The escaping grey-streaked witch was burrowing into the ground like a desert fox, digging at witchery-assisted speeds, and Kisia, incoherent with fury, *followed* her. Rasim thought she might chase her all the way to the center of the earth, but Nasira, up above, yelled, "*Journeyman!*" and Kisia stopped with a furious glare at their captain.

Nasira snarled, "Wipe that look off your face and take Lars's hand, Journeyman, or else!" and Kisia, sullenly, moved toward the round-shouldered Northerner.

He was well into the pit, but as part of a rescue crew, not because he'd fallen. He held Endat's hand as the Sunmaster lay on his belly with most of his weight on the solid ground. Kif was sitting on Endat's legs, pinning him in place. Lars seized Kisia's arm, almost throwing her out of the gaping hole before reaching for another Shenryalan woman. She scrambled toward him, and he hauled her upward as easily as he'd done Kisia, reminding Rasim that he'd spent most of his life in back-breaking labor in the mines. Hands caught her, pulling her the rest of the way up. Lars grabbed Rasim by the scruff and yanked him out of the ditch, too. He cried out in protest, trying to grab Bayar as Lars pulled him up, and missing by scant inches.

The grey-streaked woman's daughter turned from staring after her mother, and carefully moved toward Bayar instead of taking the reaching hands from above. He was too short to reach them himself, until the girl made a stirrup of her hands and whispered, "Go," beneath the shouts around them. Rasim saw him cast her an agonized look, but he stepped into her hands and she lifted him upward with a shouted bellow for strength. She sank into the soft exposed earth as she did so, ankle-deep in roots and dirt, and just barely missed the fingertips now reaching for her.

The rift slammed closed, the earth's surface rough but the gaping hole in it disappearing like it had never been.

Endat and several Shenryalans were stuck in the ground to the shoulder, and one man's head had been closed into the earth. Lars, the girl, and another Shenryalan woman were buried entirely as the rift closed. People started to scream again as they realized what was happening, falling to their knees to begin digging helplessly with their hands.

Desimi bellowed, "*MOVE!*" with such power that people scattered to the walls of the tent, gazes locked on the Ilyaran journeyman with obedient confusion. Rasim stood still, arrested with astonishment as Desimi, lip curled with concentration, spread his hands and repeated, "Move," into the sudden, overwhelming silence.

The earth pulled apart again.

CHAPTER EIGHTEEN

In the silence, under dozens of gaping gazes, Desimi shaped the earth as though he'd been meant to all along. Where it had torn and ripped violently under the woman's power, it now flowed, piling up like sand pushed by water as he delved deep enough to save those who had been buried. It was strangely beautiful.

Endat's shoulder and arm came loose, but he stayed where he was, still holding Lars's hand as the earth rift opened to first expose, and then free him. The Sunmaster hauled the Northman upward and Lars came to the surface coughing and gagging as a shout of relief went up around the tent. Moments later, the others were free, weeping and spitting dirt as they struggled for air. Rasim thought Desimi would shape steps or ramps from the earth to let them climb out, but the people on the surface were faster, helping their friends up. Irlin herself pulled the girl who had helped Bayar from the crevasse, but Bayar shouldered his mother aside and held the Shenryalan girl as she wept.

Desimi said, "Move," again, and this time lifted his head long enough to meet Rasim's eyes.

Rasim had known Desimi their whole lives, and even more, knew the look of a boy with a dangerous plan. He blurted, "Are you sure?" and got the faintest flicker of a smile, and a much more certain nod, in response. Rasim nodded back, and this time he lifted his voice, assisted by sky witchery, to cry, "Move!" in Shenryalan. He turned to the translator, talking as fast as he could, and as the interpreter echoed him, Rasim carried the translated words over as much of the camp as he could reach with his skymastery.

It amounted to 'pick up the babies and move the horses, the ground is about to open beneath you,' and that's what happened. Desimi worked with his eyes half closed, hands spread like he was pulling the earth apart between them, and his lips parted, moving with concentration. The rift he'd opened in the great tent spilled out its door, bending as his witchery followed the Shenryalan sorcerer's.

She had gone deep, like a burrowing desert spider. Her power had ripped the earth apart, but only where she'd meant it to, in the tent for her initial escape. Desimi was much more destructive, ripping the earth open from the surface all the way down, although he was clearly trying to be careful with his witchery, letting it run slowly enough that people had time to get out of the way. Rasim could almost see him learning the magic, figuring out how to make the earth move at his whim. All at once the rumbling broken surface of ground that he'd been tearing apart submerged, like he'd figured out how to do what the Shenryalan witch was doing.

By that time Milu and Telun were there, outside the great tent, both of them gaping. Milu knelt, putting both hands on the ground and tilting his head like he could hear inside the earth itself. Then a sharp grin shot across his face and he yelled, "Everybody brace!"

Rasim lifted the warning to all ears, watching people grab onto each other or drop to their bellies in order to ride out whatever was about to happen. Almost instantly, there was a deep snapping surge and the ground shook like something massive had hit it. Milu groaned and lay on his face, but Desimi cackled and said, "Good," then made a fist of one hand.

Not very far away, the ground broke apart and the Shenryalan witch rose from it. She was limp, not quite unconscious, but obviously not able to fend off the guards who rushed to seize her. Irlin, who had come to Rasim's side at the great tent's door, said, "Does your ship mother have any more of the drug you call heartbreak?"

Nasira, who was only a step or two behind them, still inside the tent, said, "I don't, I'm sorry. Lorens used the last of it weeks ago."

A spasm of doubt shot through Rasim as he recalled the cascade of certainties he'd felt about the Northern prince's hand in so many deaths. He looked for Lorens's yellow hair, and didn't see him, but before he could say or really even think much of anything, Milu said, "I think I can cut her off from her witchery," and Oyun, hobbling out of the great tent, snorted.

"Old Oyun *knows* she can." She spoke Ilyaran, gaining sharp glances from everybody but Rasim, who crooked a grin as she revealed her secret, then said, "Oh!" a little stupidly. "You have zjhala, don't you. That's what you gave me the first night."

Oyun clicked her tongue. "Too many secrets, sorcerer-boy. You learn too many of old Oyun's secrets. Shaman's secrets. The Great Spiral will bring you back here, one day." She paused, taking her attention from him to examine Desimi with a sort of critical but satisfied gaze. She thumped the big Ilyaran boy with her stick and he jumped, then rubbed his shoulder, half offended until Oyun met his eyes and nodded once.

Not at all to Rasim's surprise, Desimi's hand went to the necklace that King Taishm had given him for his efforts in service to the Ilyaran throne. Oyun's single nod felt like that same kind of praise, even to Rasim.

Enormously to his surprise, Desimi grinned crookedly and bowed to the old shaman, his hand still over the necklace and, not exactly coincidentally, over his heart. Oyun chortled, then snapped, "Bring her," in Shenryalan, and the earth witch's captors dragged her toward Oyun's tent. The old shaman led the way, leaving the Ilyarans temporarily gathered together, and more or less alone within the Shenryalan camp.

Everybody turned toward Desimi.

The big journeyman's shoulders hunched uncomfortably and he cast a helpless look at Rasim, as if Rasim might be able to explain what he couldn't. He mumbled, "It was important," and Nasira let loose a sharp, incredulous laugh.

"If *importance* gave us the ability to wield new witcheries at will, Journeyman, Ilyara never would have burned! What *was* that?"

Desimi, defensively, yelled, "I don't know! I've been watching Milu work earth since we got here and all of a sudden it was important and it didn't seem so hard so I did it! And Skymaster Arrat spent weeks trying to teach me skymastery on the *Wafiya* so maybe that helped? I don't know? Rasim!"

Rasim nearly startled out of his skin. "I didn't do anything!"

"I know, but you're the one this keeps happening to, so why did it happen to me?" Desimi wasn't *quite* whining, but Rasim couldn't think of another word for his tone, either.

"And *earth* witchery," Sunmaster Endat burst out. "Ilyarans don't work *earth* witchery, Desimi!"

Milu cleared his throat, and Rasim said, "But you were unbalanced," to him, which made everybody's heads whip back in his direction. "Oyun said Milu was kind of like me. Earth witchery might have even been more natural to him than stone witchery, but he only learned stonemastery because that's what Ilyarans do. They're close enough that he probably wouldn't have ever—" He stopped abruptly, not really wanting to admit the dragon's arrival had been caused by his unbalanced magics.

"What do you mean, kind of like you?" Nasira's voice held a dangerous note, but Rasim was almost relieved. At least the question of dragons didn't have to be answered right now.

Or maybe it did. He sighed and slumped and wondered how, exactly, the moment had gone from everybody being stunned at Desimi to the captain being mad at *him* again. "Oyun thinks my sea witchery was so weak because the Great Fire scared me so much that I suppressed all my magic. And then I met Siliaria—"

"You mean she kissed you," Kisia whispered in a sing-song. Nasira shot her a daggered glare and she went guiltily quiet. Rasim had never been so grateful for the captain's ability to silence someone with a look.

"—and Oyun thinks that unlocked the potential I had. Not just for being a sea witch, though. Because she thinks that if I..." Rasim sighed. Trying to explain the old shaman's beliefs when it was exactly the opposite of how the whole Ilyaran guild system was set up seemed practically impossible. "Basically everything that's happened unbalanced my magic and she helped me straighten it out and Milu was like that but less so. So is Telun," he added abruptly, which made the older Stonemaster journeyman blink in surprise.

"Me?"

Rasim waved his hands in the air, wishing he'd kept his mouth shut. Wishing he'd done that most of a year ago, and hadn't gotten himself into any of this, although he couldn't ever regret sailing on the *Wafiya*. "She said sniffing you told her that you'd been born with the potential to hear Tilarea, but that becoming a Stonemaster apprentice had silenced the air goddess's voice in your spirit. She didn't know if it could be reawakened."

Telun's jaw fell open. "I'm not a very good stone witch, you know."

Milu made a sound of protest, but Telun shrugged it off. "I'm not, love. It's fine, you've power for the two of us and half the guild besides, but…you weren't a good sea witch, Rasim. Does that mean you were born with the potential to hear a different god?"

Everyone turned their attention to Rasim again. He said, "I thought we were talking about Desimi now," but Nasira's face hardened, and he sighed. "Riorda. But the Great Fire scared the sun witchery right out of me, until Oyun…" With another sigh, Rasim turned his palm up, and, with care, called fire to life in his hand.

A sound of disbelief went up from the Ilyarans gathered around him, although Kisia whispered, "I *knew* it!" and Sunmaster Endat surged through the little group to seize Rasim's wrist.

"You've learned to find it! And call it from nothing?" Incredulity and possibly envy filled the sun witch's voice. "Do you know how rare that is?"

Rasim looked for Pynda, who had followed Milu and Telun from their tent when Desimi started using earth magic. Her jaw was set and tears glittered in her eyes like she was defying him to call her out on it. Instead, much more to her than the master, Rasim said, "I do," very gently. "Daka could do it, and I knew she was among the best of you."

Pynda's jaw clenched harder, but the tears spilled, and Kisia went to put her arms around the older girl. For long seconds, Pynda stayed as she was, rock solid and defiant, but then with a choked sob she collapsed into Kisia's hug, and for the first time that Rasim knew about, cried over the death of her friend. He closed his hand around the flame he'd called and turned his attention back to Endat. He felt very old and very tired in that moment, and Endat released him with an apologetic frown that suggested that burden of weariness was somehow in Rasim's face.

"You've done it, then," Endat said slowly. "You've become what King Taishm hoped. A master of all our witcheries."

Rasim winced. "A journeyman at best. And I'm never going to get beyond apprentice as a stone witch."

Kisia hummed with disagreement, but didn't argue aloud, and either way, Endat fell back a step, expression deep with thought. Rasim said, "But what about Desimi," and the bigger journeyman looked betrayed as everyone's attention returned to him.

"We should put the ground back," he mumbled. "Especially where you dug the rock up, Milu." They had, in fact, settled most of the rest of the earth already, but Nasira, in a tone of bewildered exasperation, said, "The rock?"

Milu and Desimi, both looking faintly ashamed of themselves, exchanged grins that were also exceptionally pleased. "There's a huge boulder under the surface," Milu said. "Their earth witch was tunneling toward it, but she would have passed over it, or gone around. I moved it into her path faster than she could react. She smashed right into it."

"Then when she was stunned I brought her to the surface," Desimi said cheerfully, although his humor slipped quickly. "I couldn't figure out how to get ahead of her to stop her, or grab hold of her to drag her up. I'm sorry, Captain."

Nasira's jaw worked as she searched for a response, and Milu clapped Desimi on the shoulder. "You did well for someone who's never used the power before. Exceptionally well. No one was even hurt when you tore up all that earth. I'll teach you." He paused, glancing around their surroundings, and shrugged. "Or their witches will."

In the wake of that, Nasira said, "You have nothing to apologize for, Journeyman," in a slightly strangled voice. "You have, in fact, done well. We'll arrange for lessons as soon as we can. Earth witchery," she said beneath her breath. "What is the world coming to?"

Oyun strode out of her tent, a look of satisfaction on her wrinkled face as she returned to the greater one. The Ilyarans followed her in, mostly, Rasim thought, because nobody wanted to miss anything, at this point. Not even Captain Nasira.

People were still setting the tent's interior to rights, making Rasim realize it had really only been a few minutes since Alsari's sister had torn the ground to pieces. Despite Desimi's best efforts, Bikat and Irlin's thrones were half sunk in the earth, and the chair Bayar usually sat in was gone entirely. Someone scurried to put Oyun's chair on its feet as she entered, but she stopped in the middle of the tent, at the heart of where the magic had started, and thumped her stick down. "Qyacha will work sorcery no more. Her anger is great, and until it begins to fail to despair, she will answer no questions."

"I have some guesses," Rasim said very quietly, almost hoping no one would hear him.

Instead, *everyone* heard him, as if he'd lifted his voice with sky witchery and boomed it out across the whole encampment. Those tidying up stopped and turned to him as the translator interpreted his words, and Bayar, who was still sitting on the floor comforting Qyacha's daughter, raised his head. "Tell us what you guess, Rasim al Ilialio."

"Alsari said she stole the knowledge of sky witchery. Is it possible—" Rasim's gaze skittered around the room, finally coming back to Oyun for answers. "Are your sorcerers trained in secret? It doesn't seem like Milu's training has been hidden, but I don't know what was happening before we got here."

"They took me away from the camp every day," Milu reported. "I showed Telun what I'd learned when I came home, and you when you got here, but they did take me somewhere else."

Rasim nodded. "If that's how it's usually done, I think she followed someone to a training place, a long time ago, and learned from in hiding. I think...you travel a lot, all of you, don't you? All Shenryalans. I think she must have gone far to the east, maybe even out of Shenryal, and found Northern sorcerers to teach her more, or to teach others like her, who wanted witchery but weren't chosen to learn it."

"Yes." A small voice broke in, and with obvious reluctance, the girl who had saved Bayar got to her feet and bowed unhappily toward Irlin and Bikat. "I am Jerial, daughter of Qyacha, granddaughter to Nirjeran."

Irlin smiled briefly. "You are known to us, Jerial. Speak."

Jerial whispered, "Thank you, Great Mare," but hesitated before going on. Everyone's attention was on her, and although Rasim had seen her in the great tent and helping with clear-headed efficiency during the poisoning, he didn't think she was accustomed to using her voice. He thought her actions were usually enough. She was still dirty from having been buried, and now brushed at a little of the mess, like she'd only just noticed it. Then she made herself stop, lifted her chin, and spoke with a clarity bordering on defiance. "Alsari is my aunt, and Darracha my cousin. They haven't ridden with us for a long, long time. I thought they had fought. Mother is the oldest, and Alsari's absence hinted of banishment. But that's not what happened, is it?"

The formality she'd been trying to hide behind melted away as she looked from Irlin to Rasim and, miserably, back to Irlin. "Mother is ambitious. I know that. And Bayar is your only son, Great Mare. If he could be removed, then the mantle of Great Mare must be worn by another clan mother."

"Yes." Irlin's voice was gentle. "What do you know, little mare?"

"Nothing that meant anything to me at the time," Jerial whispered. "Please believe me, Great Mare. I didn't know, and I hadn't thought about it for a long time. But when I was a child, Aunt Alsari came with the skins and teeth of a hundred vipers. Together she and Mother milked their teeth into a bowl and boiled the milk over a fire until the poison smoke made the cattle that breathed it in sway and sicken. They—"

"Stop," Oyun said, so sharply that for a moment no one even breathed. Then her voice gentled, almost as much as Irlin's had. "Stop, little mare. I know what they did next, and no one else needs to. You and I will talk, horse-daughter. You and I will see what is to be made of you, now."

CHAPTER NINETEEN

Bayar, with an undercurrent of threat, said, "Jerial will *not* pay for her mother's crimes," and drew everyone's attention. His jaw set more belligerently than Rasim had ever seen, and he spoke as if he was aware of defying rules that he would crush under his feet, if need be. "No one who sided with the earth witch would have saved me that way." Slightly less ferociously, he added, "That was the most foolishly courageous thing I've ever seen anyone do," to Jerial, who smiled at him with wet eyes, then laughed hoarsely when he added, "And you wouldn't *believe* some of the foolishly courageous things I've watched Rasim do."

Rasim said, "Hey," feebly, but Kisia said, "You jumped on a sea serpent, Rasim."

"Yeah, but Bayar didn't see that!"

"I did see you jump on a dragon."

That was hard to argue with. Before Rasim could come up with a response, Jerial squared her shoulders and faced Irlin. "Your heir is right, Great Mare. I would never harm Bayar, or agree to lift my mothers by hurting someone else. I can't make you believe me, but—"

"We all know you're telling the truth," Kisia interrupted softly. Jerial's eyes jerked to her and Kisia shrugged, as helpless as Rasim had ever seen her. "You didn't have to help me when we were poisoned. I bet your mother was furious with you. I bet you knew she'd be furious, too. But you helped me anyway."

The Shenryalan girl blushed again, and beyond her, Rasim saw Irlin smile. Jerial, though, said, "Yes, but...I heard the sorcerer-child speak of a healer."

Resigned offense flashed through Rasim. It was one thing for the adults to call him a sorcerer-child, but Jerial wasn't *that* much older than him. Oyun gave him a sharp grin, and Nasira, like she was aware of both his objection and Oyun's amusement, shot a warning look in his direction. Rasim wanted to protest he hadn't done anything, but then he would have done something, so he bit his tongue as Jerial finished her confession. "I thought if the outsiders had a healer who could save one of their own, if I helped Kisia, they might be willing to help me. To help Bayar," she corrected herself.

Oyun said, "Hnf," in mock indignation. "You don't trust your shaman, filly?"

"It was hinzjha," Jerial said, bold with sudden anger. "How many hinzjha deaths have you prevented, old mare?"

A hiss went around the tent, shock and dismay and, Rasim thought, something else. Awe, maybe. He suspected people didn't often challenge the old shaman. Oyun's grey eyebrows flickered upward, and although clearly there were a lot of Shenryalans outraged on Oyun's behalf, Rasim didn't think Oyun herself was. Neither was Irlin, although Bayar's eyes had widened at Jerial's defiance.

"One," Oyun said. "Bayar's. His is the fifth life I've tried to save from hinzjha, and each time before, it has been quicker than I. So perhaps you were very wise, little mare." She was quiet a long time, studying Jerial, who stood with her hands fisted and her jaw lifted like she was daring the old shaman to do her worst. After a long, thoughtful pause, Oyun, with great deliberation, said, "Your mother is not worthy of her daughter."

Silence rang out from that statement, silence so loud it might have been a gong struck in the middle of the tent. It was followed by another hiss that ran around the tent, the gathered Shenryalan councilors all coming to attention, their gazes sharp and bright on Oyun and Jerial. Even Irlin looked astonished, but Oyun's eyes glittered with certainty. Rasim shot a glance toward Nasira, Karluk, all the adults in the Ilyaran-heavy contingent, but they clearly had no more idea what was going on than he did. Not even Kisia, who had learned more about Shenryalan custom than any of them, looked like she knew what was happening.

Jerial, though, obviously did. She stood so still she swayed, and her eyes were huge as she whispered, "Wise mare..." to Oyun in a half-protesting whisper.

"How many aunts have you, little mare?" Oyun

asked the question like she knew the answer, and like it didn't matter. Rasim felt suddenly as if he and the other outsiders were watching something they had no business witnessing, but Oyun evidently didn't care, and it appeared no one else in the tent was going to gainsay the old shaman.

Jerial whispered, "Three, wise mare, and their daughters number seven among them."

"And who is oldest, among you?"

"Qyacha is first of her mother's daughters, and I am first of hers, and first before all her sisters' daughters." Jerial's hands were a nervous knot in front of her stomach, but her voice had steadied as the Shenryalans gathered close, surrounding her with men on one side and women on the other, all but blocking Rasim's view. The outsiders were neither necessary nor invited to what was going on.

"We know Alsari's heart already," Oyun said with cold dismissal. "I will look into the hearts of your aunts, and their daughters, and decide their fates when the time comes. But *your* heart is known. Three times and more you have chosen, and each time you have chosen the most courageous path through the Great Spiral. Today, you have no mother save the clan." The old shaman closed her hands on Jerial's shoulders, lifting her voice until Rasim was sure it carried outside the tent, too. "Speak your name, Jerial."

"Jerial." Jerial's voice shook, and beyond her, Rasim caught a glimpse of Bayar's eyes, bright with tears as she whispered, "I am Jerial, daughter of Shenryal, granddaughter of Nirjeran. I have no mother save the clan."

A SONG SPRANG up around them, deep and sad and celebratory all at once. Beneath, and then over it, Oyun spoke, her voice first soft, then thundering as sky witchery carried it far beyond the tent. "Hear this! The spiral carries on! A new clan is born today! All mark Jerial, daughter of Shenryal, leader of her family's herd, however large or small it may prove to be!"

Her proclamation was carried beyond the tent not just by her own words, but by other voices rising in astonishment as they shared what was obviously stunning news. Rasim edged his way closer to Kif, hoping the old Northern adoptee into the Shenryalan tribes could tell him what was going on. The old man glanced down at him, eyebrows furled, and Rasim whispered, "Did Oyun just exile Jerial's mother?"

"No. This is worse than exile." Kif's face was lined in scowls. "She *unmade* her. No one will ever claim her name again as part of their ancestry. She doesn't exist anymore."

"Holy seas. What will happen to her?"

Kif shrugged. "She'll live out her days alone and die forgotten. The King Horse won't welcome her back to the Great Spiral as she is, although he might accept her as a worm or a bug or something useful to the spiral. Her journey toward a human spirit will begin all over again, and she may never be worthy of it."

"Kif..." Rasim touched the old man's arm uncertainly. "Is that what happened to you?"

The faintest smile creased the corner of Kif's mouth. "No. I was only sent away. My name remained on my daughters' lips, and my language lived with them even here. If I'd been unmade, I could never have become Grandfather Winter."

A sour knot untwisted in Rasim's belly. "I'm glad."

"Me too." The old man examined him briefly. "I've heard them tell you how much trouble you make, Ilyaran. Remember that you've brought a family back together, too. More than one. That wouldn't have happened, without you and your trouble-making."

A new knot formed, this time in Rasim's throat, and it squeezed tears into his eyes. "Thank you."

Kif nodded, then moved closer to the Shenryalan elders and the complex congratulations they offered Jerial. Rasim, chewing his lower lip, squirmed back to his friends, and then, not quite letting himself admit he had a plan, started working his way toward the door. Jerial's mother had to know something about how the Northerners had gotten delzjha. If he was right, if Lorens *had* had some with him, if he'd given it to the stone witch Cindu as they were fleeing Moran, then maybe Jerial's mother could make the link for him. Maybe she could verify, if not quite prove, what Rasim feared. He just needed to talk to her.

He crept outside, and got about five steps toward Oyun's tent before a hand landed on his shoulder, and Captain Nasira's cool voice said, "And where do you think you're going, Journeyman?"

For a heartbeat, Rasim hoped if he sagged enough maybe he would just turn into mud and slide right out of Nasira's grip. It didn't happen. Disappointed and guilty at getting caught, he straightened and turned a bright hopeful smile on his captain. "To the toilet?"

"You're going to sneak into their spiritmaster's tent to talk to that girl's mother," Nasira said in a tone that dared him to defy her.

"Someone has to," Rasim said desperately. "She could have all the answers, Captain. Answers we need!"

"And you don't trust Bayar's people to get those answers?"

"Not fast! We need to know who we can trust, Captain, and we need to get home soon, too. The more we can tell King Taishm about what's been going on all over the continent, the better prepared Ilyara will be for whatever's coming. And if I'm right about the renegades here working with Northern witches, then we need to know who's coordinating that! We need to know if it's one of our allies!"

"You mean, whether it's Lorens." Nasira walked Rasim away from both the great tent and Oyun's, taking him toward as much privacy as could be had in the busy camp, even if they were speaking Ilyaran.

"What if he gave Cindu delzjha instead of heartbreak, Captain?" Rasim blurted the question and Nasira stopped cold, staring the little distance down at him.

"What?"

A shiver ran over Rasim's skin as the chill in her voice, although he thought he knew her well enough now to trust she wasn't mad at *him*, but rather at the idea he'd presented. "We thought he gave Cindu heartbreak, but after that, Cindu wrecked so much more of Moran. What if he slipped him delzjha instead? We *know* someone in the North had it, and the Shenryalans make it, and Missio died in Lorens's arms before she could tell me anything about who'd given her the drug. Captain, I might be wrong, but what if I'm right?"

A muscle ticked in Nasira's jaw. "I want to say we could just ask Lorens. I want to believe the answer he'd give us would be the truth."

"Well, I want to captain the *Wafiya*, but we don't always get what we want, do we?" Rasim retorted, then bit his tongue so hard his eyes bulged.

Nasira's face contorted like she was genuinely shocked but also struggling not to laugh. It took a few seconds before she gained enough control of her voice to say, "No. No, we do not, Journeyman. Very well. But I will *not* countenance sneaking into Oyun's tent. You go in with her permission or not at all."

Rasim whispered, "Yes, Captain," and slunk back to the great tent with Nasira in his wake, making sure he went where he said he'd go.

CHAPTER TWENTY

They returned to an appalled silence that seemed to be centered on Bayar, although they hadn't been gone for more than a few minutes. Rasim sidled up to Kisia, who whispered, "Bayar just asked to come with us when we leave. Where were you?"

Rasim started to answer, but Irlin, in granite tones, said, "My son, you can't possibly expect—"

"Me to stay where someone is actively trying to kill me, when I might be of use as an ambassador to the Ilyaran king?" Bayar asked smoothly.

Bikat's mouth actually twitched as if he was impressed with Bayar's audacity and logic, but Irlin's expression darkened. "You've been away from the plains for most of a year already, Bayar. If you leave again you may return no longer one of the people."

"The King Horse's spirit is strong in him," Oyun said with great serenity. "Bayar has stood trials unlike most of us ever imagine and has returned unbroken, his heart unscathed. His place among the people is forever secured. I have no fear for him."

"*If* this is to happen, we will send an escort," Bikat said.

Nasira's head jerked up and her voice rose and broke on two words: "With *horses*?"

Bikat regarded her blandly. "We are riders."

"The *Wafiya* is not well suited to carrying livestock! And I'd bet your horses aren't used to sailing!"

Bayar, as blandly as his father, said, "Shenryalans are not accustomed to sailing," and managed to remind everyone who'd been there how difficult finding sea legs had been for him. Nasira rubbed her hands over her face, then lifted a grim look on all of them, clearly prepared to take a stand.

Bikat, however, spoke before she did, with the air of a man who had solved everything. "Our Great Mare is not wrong. Bayar has been long, *long* away from us, and while I would never doubt Oyun, I propose we find a middle road. Bayar will ride with us."

Bayar took one short breath, considered his mother's dire expression, and silenced himself as Irlin said, "*Us?*"

Bikat turned his mild gaze on her. "I cannot ask the gathered clans to send emissaries to distant Ilyara without leading them myself, my love."

"How long does it take to ride a horse from Shenryal to Ilyara?" Rasim asked, drawing attention again.

Bikat gave him a rather sharkish grin. "That depends greatly on how much of a hurry we are in, sorcerer-child. Two months. Perhaps three, but the weather will be in our favor."

"And how long does it take to march an army from Moran to Ilyara?" Rasim asked Nasira.

She glared at him. "How would I know? I'm a seamaster. We *sail*."

"You're the one who said we didn't have time to sail home before the Moranese army got there!"

"Well, I assume we don't!"

Karluk, the formerly enslaved Ilyaran sky witch, said, "Some three months," and drew attention much more sharply than Rasim had. He shrugged, his jaw set hard. "It will take some three months for them to make the march. The man who enslaved me enjoyed travel, and usually did so with enough protection to be considered a small army, so I know something of the speed that can be made on those roads. And there will be more of them than he had, and there are mountains to cross, which will slow them further, even in summer."

"Thank you. So we can be home in a month, Bikat can be there in two, and the Moranese, who have a head start, can be there in three." Rasim inhaled deeply, turning to Nasira. "Captain, we might all get there at the same time. The Moranese will have a cavalry and I'm *not* trying to get you involved in what might be our war, King Horse—"

"I believe we're already well embroiled, sorcerer-child. Go on."

"—but Shenryalans are known all over the continent for their riding skills. The Moranese cavalry may back off from conflict if there's even a chance they have to fight you. If we're trying to avoid a fight, having them on our side would probably be really helpful."

Endat shook his head. "But I can't condone asking the Shenryalan people to join us on this journey. It may end very badly."

"Luckily, you didn't ask," Bikat said.

Jerial, almost at the same time and in a very soft voice, said, "I would like to join Bayar on the long journey."

"No." Irlin's tone brooked no argument this time, although Rasim hadn't thought there was much to argue about before, and yet it appeared Bayar and Bikat were both getting something resembling their own way. "You're newly made the head of your family, Jerial, and have older aunts who won't like that, even if their hearts are true. You can't afford to leave now, and even if you could, I have other reasons to keep you here." Her gaze flickered to her son.

So did Kisia's. Rasim's stomach twisted again and he scowled at the carpets on the big tent's earthy floor. A few of them were half stuck in the dirt. He wondered if someone would dig them up when the camp moved on, or if they'd be left there as a reminder of a very strange day.

Without warning, Nikki, the Moranese beggar woman, said, "I will stay," in Shenryalan. Nearly everyone in the tent turned her way, with Oyun and Irlin's gazes both interested and compassionate. Nikki repeated, "I will stay," then lapsed into Moranese, which Captain Nasira began to translate when it became clear the Shenryalan translator couldn't. "I'm old," Nikki said, with Nasira echoing her. "No one ever wanted me in Moran, and it was a hard enough place for the unwanted before the sea walls came down, so I left Moran with these magic-laden heathens and they brought me here. Not to Golden Ilyara, but to a place where old women have power."

Every sea witch in the tent drew a soft breath like they wanted to mention Guildmaster Isidri as an example of old women with power in Ilyara, and then all exchanged faintly amused glances as they heard each other beneath Nikki's continuing speech. "I don't expect power. A little respect would be nice. So I'll stay," she said, again in Shenryalan. "If I can."

"You are welcome, ancient sister," Oyun replied, and Nasira translated that, too.

Nikki, who had been a tense and sullen old woman for the difficult weeks Rasim had known her, relaxed for the first time since they'd left Moran. "Thank you."

Oyun nodded, then turned her attention to Skymaster Karluk and his wife Zyterna. Neither of them had spoken in the time Rasim had been in the tent, except in relief when Lars and the others had been pulled from the gap in the earth. Karluk's dark knuckles were white with the strength he held Zyterna's hand. "And you?" Oyun asked.

"I would like to go home," Karluk said in a low voice. "But Ilyaran custom is that guild members don't marry or have children, and I'm not prepared to give up either my family or my witchery. Not now. Not after all we've been through."

"Nor should you." Nasira had made that choice herself long ago, before losing everything to the Great Fire, and old anger dripped through her voice now. "I might have saved my family, if I'd had access to my witchery. I won't ask anyone else to face that hardship themselves."

"But will the king?" Karluk sounded like he knew the answer, and like it was too much to bear.

Rasim drew breath, but Desimi beat him to it, sharpness in his deepening voice. "The king better not. He's the one who wants to build the King's Guild out of witches who can master more than one magic. If that's really what he wants, he can't punish witches who want to break other Ilyaran rules, right?" He shot a quick look at Rasim, as if hoping he'd said the right thing, and Rasim grinned back at him. Desimi's shoulders loosened and he stuck his jaw out at Sunmaster Endat, who regarded him with a look very like the one people usually gave Rasim.

Karluk slumped, his hand still tight around Zyterna's. "Still, it might be best if we stayed in Shenryal, at least until we know. If the King Horse and Great Mare will allow it."

Irlin smiled. "Perhaps Jerial might find space for you in her tent."

Hope lit not only Karluk's face, but also Jerial's as Irlin went on. "I understand, however, that Ilyarans do not ride. We cannot make Shenryalans of you if you do not sit on a horse, sky-sorcerer."

"I'm sure our children will come to it naturally,"

Karluk said in a thick, grateful voice. "Zyterna and I may be a little slower, but we'll try, Great Mare."

"I would be honored to teach you the way of the horse." Jerial pulled together a watery, emotional smile, her eyes bright as she added, "Perhaps you'll even learn the King Horse's path," and Karluk laughed, but it was Zyterna who answered.

"I think my husband's Ilyaran goddess wouldn't forgive him for that, but the only gods I've known are those who look away from slavery. I would like to learn more of the King Horse and your Great Spiral, myself." Her Ilyaran had improved considerably since Rasim had met her. He wondered how much time she and Karluk had been forced to spend apart during their marriage, if only a few weeks of speaking it regularly had made her that much more comfortable with it. They must have been apart far more often than they'd been together, in Moran.

For a hard, wrenching moment, he not only approved of Cindu tearing down that city's river walls, but wished he'd been the one to do it. He closed his eyes, trying to move past that dark impulse. When he opened them again, he found Sunmaster Endat's steady gaze on him, like now he thought maybe Desimi was rubbing off on Rasim, instead of the other way around. Rasim didn't know if it was good or bad in either case.

Nasira sighed explosively. "All right. Is anyone else staying or going or changing plans to suit themselves? No? Then, Spiritmaster Oyun, we have a request to make. Rasim would like to talk to your captive about how the Northerners got your drug delzjha, and..." She trailed off, looking around with an expression that slowly grew so dark that all the other sound in the tent gradually faded away as the people gathered there tried to figure out what she was looking for.

"Where," Nasira grimly asked into the silence, "is Prince Lorens?"

"HE BROUGHT dinner to the tent last night," Kisia said after a moment.

"He was there when I fell asleep," Rasim added. "Did anyone see him at breakfast?"

"I thought he was sleeping." Nasira spoke through clenched teeth. "But he would have woken before we came to see Irlin and Bikat. Someone go ask Pynda if she saw him leave."

Milu shook his head. "He wasn't there. Telun and I were with her until the earth witchery started. Lorens's bed was empty."

Nasira sounded like she was working the ship's ropes in a hard wind, her voice was so tight. "Can anyone think of a good reason for him to have left without warning, apparently in the middle of the night?"

Rasim could, but it wasn't a nice reason. As the silence from the rest of their group drew on, Nasira's gaze landed on him. The suspicions were, and had been, his all along. Evidently that meant he got to voice them. It could be argued that she meant it as an honor, but it felt more like a punishment. "He left as soon as I was rescued. The only reason I can think that he'd do that was he was afraid I would come back with information that could…"

"Implicate him," Nasira said when Rasim ran out of words. "Rasim believes Lorens may have something to do with the drug trade that's brought delzjha into Northern hands."

"That doesn't make sense," Kisia protested. "He had to have known that Milu and Bikat were going to get Rasim. Why wouldn't he have left then?"

"I don't know. Maybe he hoped I was dead. There wouldn't be any point in running if I was dead."

Kisia squinted. "You're right. He should have gone with them and made sure you were dead." Rasim stared at her, and she spread her hands. "Well, he should've! He could have gathered you in his arms and suffocated you or something."

"Only," Bikat interrupted in a very dry tone, "if he got to Rasim first, and I will take it as an insult to all the Shenryalan people if you suggest a lanky Northerner can out-ride even a single one of my guard."

Kisia went from contemplating how best to make sure Rasim was dead to contrite in a single blink, and bowed. "I would never suggest such a thing, King Horse."

Bikat made a sound like he accepted her apology, although Rasim suspected the Shenryalan leader might think they were amusing. Whatever humor he might have shown, however, faded as he said, "Many of us have close bonds with our horses, but I fear there are far too many horses in the camp to be certain whether a few have gone missing. And while I have confidence in our ability to find even a single rider on the plains, we need a place to begin looking. I might suppose we should start with the direction we found you in, sorcerer-child, but if I were a fugitive and at all wise, I would not take that path myself."

"Me either, so I don't know," Rasim said grimly. "Let's ask Qyacha."

CHAPTER TWENTY-ONE

They brought Qyacha to the central tent, instead of bringing everyone in it to her. Jerial, supported by Bayar, left before her mother was brought in, and the new members of her family went with them. Rasim imagined Bayar would be doing a lot of translating for the next few hours and days.

Qyacha did not look like a dangerous woman as she knelt in the middle of the great tent. Most of the stern anger was gone from her face, and she glanced around as if a little disconnected from her own body. Rasim knew exactly what that felt like, but couldn't find any sympathy for her.

Too many people were debating what to ask, and who should do the asking. Rasim hadn't exactly thought it out that clearly, but that was why he'd wanted to talk to her on his own. Extra people complicated things too much. After several minutes of listening to the adults debate, Rasim, knowing he shouldn't, wove a little sky witchery and spoke directly in Qyacha's ear. "Did you know Lorens before he came here with us?"

Her gaze went very focused for a moment, but the way her head bobbled as she looked for the person who'd spoken to her told him that she wasn't nearly as alert as she appeared for those few seconds. Then her eyes met his, and the clarity of anger burned in her gaze for another heartbeat or two. "Did you know Lorens before he came here with us?" Rasim asked again.

"Alsari did. Where is my sister?"

"I don't know," Rasim admitted softly. "There was an attack. People died. I don't know if she did or not. The younger woman who took me did, though."

Qyacha's lip curled, but then a wave of detached grief rolled over her. "Darracha?"

"I hope she's all right. I didn't see her again after the attack. Did Alsari give Lorens delzjha?"

A sneer washed over Qyacha's face, slow but sure. "For sorcery, yes."

Rasim's heart clenched. "Is Lorens a sorcerer?"

Qyacha actually laughed, and Rasim, not expecting that sound, didn't catch it well with his witchery. He was suddenly very aware that everyone around them was now trying to pretend like they didn't know he was questioning the earth witch. Maybe they thought she'd stop talking if she realized they, too, were listening. Or maybe they just thought she wouldn't answer if anyone else spoke to her. "Not him. His people." She leaned toward him clumsily, like she wanted to whisper a secret. "The pale ones have hidden sorcery for—"

The next word was well out of his vocabulary, but Rasim thought it must mean a long time. He nodded. "Do you know where Lorens has gone?"

The woman's lip curled again and she looked away with a disdain that would have been cutting, if her drug-slowed actions had been crisper. "Where is my daughter?"

"Free," Rasim said softly. "Found not guilty of your…" He wanted to say 'crimes,' but that was beyond his vocabulary, too. "Mistakes."

"Nnnn. Weak daughter. Bad blood."

"If she has bad blood," Rasim said carefully, trying to get all the words right, "it must be her mother's, because I haven't heard any Shenryalan claim their clan by their father's name."

A low hiss went around the tent from those who understood him, so he thought he'd spoken clearly enough. Qyacha, suddenly furious, threw herself toward him. It worked about as well as his own outraged attempts at violence had when he'd been given zjhala: she lost her balance and began shrieking with anger. Guards stepped in to pick her up and carry her away, and in the aftermath, Rasim felt all eyes on him again.

He sighed and stood up, meeting Nasira's exasperated gaze. "You all would have kept talking about what to ask forever."

"Probably not *forever*. What did she say?"

"Her sister knew Lorens and traded him delzjha for

knowledge of more sorcery. She says the Northerners have been keeping their magic secret for a long time now. Why did they stop using it, if the secret is still known?"

"Dragons," Oyun said. "Dragons go where the sorcery is strong."

"They don't, though," Kisia said. Oyun's eyebrows rose, but Kisia spread her hands. "Ilyara's stronger with witchery than anywhere else in the world, and we don't have dragons."

Oyun's eyebrows flickered back down into a frown, and although her face said she wanted to, she didn't argue. Instead she inclined her head, then left, still frowning at the Ilyarans. Rasim muttered, "What was that about," not really meaning it to be a question, but Nasira, close enough to overhear, shook her head.

"I'm not sure I even want to know. Did she say where Lorens had gone?"

"No. We were trading answers, but she wouldn't answer that one. Maybe Oyun can make her tell the King Horse."

Nasira bared her teeth briefly, then nodded and tucked her hair behind her ears more firmly as she turned to Bikat and Irlin. "King Horse, Great Mare… we may have gained more answers than we expected, in coming here, but I think we had better prepare to leave. If your spiritmaster can't convince Qyacha to tell her where Lorens has gone, or if she doesn't know, then we need to return home as quickly as possible to warn our king that there may be trouble coming from the North, as well as Moran. Will you forgive us for a hasty departure?"

Irlin smiled. "There's nothing to forgive, ship-mother. You have brought our son home to us, and even here, helped to keep him safe from those who worked against him. Shenryal, and our family in particular, is in your debt."

To Rasim's utter astonishment, the two women hugged, and then Nasira led them out of the great tent to begin their preparations to go home.

DESPITE NASIRA'S BEST EFFORTS, it was two full days before the Ilyarans were able to leave. There was ceremony around bringing the outsiders into Jerial's new clan, and because Karluk was Ilyaran, Irlin thought it was important that the *Wafiya*'s crew attend. An overwhelming number of people from the gathered tribes also came to celebrate, which Rasim thought was probably on purpose. It would make it harder for her aunts to object, if for no other reason than a big party meant everybody knew about the change in Jerial's status.

He knew that they'd set Qyacha free, hoping that she would go wherever Lorens had gone. Rasim thought she should be smarter than that, but people often weren't, so like everyone else, he waited to hear word from Bikat's riders that the Northern prince had been found. He fretted in their tent the evening before they were meant to leave, pacing and waiting for news of Lorens, or even of Darracha. It was possible she'd survived the stone snake's attack. If she had, he wanted to introduce her to Sesin.

Desimi threw a pillow at him, trying to get him to stop pacing. "Imagine how bored you're going to be when this is over and all you have to do is a journeyman's work."

Kisia snorted. "Rasim won't be bored. He'll end up in the palace with King Taishm."

Rasim shifted his shoulders uncomfortably. "I know I'm going to have to tell him about the witchery and I guess I'll be in the King's Guild, if that happens, but I don't think it'll be in the palace."

"I didn't say you'd be in the palace with the King's Guild," Kisia said cryptically.

"I don't know where else it'd be, but I just want to be in the guild. *Our* guild."

"Captaining the *Wafiya*," Desimi said, for once not sounding entirely rude about it.

"Or sailing under Kisia's command."

"Nah. Kisia's going to become Guildmaster."

"I'm going to have to captain the *Wafiya* first, then, aren't I!"

Both the boys turned to look at her and Kisia raised her chin defiantly. "You've both thought about it too."

"Not me," Desimi said. "Being Guildmaster sounds like too much work."

Rasim hunched his shoulders. "I'm not thinking about anything except going home and getting this whole mess sorted out."

"And becoming Guildmaster," Desimi said to Kisia, and she grinned.

"Not for ages. Captain Asindo's got a lot of years ahead of him."

"I just want to sail on the *Wafiya*!"

Kisia said, "And captain it," and Desimi said, "And *then* become Guildmaster," and Rasim hid under the pillow Desimi had thrown at him.

"I might stay here in Shenryal," Pynda announced unexpectedly, from where Rasim suddenly guiltily realized she'd been trying to sleep. Her voice muffled by a pillow, but didn't sound very serious. "That way I'll be as far away as possible from the three of you and all the trouble you're going to cause back home."

"You're wiser than any of my journeymen," Nasira said as she came in. "Pack up, all of you, but Oyun wants to see you three first."

"See," Pynda said. "Trouble."

"I didn't *do* anything!" Rasim sat up, raking his fingers through his hair like he could get the loose curls under control that way. Kisia tossed him a wide-toothed comb and he pulled his hair back, trying to see if it was long enough yet to tie into a knot at the base of his neck. It wasn't nearly, and he gave up, letting it spring free again as he muttered.

"You look fine," Kisia said. "Let's not keep her waiting." They hurried out of their tent over to Oyun's, exchanged brief, curious glances, and waited when Kisia said, "Daará?"

Oyun called, "Daari," back, and they filed in, squinting at the comparative darkness inside. The tent wasn't *as* hot as it had been when she'd taken Rasim on the spirit journey, but it was still much warmer than outside. It made Rasim miss the Ilyaran heat.

Before they could say anything, another voice outside said, "Daará?" and Oyun repeated the welcome, allowing Bikat and Irlin to enter. They were both dressed formally in the same elaborate robes they'd worn to greet the Ilyarans at their first arrival. Bikat had silken colors wrapped around his palms again, although Irlin didn't, this time. Bayar, not quite as formally dressed, came a step or two behind them. Kisia's hands twisted before she dropped her eyes, mustered a smile, and looked up again as if nothing was bothering her.

Irlin saw all of that as clearly as Rasim did, and gave Kisia a surprisingly sympathetic look. "You've been very brave for us, Kisia, with little to show for it so far. The clan owes you a debt of gratitude."

"No." Kisia kept her smile in place, although Rasim thought her eyes looked sad. "I'm just glad—" She made a little face. "I'm glad I was there to get poisoned, I guess, because two of those darts would have killed Bayar."

"The King Horse gave us a great gift with your presence and strength," Bikat said. "It is almost unheard of, that a stranger to our camps would sacrifice so much for one of our own. We are, as Bayar told you, an isolated people, unfriendly to outsiders, but in the days you've been with us, we have taken in a great number of strangers. Karluk, Zyterna, their children, Nikki, and even Grandfather Winter, the one you call Kif. We would like to adopt one more stranger into our tribe, Kisia."

"Into our family," Irlin corrected. "I have no daughters, Kisia, which is considered a great shame—not an embarrassment, but a misfortune—among the clans. I have no regrets about it myself, but I wonder if you might allow me to add my name to your lineage, and call you daughter of the heart, myself."

"Oh." Kisia put her hands over her mouth, eyes bright with emotion. "I'd like that very much. I would be honored."

A surprising amount of relief lit a smile across Irlin's face. "There's a ceremony, if you wish to partake, or it can be a truth kept between ourselves. The ceremony involves a...marking, a..." She hesitated, then pushed the sleeves of her shirt up, exposing dancing animals inked into her skin.

"Tattoos," Kisia said. "Oh. They're beautiful, Irlin. How long does it take?"

"For you, it would be..." Irlin pushed her sleeve higher, showing a tattoo of an outlined horse's head with a wild arc of mane encircling her left shoulder. "It takes long hours, and is painful, but is not so long that you would be unable to sail with your ship in the morning."

"We thought Sesin might be able to speed the healing," Bayar said, and Kisia, who's expression had gone uncertain, suddenly cleared with relief.

"Oh, that's a good idea. Yes. Thank you. I'd be honored," Kisia said again.

"As would I," Irlin said in a low, intense voice. "Kisia,

daughter of Rahael, granddaughter of Isidri, you have offered much and had much taken from you in the name of helping my son, my family, my clan, my tribe. You would be a daughter to do the Great Mare proud."

"Then that shouldn't be kept secret, should it?" Kisia smiled a little nervously. "Let's do the ceremony."

Real joy lit Irlin's face. "It will be done tonight. We'll go from here to prepare. The women of your tribe—ah, your ship—are welcome to join us."

Rasim felt his face fall, and Oyun laughed at him. "Some things are for the mothers and daughters, sorcerer-child. You don't need to be part of it all. You should return to the People," she added more seriously. "When this turn of the spiral is over, return to the plains, Rasim. Your spirit is not a quiet one, and I fear peace will elude you. Take this." She pressed a length of hair into his hand, and for a moment Rasim thought it was her own. Then he realized it was horse hair, a long enough section to be braided, and guilty relief ran through him. "If you return through the Crack in the Bowl, and climb high onto its cliffs, then burn this with the power you found on the plains, it will lead you to us, no matter where we may be. I'll look for you, sorcerer-child."

Rasim curled his fingers around the braided length of hair. "Thank you, spiritmaster."

"I like that word," she said with evident satisfaction, then turned to frown up at Desimi critically. He gave her a cheeky grin in return and she laughed, patting his cheek, then stepped back and let Bikat come forward.

The King Horse lifted his silk-wrapped hands to

Desimi the same way he had when they'd met, then lifted his eyebrows, clearly waiting. Desimi shot Rasim a bewildered look, then, awkwardly, raised his own hands, palm out, like Bikat's were. Satisfaction darted across the King Horse's face. With long-practiced skill, he unwove the silks from around his palms, one at a time, then rewove them around Desimi's hands and wrists in a different style, until they were almost gloves. Then—also unlike how he wore them—he tucked the ends in, blending thc silks together so they looked stitched instead of just wrapped. "Wear them with wisdom and honor," he said very formally.

"Uh." Desimi's gaze darted to Rasim again, then back to Bikat. "I will?" His eyebrows drew down, and, less uncertainly, he said, "I'll try," and Bikat smiled.

"The King Horse can ask nothing more of us. Let it be known that you are seen in his eyes, Desimi, son of —" He paused. "We have learned no names for your mothers."

"Oh." Desimi smiled crookedly again. "We're orphans, King Horse. Not Kisia, she's different, but Rasim and I, we're children of the river. Son of the Ilialio, and I guess maybe grandson of Siliaria, if the goddess doesn't mind too much."

Rasim liked that better than the answer he'd given Darracha, and Kisia said, "That's how the legend goes, anyway. The story is that Ilyarans are all the descendants of our gods, and that's why we have so much magic."

Bikat's eyebrows went down and up again, and after a moment, his shoulders rose, too. "Then you are seen in the King Horse's eyes, Desimi, son of the Ilialio, grandson of Siliaria. Safe travels to you back across the wide waters to your homeland, and let it be known that the Shenryalan clan is a friend to you."

"Thank you." Desimi still sounded bewildered, but at least he was polite. Then Irlin drew Kisia to her side and smiled at the boys.

"We have much preparation to do for the ceremony. Kisia will join you when you ride to the mountains, in the morning."

Kisia made big eyes at Rasim and Desimi as Irlin turned her away from them, and a little to Rasim's surprise, Bikat and Bayar joined them as they left the tent. "Women's business," Bikat said firmly. "We have no place in it. Sleep well tonight, if you can. Kisia will be very tired tomorrow, and having friends who are awake and sympathetic will help." He and Bayar walked away, leaving Rasim and Desimi both staring at the wraps around Desimi's hands.

"Am I supposed to leave these on forever, do you think?"

"I don't know. What was that *about*?"

"*I* don't know. Kisia's getting a tattoo and you got the horse hair thing. Maybe they just didn't want me to feel left out."

Rasim shrugged. "Maybe. I guess that makes sense."

"Well, I'm not leaving them on forever. They'll get torn up by the ropes shipboard, and it's nice fabric, so I don't want it to get wrecked."

"And your hands will sweat."

Desimi made a face. "Yeah. Oh, I know. I'll put them

in my pouch with Siliaria. They can keep each other safe."

"Oh, that's a good idea." They went back to their tent, and to Rasim's surprise, he slept quickly and well, until Desimi woke him up when it was still dark.

"C'mon, Sunburn. They've got the horses all saddled for us."

Rasim croaked, "How can you be so awake?" but staggered out of bed to pull on the warm Shenryalan clothes they'd been provided with, and stumbled sleepily after Desimi to find half of their people already on horses and waiting for them. Bayar rode with them to say goodbye.

Kisia, Nasira and Sesin joined them at the edge of the encampment spiral, with two of them looking tired and Kisia giggling like a loon. Sesin's rider brought their horse close enough to Rasim for Sesin to say, "They gave her some kind of intoxicant that helps with the pain and maybe helps the tattoo set, I didn't quite understand that part, but either way, she's been higher than a crow's nest since sunset. Oyun says the hangover is awful. The tattoo is beautiful, though."

Rasim laughed. "Oh, good, I guess?"

Sesin grinned back, and they rode on, mostly in silence punctuated by Kisia's giggles or occasionally a burst of cheerful song that made the Shenryalans either laugh or wince, depending on their nature.

Her humor faded well before the end of the second day, when they finally reached the foot of the flat-topped mountain that they'd crossed to enter Shenryal. Bayar, who had ridden with them, slid from his horse and examined the mountain before turning to his Ilyaran friends with a studiously thoughtful expression. "I think I'll say goodbye down here."

Rasim laughed as Desimi helped Kisia down from her horse. "Not going mountain climbing with us?"

"Last time I did that, a dragon tried to eat me," Bayar replied solemnly. "I feel it's a bad risk. Goodbye, my friend. Travel safely."

"You too, Bayar. I hope we'll see you..." Rasim sighed. "In Ilyara, without a war."

The Shenryalan prince bowed his head, embraced first Rasim and then Desimi, then, as the Ilyaran group began to climb the mountain, walked a little distance away with Kisia. Rasim tried not to watch as they spoke quietly for a few minutes, until nearly everyone was on the mountain and Kisia reluctantly broke away from Bayar. She didn't look back until she'd caught up with Rasim, not too far up the mountain, but far enough.

Bayar was watching them still. When she turned, his beautiful smile bloomed. He bowed, and then, as if with effort, finally turned away.

Rasim, unsure she'd accept it, offered Kisia his hand. She took it and squeezed it, then, without saying anything, climbed ahead of him, hurrying to catch up with the others. Rasim thought she might be afraid she would stay, if she looked back again.

He looked back once more himself, watching the Shenryalans gather themselves to ride away, then began to climb, holding the idea of the *Wafiya*, and home, in his mind.

CHAPTER TWENTY-TWO

They missed the evening tide, but Nasira muttered that they were sea witches and could put themselves out without the help of the tides, and after a brief exchange of glances, Hassin, the crew set to doing just that. Nasira stalked the captain's deck, twitchy with impatience, until the Shenryalan mountains were well faded on the horizon. She gave command to the first mate, Hassin, and went below.

He waited less than two minutes after her departure to say, "*Well?*" and every member of the crew who wasn't actively involved in sailing the ship crowded close to hear about their adventures. Kisia's tattoo was much admired, not just the evening they left, but in the days that followed, and she kept her arms bared, letting the tattooed horse on her shoulder heal. Most of the crew eyed it with envy as the redness settled and the blue-black lines grew more distinct. "I'd want a sea bird," Sesin said, and Desimi shook his head.

"There's nothing I want enough to have it stabbed into my skin. Rasim could get a dragon, though."

"You just want *me* to get stabbed thousands of times."

Desimi looked innocent and Rasim couldn't help laughing, although he'd never admit aloud that maybe a sea serpent sounded kind of appealing. He'd end up with tattoos all over, though, if he tried to mark his adventures with them.

Some part of him thought that if he kept a close enough eye on the horizons, he might catch a glimpse of Northern longships, and that they might find Prince Lorens. He had no more luck than they'd had on the steppes, but hope kept running through him, until it turned into a sudden dire thought. The kind of thought, he knew, that had to be shared with the captain. He slogged past Desimi, who was unsuccessfully studying with Skymaster Arrat, and the bigger journeyman gave him an odd look.

"You look like you're going to your own execution, Sunburn."

"I had a bad thought I think I need to tell the captain."

Desimi's eyes widened. "I'd start by telling Hassin, then. Or at least keep him between you and her."

"Heh. I don't know, Desi, I think maybe you're turning out to be smarter than you look."

Desimi said, "Thanks," and then, "*Hey!*" as Rasim walked away, first grinning, then chortling, even if Nasira wasn't going to like what he wanted to say. He hesitated at the steps to the captain's deck, and Nasira glanced at him like his very existence promised frus-tration.

"Come up here and just get it over with."

"It's just that I had a thought, Captain." Rasim climbed the few steps to join her on the quarterdeck. "If Lorens got away from the steppes, if he's part of an enemy movement, then he could come to Ilyara with a whole fleet of his own."

Nasira's lip curled. "The loss of half our fleet doesn't make the Seamasters useless, boy. The guild can protect Ilyara from shore, if need be."

"Not as well as we can from the seas." Rasim braced himself for her ire. "I have an idea."

The captain barked laughter and spread her hands. "Of course you do. Of *course* you do. Spit it out, lad. Let's hear this idea."

"The Islands pirate, Donnin," Rasim said in a small voice. "Lady Donnin, who we helped get her lands and her daughter back. She said her ships were ours if we ever needed them."

Nasira stared down at him, as if the weight of her gaze might squish him into the deck. He put some effort into straightening his spine, and Nasira squinted at him as if he'd done something unexpected. Then she shook her head. "So what do you want me to do, Rasim? Sail east to the Islands and collect a fleet before going home? What makes you think a pirate is as good as her word? What makes you think they can muster their ships as quickly as we'd need them to? And what makes you think they'd sail under Ilyaran command, because," she said, her eyebrows rising, "I assure you, Ilyarans will not sail under theirs."

"They know we're better sailors," Rasim replied. "And we're the ones with the skymasters who can fill their sails and send them to Ilyara faster than any natural wind, so I think they'd sail for us. I think Donnin would tell them to, and I think she owes m—us —enough to keep her word."

The captain's eyes glinted and Rasim knew he'd made a mistake, even if Donnin *had* said her fleet would sail to his call. "She owes *you*," Nasira said pointedly, and Rasim made an explosive sound of frustration.

"I don't think she meant *me*, Captain. I'm a guild journeyman, not somebody you make treaties with. If somebody says they're going to help *me*, they must mean they're willing to help Ilyara, because otherwise—"

"Because otherwise you're a very dangerous young man," Nasira finished softly.

Rasim sagged and looked away. "I don't want to be dangerous. I just..." He laughed unhappily. "I just want to sail on the *Wafiya*, Captain. I swear on Siliaria's bones, that's all I've ever really wanted."

"I know." The captain sounded weary. "I've been sailing with you a while now, and we both know I wasn't happy about it, but for what it's worth, I've come to believe you. I don't think you wanted any of this, and I don't even think you've sought it out. Trouble finds you like sharks find blood in the water, but Siliaria's *fins*, boy, you are *terrible* at letting it lie. What on all the seas is Taishm going to think if I sail into Ilyara at the head of an Island fleet? The guild was nearly disbanded for treason once."

"I think if we get there ahead of an invading army he might understand," Rasim mumbled, and a little to his surprise, the captain laughed.

"There's that." Nasira scrubbed her hands through her loose hair, then tucked it behind her ears again as she scowled at the approaching mouth of the river. "Did you go behind my back to talk to Hassin about this first?"

Rasim glanced toward the first mate, working ropes halfway down the deck. "No, Captain. Desimi thought I should, but—I know," he said, at Nasira's sharp look. "He's getting sneaky."

Nasira groaned. "Just what the guild needs. You with your righteousness and quick thinking, Kisia with that iron will and calculating heart, and now Desimi, with all that power, turning devious. Siliaria preserve us. They like you, you know. The crew. Hassin. People want to follow an honorable leader. The problem, Journeyman, is that power corrupts."

"I'm not a leader! I'm thirteen! And I don't want power. Not except this." Rasim extended his hand toward the sea, calling up a funnel of dancing water. An offended fish leaped from it and flopped onto the deck at Nasira's feet. Rasim, dismayed, scooped it up and threw it back overboard while the captain stared at him with an expression that suggested he'd just soiled her personal territory with something unspeakable.

The expression didn't change much as she said,

"And yet," and cast her gaze toward a half-furled sail, then gave him an expectant look. Rasim sighed and lifted his eyes to the sail, then closed them, feeling the dance of air against his skin. It moved so much like water, swirls and eddies, even weighted, in its way. Now that he knew how, it was easy to shape it, to spend it spinning toward the sail and let the cloth billow and fill.

Skymaster Arrat bellowed, "Hey!" and Rasim guiltily let the sky witchery go.

"The only stone I've to hand is my icon of Siliaria, and I'd rather you didn't shape her, or set fire to my ropes again," Nasira said dryly. Rasim swallowed a protest, and the captain went on without a change in her tone. "Whether you want power or not, Journeyman, you're lousy with it. It's what the king hoped for, so I suppose there's some value in it, but bear it in mind, Rasim, that it's an easy step between doing what's right for your people, and doing what's right for you."

"Do you think I think we should ask Donnin for help for *myself*?"

"I don't," Nasira replied steadily. "But I think it would be easy to take that step, maybe without even meaning to. You've probably gotten us all into a war without meaning to. It raises concerns about what you might do on purpose."

"Desimi will sit on me if I try..." Rasim didn't even know what he might try. "Anything. And Kisia would squish all the blood out of my heart."

Nasira barked a sharp laugh. "You may be right

about Desimi, but Kisia would captain you and your witchery all the way to the throne. That girl is made of ambition and she worships the seas you sail on."

Rasim squinted at her, confused. "We all worship the sea, Captain."

For some reason the captain laughed yet again, and waved him away. "Go. Get back to your duties, Rasim. I'll think on what you've said."

FOR TWO DAYS, Nasira thought while Rasim and Desimi practiced sky witchery under Arrat's tutelage. Or rather, Rasim practiced while Desimi failed, time and again. On the third morning, he threw himself on the deck next to Rasim and muttered, "I don't understand what you're doing differently from me. I want you to show me how you do it."

Rasim tried to fling his hands in the air, but he was leaning on his elbows, so he just collapsed back to the deck, hitting his head for his efforts. "Skymaster Arrat has been trying to teach you!"

"I know. But you're the one who's learned to do it, so you must know, or feel, something that he doesn't." Desimi scooted up to sit cross-legged beside Rasim. "So how did you learn?"

"I don't know! How did you learn earth witchery?"

"I don't know! It was important that I get it right, right then!"

"Well, that's how it's all been for me!

"Ugh!" Desimi glared at everything, but Rasim most of all. "Well, what does sky witchery feel like?"

That, at least, Rasim could answer. "A lot like water, actually. It's heavy. I didn't know air was heavy. But it's light, too, in a way water isn't. It moves the same way, though. It..." He sat up, pulling a little funnel of spinning wind together between his hands. There wasn't much dust on board, so it was hard to see, but he could at least feel the speed of moving air, and said, "See, can you feel, put your hand out."

Desimi did, palm out, close to the funnel, and nodded. "Like a water spout."

"Right, so put some water into it. Just a little, so it turns into a water spout but not so much that it collapses."

Droplets rose from all around them, glimmering in the sun before they landed lightly in the funnel. The air's speed spun them out, stretching them into an isolated whirlpool in Rasim's hands. Anybody could see it now, the water giving weight and shape to what had been empty, if hurried, air, and Rasim nodded. "So they're a lot alike, right? They work almost the same. But I'm spinning it, right? You just put the water in. Can you feel it spinning?"

"The water? Sure."

Rasim nodded again. "Close your eyes and just try to keep feeling the spin."

"Sunburn, I can spin water in my sleep."

"Just do it, Desimi!"

"Ugh, *fine!*" Desimi closed his eyes but left his hand extended toward the little whirlpool. Rasim, drop by drop, began to take the water away, until Desimi's eyebrows furled in a tight frown. "It's getting lighter."

"Just concentrate on the spin. Keep it going and ignore what I'm doing." He immediately felt Desimi take over the water, whirling it at speed, which wasn't exactly what Rasim had hoped would happen, but he kept stealing droplets, whisking them out of their whirlpool. Desimi said, "It's getting *lighter*," through his teeth, like he trusted neither Rasim nor the witchery, but he kept it going, frowning so hard it looked like he'd give himself a headache.

There was almost no water left in the funnel by then. As slowly as he'd taken the water away, Rasim tried to let the sky witchery go, muttering, "Keep it spinning," with as much concentration as Desimi used. It felt like forever before he was pretty sure he wasn't using skymastery anymore, and took the last few drops out of the funnel.

"It's too light." Desimi's voice rose in alarm. "It's too light, water weighs more than that. It's too quick, it's too—" His eyes popped open and the funnel wobbled dramatically as he saw Rasim sitting on his own hands, a grin spread across his face. "Is that—am I doing that?"

Rasim whispered, "What's it feel like?"

"Light. Quick. Like water but—delicate." The little funnel fell apart, but a huge grin crawled across Desimi's face, too. "Did I do that?"

"Wreck my funnel? Yeah, you did."

"Yaargh!" Desimi flung himself on Rasim, knocking him over, and the two of them rolled across the deck, pounding on each other and howling with outrage and delight. They didn't come to a stop until they crashed into someone's shins and found the captain glowering down at them.

"I thought you were past this kind of fighting," Nasira snapped. "I don't have time for this on—"

Rasim yelled, "Desi's a sky witch, Captain! He did it! He used skymastery!" and punched Desimi in the shoulder again. "We've been doing it wrong! The masters have been trying to teach us like we're first-year apprentices, but we're too set in some of our ways already. It might work for the little ones, but for journeymen we need to find what's familiar, what's similar from one witchery to another, and glide into it! It'll work, Captain. It'll work!"

Sunmaster Endat hurried up, catching the end of that and saying, "Of course, of course, I should have realized. Rasim, I want you to do whatever you just did to teach Desimi skymastery and try to bring a flame into i—"

Nasira roared, "Not on the ship!" and no one dared mention sunmastery again for the rest of the voyage.

THE NEXT MORNING, the Wafiya passed through the Eastern Straits that separated the Northern Sea from the broader ocean. Nasira called out orders, and instead of turning south, they carried on eastward toward the scattered archipelago that made up the island nations. The crew sailed with an air of almost vicious anticipation, as if even the prospect of a fleet to defend Ilyara with brought out the warriors in them.

The nearer they came to the Islands, the more nervous Rasim became. It had seemed like a good plan —or at least a necessary one, likely to succeed—when he'd proposed it to Nasira, but as the days slipped away he became increasingly convinced that he'd lost his mind. Maybe Donnin owed him, maybe she'd promised her fleet was his if necessary, but the idea that he was going to ask her people to join a possibly continent-wide war lay heavily on him.

"Cheer up," Desimi told him the morning the outlying islands came into view. "At least there weren't any serpents this time."

Rasim gave him a hard look. "You're not helping. What if I get people killed with this?"

Desimi leaned on the rail beside Rasim, watching ship fish breach around the prow. "You will. If there's really a war coming, you will. You're going to have to get used to that idea, Rasim."

"How? How can you be so calm about it?"

The bigger boy shrugged. "Probably partly because it's not my idea. But even if it was, it's what happens when you push big ideas around. People don't just change. They fight to keep things the same and they get mad if they find out they have to change anyway. Especially if they're not sure the new way is going to be better for them."

Rasim scowled at him. "When did you get so smart?"

Desimi shrugged, staring at the water. "I dunno. Maybe when Kisia and I got out of the sewers in

Hongrunn and found out while we'd been messing around a bunch of our friends had died and even more had been kidnapped. And you weren't there anymore. This whole past year has been…everything's changing. More than I thought it ever would. I mean, we saved King Taishm."

"Mostly you saved him."

"I guess. The point is, we were just apprentices and we got pulled into the middle of all that. That wasn't supposed to happen. That's bigger than I ever planned on."

"What did you plan on? I always thought you would captain the *Wafiya* and become Guildmaster someday."

"Everybody thought that." Well off the ship's side, water danced upward in a graceful show of witchery, spinning itself into replicas of the leaping ship fish, then into vast whales that were chased by a watery serpent. Even now, with power of his own, Rasim couldn't help but be impressed by Desimi's easy, casual skill with seamastery. Other crewmembers paused, watching the display with smiles and, when the water fell back down to become one with the ocean again, applauded or cheered before going back to their work. "Because of *that*. And I guess I did too, but the more we've been out here, the less I like the idea. I don't think I want a Guildmaster's responsibility. I don't think fast enough. I'm not like you. It's taken me a long time to even figure out what being a captain or a guildmaster is even really about."

Rasim squinched his face, almost afraid that if he

asked, Desimi would stop talking. But Desimi stopped anyway, so Rasim, cautiously, said, "What's it about?"

"I thought it was just about power. But it's really about being decent, and learning to take care of other people instead of just yourself." He glanced at Rasim. "You'd have made master, even if Siliaria hadn't kissed you."

Rasim choked on a laugh. "I don't think so."

"Yeah. You would have. Because you care, and you try hard. I really hated that about you. You were terrible but you kept *trying*, and you'd help even if you were bad at it, and people didn't mind that you were terrible, because you tried. And I was good, but they only put up with me instead of…admiring me, I guess. And I didn't get why."

Rasim's eyebrows shot up and he pressed his lips together, keeping every single thought he had firmly behind them. Apparently he didn't have to mention any of Desimi's unkind behavior out loud, though, because the bigger boy laughed roughly. "Yeah. All of that." He set his jaw and shrugged. "But I guess I was jealous, and that's why I hated you so much. It didn't really have anything to do with the fire and you being part Northern. That was just the easy answer." He sighed, dropped his head, and mumbled, "It's a lot easier to just go with the easy answers."

"I know."

"Do you?" Desimi looked sideways at him. "You never seem to take the easy path."

"I never got the chance." Rasim lifted his chin, watching the water again. "I couldn't, when we were little. I didn't have enough witchery, and I wanted to sail on the *Wafiya* so much. But the last year, I mean, I don't just see the right answers, Desi. I can see how much easier it would be to not...I don't know, start slave rebellions in Moran? Not yell at the crown princess of the Northlands about it being wrong to enslave people? Not nag the captain into sailing for Shenryal?"

"You had help there," Desimi pointed out. "If Bayar hadn't turned out to be a prince, she wouldn't have done that."

"Maybe not, but I can still see that it would have all been a lot easier if I'd just...I don't know. Given up during the sea serpent attack."

"Well, then you'd be dead," Desimi said irritably. "That's not easier, that's just dead."

"The point is there's lots of times I've thought it would be easier to not do the right thing!"

"Yeah, well." Desimi straightened, scowling at the water again. "I wouldn't have learned half as much if you'd done that, so for what it's worth, it was worth something to me."

He stomped away, but when Rasim said, "Desimi," he looked back. "Thanks."

Desimi made a horrible face. "Whatever, Sunburn."

Rasim ducked his head and grinned at the water, so he was looking in the right place to see a bolt of lightning careen across the ocean's surface and crack the *Wafiya*'s keel.

CHAPTER TWENTY-THREE

There were two sounds: first, the keel cracking like thunder, then, like a long-forgotten afterthought, the lightning's crackle, like it moved so fast the noise of it couldn't keep up.

Between those were shouts of horror, screams that spoke of injury, and a huge surge of witchery from every seamaster on the ship. The ocean below them became a bowl, cradling the broken ship as suddenly-frantic sailors darted over the sides to examine the damage. Rasim stayed on board, staring in bewilderment across the sea.

There were clouds scattered across the sky, softening the horizons and skimming high above them, but none of them had the heavy threat of rain, much less the thunderheads that brought lightning. And lightning didn't skitter across the ocean's surface like a stone skipped across a lake. Even if the distant Islands somehow could produce a charge of lightning and shoot it outward instead of up or down, they were much too far away for it to reach the *Wafiya*. Rasim didn't know how far lightning could travel, exactly, but he was fairly sure it was more than the hundreds of miles they still had to go before they reached the Islands.

"Journeyman!" Nasira's furious voice cut through the rest of the chaos. "Rasim, what by Siliaria's blood is *happening*? Did you do this?"

"No! I don't know what happened! We're under attack!" Rasim knew it was true as soon as he said it, although he had no idea who was attacking, or from where.

"With what?" Nasira bellowed. "*Lightning* witchery?"

"I guess?" Rasim finally jolted into motion, but long before he reached the main mast, he saw others were ahead of him, scrambling high to scout the horizons. Someone shouted hoarsely, pointing north, and those who could spun to look just as another arc of lighting shot across the water. It burned bright in Rasim's vision, barely visible before it slammed into the *Wafiya*'s hull. Explosive fire erupted around the edges of a suddenly-gaping hole, and more screams shattered the air. Rasim closed his hand and the fire went out, sun witchery responding even if he'd had no practice with it.

Nasira, incandescent with rage, snarled, "Someone find that witch and *stop them*." Rasim spun again and rushed for the railing, but Desimi got there first, and Hassin, was there before both of them.

"Stay," he snapped in the harshest tone Rasim had ever heard from him. "Keep the ship afloat. I'll deal with this." The first mate dove into the water without waiting to see if he would be obeyed, and the water rippled a moment as he propelled himself through it with witchery, moving faster than anyone Rasim had ever seen. In a heartbeat he was gone, throwing himself toward a distant ship all alone.

A third blast arced toward them, shattering the small aft mast into a shower of splinters and Nasira roared with frustration. "What stops lightning?"

"I don't know," Rasim said helplessly. "Earth?"

"We don't have any earth, Journeyman!"

"Wood!" Rasim said. "Wood, Captain, the aft mast is already broken, if we—Arrat! Skymaster Arrat! We need to lift the aft mast into the air, off the ship, we need to—"

"We can't hold that much weight," Arrat shouted back, neither of them using the sky witchery that would make a conversation over several meters easier. "Not without creating winds that will sink the *Wafiya*."

"We can hold it *with* water," Desimi yelled, drawing everyone's startled attention. "We can lift it out of the water, we can hold the water separately, argh, Rasim, you know what I *mean*!"

"Yes, yes, right, like the little fire in Ilyara, but we need metal to draw the lightning—"

Another bolt slammed into the ship. Rasim screamed along with everyone else, and Nasira's face went grim as she took a few seconds to survey the damage. There were two vast holes in the *Wafiya*'s hold now, both more or less above the waterline, but precariously close to it. The second fire went out without

Rasim's help, although he felt a touch of sunmastery and knew Endat or Pynda had taken care of the situation from below decks. Nasira, sharp with fear, said, "We can't take another hit like that. We'll go down."

"Oh." Rasim spoke in a small stupid voice and closed his eyes. "That's what we need to do, Captain. We need to go down. We need to bring the *Wafiya* deep. I bet they can't hit us if they can't see us."

"The main mast is forty meters tall, Journeyman," Nasira said through her teeth. "That's a long way down, and not all of our crew are seamasters." Her voice lifted, though, and she bellowed, "Lower the sails and prepare to *sink*," although the last word turned to a snarl.

"Dive," Rasim said hopefully. "It's on purpose. We're diving."

"Gnaargh! Get! Go! Pair up anybody who isn't a sea witch with someone who is and if anybody panics I will drown them myself!" Canvas began to fall in huge waves and at incredible speed, the skymasters frantically trying to keep them under control as they came down much faster than they were supposed to. Before they'd touched deck, the bowl of water cradling the *Wafiya* began to deepen, slowly at first, then much more quickly as the crew's witchery harmonized and they became more sure of themselves.

Pynda and Endat appeared on deck. Pynda's eyes were wild with alarm, and even Endat, whom Rasim thought of as unflappable, was visibly tense around the jaw and shoulders as the ship dropped again. A couple of the older crew joined them, muttering promises that things would be all right. Rasim admired that they could even imagine that was true.

"I can keep the water out of below decks, if you want me to, Captain," Desimi said abruptly. "The buoyancy will make it harder to keep the ship deep, though."

"Yes." Nasira hissed the word. "Yes. Do that. Not a bowl, but a sheathe. Do you hear me, Seamasters?" she called. "Let the water close around us and take us down."

The shape of the sea changed around them, surging closer. Desimi's hands spread, his gaze gone dark with concentration as the rising water cloaked the *Wafiya*. Even knowing Desimi's power, watching it rush up to the holes in the hull and then stop there as if glass held it at bay took Rasim's breath away. Air bubbled upward furiously as the ship went deeper, although the deck, and all the witches on it, remained inside Desimi's circle of witchery. Sailors furled the sails at a frantic pace, getting them under control as the ocean closed over their heads and the light changed to the eerie, shimmering blue of shallow water.

Lightning shattered the main mast when it was still well above the water's surface, chunks of wood raining down in rippling splashes. The witchery being worked trembled as panic ran through the crew, but steadied again as Nasira called a reassurance. The ship drifted deeper, light changing from light blue to dark, and a cold trickle of dread threaded its way through Rasim's gut.

The only time he'd been this deep in the ocean, a sea serpent had been pulling him down. The light had all but gone before he managed to kill it, and the swim back up through the darkness had lasted a lifetime.

The last time he'd been deeply submerged at all, it had been in Hongrunn's salt-filled lake, and a third of their crew had died.

He wasn't the only one remembering that. Ilyaran faces went as pale as they could as the *Wafiya*'s broken mast sank all the way below the surface, and grim, frightened glances were exchanged. Nasira, softly anyway, but with her voice strangely muted by the hollow of air that Desimi kept carved out so the ship's crew could breathe and work without attending to it themselves, said, "It isn't the same. We're in Siliaria's embrace now, and she will do us no harm. After all." A thread of humor carved its way through the captain's voice. "After all, we carry her beloved with us. Rasim, usually I wouldn't excuse any witch from duty at a time like this, but if your lady comes calling…"

Laughter rippled through the crew and Rasim ducked his head, mortified and relaxing all at the same time. "I'll do my best to worship her, Captain."

Another laugh, much louder this time, rushed through the crew, and someone felt comfortable enough to say, "What now, Captain?"

Nasira pulled a hand over her mouth thoughtfully, studying her crew before gesturing to four journeymen whose skills in the shipyard were well-known. "Go below. Start patching the holes in the *Wafiya*'s side. There are some planks, but scavenge anything you need. The galley table should help."

"But dinner!" Dressin, the cook, wailed to the

sounds of thin laughter.

"We'll eat on the deck like savages," Nasira promised him, then turned her attention to Desimi. "Can you keep us shielded if we move under our own power instead of just with the current, Desimi?"

Desimi, through his teeth, said, "I can if it means we'll take out the dogs who broke the *Wafiya*, Captain."

A thin, sharp smile curved Nasira's mouth. "You read my mind, Journeyman. Rasim, you don't seem to be doing much. If it's not too much trouble, perhaps you'd help me turn our ship in Hassin's wake and give those wretches a right surprise when we come up under them?"

"I didn't mean to not be doing much!" Rasim began before the rest of what she'd said settled in, and with a smile as sharp as Nasira's own, nodded. "I think I can do that, aye, Captain."

A roar went up this time as the captain—and, following her lead, Rasim—took hold of the water around them and brought the *Wafiya* in a slow but graceful curve beneath the ocean's surface. Rasim felt Kisia's magic supporting Desimi's, and as the ship began a ponderous journey north, the witchery around him changed a little. A few witches turned to helping Desimi, and someone built thin tunnels through the water to the surface so bad air could be swapped for good. The air freshened quickly, sky witchery assisting an easy exchange.

Most of the crew, though, continued with the effort of keeping the huge, strangely buoyant *Wafiya* far enough underwater that its passage didn't disturb the surface. As they adapted to working entirely under-water and the amount of drag a ship the size of the *Wafiya* commanded, Rasim and Nasira channeled currents to move them along at increasing speed. Then a shudder ran through the flagship's already-weakened bones and somebody yelled at them from below as the sounds of repairs suddenly stopped. Rasim exchanged a glance with the captain before they both pulled back on their speed.

Kisia suddenly whispered, "Look," in an awe-stricken voice. Half the crew did, first at her, then followed her gaze upward until a collective gasp ran through them.

A whale, its pale belly stretching nearly the length of the *Wafiya*, swam above them. It clearly knew they were there, and just as clearly seemed to be aware it had been noticed in turn. A few massive surges of its tail sent it well ahead of the ship before it dived and rolled gently through the water to come alongside them with almost no visible effort. It slowed, exam-ining them with an eye about the size of Rasim's palm, then accidentally outpaced them and had to come back to look again.

Sesin, near the *Wafiya*'s bow, gasped as sharply as everyone else had before and whispered, "A baby. She's got a baby," as a whale barely a third the size of the larger one came to investigate, too. It was slower and bolder, spinning next to them as if inviting them to play, then diving beneath the ship to bump it. A shout of alarm rose through the crew and the young whale popped up beside them with a comically distressed expression, although how its enormous, mostly unmoving face could look either funny or distressed, Rasim didn't know.

Its mother came around again, slowing until she drifted in the water beside them, nearly close enough to touch. Kisia, eyes huge with wonder, edged up the railing and cast Desimi a hopeful look. The big journeyman smiled crookedly and nodded, and Kisia carefully put her hand into the water that Desimi was keeping back from the ship.

Rasim supposed the whale was technically holding her breath anyway, but he had the feeling she held her breath as Kisia reached for her. When she couldn't quite touch her, she twitched sideways. Nasira yelled, "Brace!" and the witch power held the *Wafiya* in place as the whale's staggeringly huge body brushed against its side. Kisia put her palm below the tremendous animal's eye, her entire self radiating with awestruck admiration. They remained that way for a heartbeat, hardly even that, before the whale moved again, the whole impossible length of her skimming along beside the ship. Then she dived, her baby following more reluctantly, and the entire ship's crew let out another collective gasp.

For a very long time, silence reigned on the submerged ship, awe overwhelming everything but the concentration necessary to keep the *Wafiya* underwater.

Then someone called, "There are ships ahead, Captain," and all attention returned to the moment, and the fight to come.

CHAPTER TWENTY-FOUR

The ships were Northern.

Rasim had swum beneath enough of the longships to know the shape of them in the water, even if the oars that struck and dipped beneath the surface weren't enough to recognize them by. There were a lot of them, more than he could count easily from below, and were mostly the narrower, longer ships meant for speed and stealth. The Northerners had cargo ships, too, broader of beam and running deeper in the water, but most of these were warships.

A fair number of them had been sunk, debris and sailors alike littering the water. Rasim could feel sea witchery surging with focused fury, and through the wavering blur of the sea, watched a pulse of foaming water smash into a Northern hull, not too far way. A hoarse cheer went up from the *Wafiya*'s crew as the punch of water broke through the hull, but no one left their duties. Several people, including Rasim, looked toward Captain Nasira, to see what they would do next.

The captain scowled upward, studying the situation from an angle none of them had ever considered before. Despite whatever magic the Northerners possessed, a noticeable number of their ships were putting distance between the wreckage and themselves. Hassin, working from underwater, was too difficult a target for the Northern warriors. Nasira whispered a curse and shook her head. "We can't surface to fight or they'll sink the ship, and I can't send you all to fight with Hassin or…"

"*We'll* sink the ship," Kisia finished for her, and while the captain gave her a look that suggested that hadn't been necessary, she also nodded.

Desimi, through gritted teeth, said, "We can't just let them get away with this," and Nasira's gaze skittered toward him.

"What would you have me do, Journeyman? There's no way to even know if Hassin stopped their lightning witch, or whether they have only one. If we surface, it may cost the entire crew their lives. If we stay below and let them go, at least we survive to show them what it means to attack Ilyaran witches. Kisia," she added, "go find Hassin. Bring him back to the *Wafiya* so we know what's been going on."

Kisia said, "Me?" not so much in protest as astonishment, then glanced around the ship. Older crew with greater experience and maybe more powerful witchery were all deep in concentration, maintaining the submerged flagship's integrity and safety. Rasim saw her realize that, and also saw her recognize that she was skilled enough to fulfill the task without being so talented her absence might further endanger the ship. "Yes, Captain."

Sea witches usually dove over the railing, letting water catch them and carry them away, when they made a quick escape from their ship. Kisia climbed the rail, then paused there, faint uncertainty twisting her expression before she shrugged and stepped through the barrier of water. Rasim had never seen anything quite like the way she went from standing on the solid deck to standing in the ocean, as if with one step she'd gone from being a land animal to a sea creature. She'd brought air with her, but still, she hung suspended in the water, effortless and enviable.

Then she visibly got her bearings and gathered more witchery before surging off through the water, as Hassin had done what seemed like hours ago now. "Steady on," Nasira said softly. "Now we wait."

More than one Northern ship sank while they waited, sailors scrambling for other ships that fled the battle site. "I don't see any lightning," Rasim said quietly. "I think we would, even from down here. Maybe Hassin did it." He sounded pained, even to himself. Stopping the lightning witch by any means necessary had to be done, but it pained him to think of Hassin killing someone.

Nasira said, "He better have," without a trace of pain.

Beyond that, no one really spoke as weariness began to set in. Most sea witches could keep themselves submerged, drawing air from above, almost indefinitely, but the *Wafiya*, filled with air as it was, wanted to pop back to the surface. Staying deep was constant, tiring work, but letting the lower decks flood would not only sweep away their belongings, but all their food. Keeping the broken ship afloat to get it home would be work enough without some of the crew having to tend to fishing and water purifying. There were no good answers, and as a bone-chilling cold settled in, Rasim realized they were going to have to act on bad ones very soon.

There was still a tight-packed group of ships above them when Kisia returned with Hassin. The young master looked exhausted and dropped from the water to the deck, shivering. Sunmaster Endat, softly, said, "If I may, Captain," and at Nasira's nod, brought a ball of fire to life between his palms. Farther down the ship, Skymaster Arrat muttered and Rasim felt a breeze spring up too, as the sky witches altered the air supply to account for what the fire needed.

It was cold enough on board that even the little ball of flame radiated distinct warmth, and changed the overall temperature quickly. Pynda went to the other end of the ship and created a flame of her own, the skymasters' breeze spreading the warming air around the ship. Hassin, still shivering, nodded his thanks, and Kisia said, "They either had only one lightning witch or they learned really fast," when the first mate's teeth chattered too much for him to talk. "Hassin dragged her overboard and drowned her, and there was no more lightning after that."

Hassin nodded again, then managed, "You talk," through shivers, and Kisia nodded.

"There are about seventy longships and another dozen shipboards with supplies. There *were* about seventy longships. Hassin took out nearly a third of them. I can't do it myself," Kisia added with chagrin. "I can't push a water bolt fast enough to break their hulls. Anyway, a lot of them retreated, but there's a handful left up there."

Sesin came down from the bow, crouching at Hassin's side to place her hand against his cheek before glancing at Nasira. "He's got the mortal chill. He'll be all right, but it'd be best if I could take him below to warm him, Captain." At Nasira's nod, she asked Endat for help, and they went below to make a warmer space for the shivers-sick sea witch.

Pynda, after an upward glance, shook her head and called, "I can't promise the Northern ships won't see the fire, Seamaster," and, with a curse, Nasira indicated she should douse the flame.

The air grew colder instantly, and Nasira cursed again. "If we don't surface soon we'll all have the mortal chill. What else did he say to you, Kisia? Did he see who's leading that brigade?"

"He didn't dare surface, Captain, and he didn't stop to interrogate any of the dying."

"Probably just as wise," Nasira muttered, then glanced toward Rasim. "You think it's Lorens?"

"I don't see how he could have gotten here this fast," Rasim admitted. His voice sounded strange and hollow in the water-enclosed bubble the *Wafiya* drifted in.

"We're ten days out of Shenryal and the *Wafiya* is faster than any Northern ship. If it's Lorens, they'd have to have been waiting for h..." He trailed off as the possibility crossed his mind at the same time it crossed his lips.

Nasira sighed hugely. "And they could have been. It's months since we left Hongrunn. Anything could have happened. All right, listen up." She waited a heartbeat until everyone's ears were turned her way, nodded with satisfaction, and said, "We have to surface before we all go numb from cold. There are a handful of Northern ships up there, but they're not waiting for us. Not for a whole crew of Ilyaran sea witches. They're waiting to see if one lone witch is going to finish sinking their fleet, and I speak the truth when I say I want to do that in the very marrow of my bones."

A rush of quiet agreement raced around the ship, and Nasira's voice sharpened. "But our priority is keeping the *Wafiya* afloat. We have a long, long journey home ahead of us, and she's battered and beaten beyond what any ship should take. *We're* battered beyond what any crew should take, although I defy those Northern dogs to say we're beaten. *If* the chance arises, *if* I give the word, then we'll fight, but I want us to live more than I want us to win right now, do you hear me, seamasters? We have a duty to Ilyara, and we can't fulfill it from the bottom of the Western Sea."

This time the agreement came as a reluctant mumble. Nasira glared around at her crew, eyes snapping with indignation. "I can't hear you!"

"Aye, Captain," came louder this time, but not loud

enough for Nasira, who snapped, "I can't *hear* you!" again.

"Aye, Captain!" The response boomed that time, crew catching each other's eyes and smiling wryly. They knew well enough she was playing to a script meant to hearten them and bring them together, but even knowing it was a script, it worked, and there was humor and appreciation in that.

"Then bring the *Wafiya* up," Nasira said with satisfaction. "Let's see what these Northerners have to offer." She called out names, assigning some crew to defensive duties, others to speed up repairs, and most of the rest kept concentrating on bringing the ship to surface slowly and in one piece. It wanted to pop to the surface like a child's toy in the bath, and keeping its ascent to a steady pace was as difficult as keeping it deep had been.

Rasim almost wished he could be on the Northern ships to see it when they breached, though. They might have seen the masts rising, he supposed, but that would only be inexplicable until the *Wafiya*, larger than even the great whale, broke the surface with a thunderous watershed. The crew shouted its triumph, and in the near distance, Northerners shouted in shocked dismay. Most of their ships began backing away, their crews leaning into the oars and the fact that both ends of a longship were slender and bow-like, making a reversal of direction little more than a reversal of an oar pull.

A single ship held the line, and a dark-cloaked person stepped to the bow, hands lifted. The air, so much warmer than it had been below the ocean, suddenly seemed to hum and hairs raised on Rasim's arms. He started to cry a warning, but before he'd done more than drawn half a breath, an arc of water slammed across the Northern ship's bow, sweeping the cloaked person away.

Another hoarse shout rose from the *Wafiya*'s crew, everyone trying to see whose witchery had taken down the Northerner. Nasira stood with her hand clenched, a sneer of satisfaction spread across her face as she held the Northerner under water, until Rasim, in a small voice, said, "Should we question them?"

Nasira gave him a hard look. "Not unless you've got heartbreak hidden in Siliaria's pouch there, Journeyman. If you want a Northerner to question, find one who isn't a witch."

Rasim whispered, "Aye, Captain," as someone else came to the bow of the stationary Northern ship. He wasn't the only one who drew in a breath, recognizing the new arrival's way of moving, his casual grace, or the bright yellow hair revealed as he threw back a cloak's hood.

"Rasim!" Lorens's voice barely carried across the distance without skymastery to enhance it. He waved cheerfully, though, as if nothing was wrong. "God's blood, Rasim," he bellowed. Even at the distance, Rasim caught a glimpse of his breath puffing steam into the air. "What are we fighting for?"

A genuine, baffled silence fell across the *Wafiya*'s deck, Ilyarans exchanging glances with each other as if they'd somehow mistaken the catastrophic blows that their ship had sustained. After a moment Rasim yelled,

"You started it!" back at Lorens, and Nasira put her hand over her face.

"We were only practicing!" Lorens shouted. "There's not usually anything to hit out on the ocean!"

"Right," Nasira said beneath her breath, as if the Northern prince would otherwise be able to hear her, "so you just happened to land four crippling blows in a row on my ship accidentally?" Anger puffed her breath on the air, a cloud that formed and dissipated just as quickly.

Rasim, uncertainly, said, "They'd have had a hard time seeing us in the distance. The *Wafiya* is taller than they are and we had to swarm the mast to see them on the horizon."

Nasira fixed him with a glare. "So they just happened to land four crippling blows in a row on my ship *accidentally*?" Rasim shrank under the question and Nasira turned her attention back to Lorens, hollering, "After disappearing from Shenryal without an explanation?"

"How long did it take you to leave, once you decided you were going to?" Lorens yelled back. Nasira's mouth twitched with acknowledgment as the Northern prince kept shouting. "I slipped out without fanfare when I knew Rasim was safe because I'd still be there saying goodbye otherwise!"

It sounded so reasonable. "I don't believe it," Rasim said, still uncertainly. "But how did they know where to aim?"

"It's a big ocean, Sunburn," Desimi muttered. He'd slumped against the hold wall, head lowered to his knees in exhaustion. Kisia sat beside him and leaned heavily against his side. They both shivered, as if cold as well as tired. "They could've gotten a scout ship close enough to see we were here and backed off before we noticed."

Lorens shouted, "Rasim? Are we still friends?" across the water.

Rasim glowered at him, probably uselessly given the distance, and didn't answer. Nasira said, "He is getting craftier," probably about Desimi and not Lorens, but left it there. "Arrat, if you would? What are you doing out here, Lorens?" Her voice lifted with sky witchery, and Lorens visibly spoke in a normal tone, then sighed and yelled back.

"You brought a Moranese army down on yourselves and your fleet is destroyed! I thought I'd come *help*, but if you'd prefer we sailed north again..." He shrugged theatrically enough to be seen across the water. "What are *you* doing here? This is not on your way home!"

"Plausible," Nasira muttered. "It's plausible, Rasim. He's behaved like an ally."

"*Someone* taught Qyacha earth witchery." Rasim didn't even know which side he was arguing anymore, and clearly, neither did his captain, who snapped, "We have no proof it's Lorens! And what little witchery we know the Northerners have has been ice, not earth or—"

"Lightning?" Rasim demanded. "He just admitted they have lightning witchery, Captain! They were 'practicing!'"

"Who taught you lightning witchery?" Nasira yelled,

then looked embarrassed as Arrat carried the words at full volume and made the distant Northern prince jerk backward in surprise.

Then exasperation crossed his face. "Can I not come aboard, Captain? This is absurd!"

"They probably won't sink us if he's aboard," Kisia said into Desimi's shoulder. She'd tucked her hands under his arm and was shivering again, like she'd caught the same mortal chill that afflicted Hassin. Rasim felt it too, a bone-deep cold that had disappeared briefly when they'd surfaced, but which was settling in again. At least the *Wafiya* was floating now, enough repairs made to the holes in her side that they weren't in much danger of taking on water. The cracked keel groaned, though, and Rasim didn't know how they were going to fix that. It wasn't *broken*, but neither was it whole, and there was no Ilyaran magic to shape it into strength again.

"No one taught us," Lorens shouted when no one on the *Wafiya* made a motion to allow him on board. "Rasim knows there have been factions experimenting with witchery. My mother routed a few of them out and put them to sea with us so we could help defend Ilyara!"

"How do they even know Ilyara is in danger?" Rasim called back. "We haven't been out of the plains long enough for you to go home and tell her!"

"Rasim." Their ships finally drifted close enough that they could speak almost normally. "Witchery pulled Moran apart. Do you think the world waits on *you* telling it what's going on? Mother's fleet met us in the North Sea so we could sail south and support Ilyara." His breath spun out on the wind, cold air carrying it into nothing. "I'm sorry about the *Wafiya*. We honestly had no idea someone was out there. You're going the wrong direction to reach home. You should be halfway to Ilyara by now, not out near the Islands."

Nasira shivered and glared momentarily at Pynda, as if it was her fault she wasn't keeping them warm, although the sun journeyman couldn't do much with open air unless she wanted to actually set the deck on fire. "We had business to attend to."

"More important business than warning Ilyara a war is coming to its doorstep?" Lorens sounded genuinely astonished, but Nasira shrugged.

"You just pointed out that the world doesn't wait on the *Wafiya* carrying news to it. King Taishm has his spies, like any monarch does."

That was probably true, but really hadn't occurred to Rasim until he heard the adults talking about it. Nasira had been eager—desperate, even—to return to Ilyara and warn Taishm, but of course someone else would have brought the news by now. Their real reason to get home quickly was to fight on Ilyara's behalf. To protect it from the sea, in case war came from that direction. Rasim shivered, wrapping his arms around himself, and frowned at the Northern prince. He had a whole fleet of warships, the one he was on sparkling as sunlight bounced off wet boards. They *might* be coming to help Ilyara, after all. In which case he'd been wrong to send them to the Islands. He'd put them in the position of getting the *Wafiya* nearly sunk.

He was tired of making mistakes. Maybe even tired of making decisions, and definitely tired of trying to get people to listen to him. Or of succeeding in making them listen to him. That was even worse. Lorens, his voice cajoling, like he hoped Nasira would tell him everything, said, "Still, it must have been important business.

"It was," the captain said coolly. Almost as coldly as the air, which hadn't been this chilly before the *Wafiya* had gone below. It was well into spring now, moving toward summer, even in the northern bits of the Western Sea. They'd been underwater a long time, but afternoon sunlight, *warm* afternoon sunlight, bounced off Lorens's ship again, catching in glittering spots. The air should be warmer. It *had* been warmer, a few hours earlier. They hadn't brought the *Wafiya* that far north.

Rasim, feeling thick and slow, said, "There's something wrong," in a low voice.

Desimi got to his feet, offering Kisia a hand, as Rasim stared across the distance at Lorens's ship. He had seen something like what was happening to it when he'd been in the North. He'd sat for a long time at a window on a cold morning, watching frost creep from a lead-lined corner toward the center of the pane. It had grown by bits, blooming shapes reaching outward, and if he leaned down to breathe against the cold glass, his breath made similar never-ending patterns as it chilled.

Something like that spread over the Northern ship's

tarred planks. It caught the light differently, duller than the frosty glass because wood and tar were darker, but it wasn't water that made the light change. It was ice, infinitely small bright crystals that didn't belong anywhere near salt water this warm, this late in the season. The air wasn't cold because they'd been submerged so long and were suffering from the first stages of the mortal chill. It was witchery, witchery that only the most powerful Ilyaran sea witches could command, but which had once belonged to Northern witches as a matter of course.

"Captain," Rasim said, much more urgently this time, "something is *wrong.*"

Lorens snarled a command in a growling breath, and ice exploded through the *Wafiya.*

CHAPTER TWENTY-FIVE

The ship wasn't a living thing, but Rasim felt it die in that moment. Boards that he hadn't thought were waterlogged burst apart as ice expanded through them. The keel, already damaged, shattered under the strain, and thick slushy salted ice slopped over the rail as the *Wafiya* lurched abruptly downward.

Lorens's longship moved away in a quick, smooth surge of oars as the Ilyaran flagship floundered. Desimi roared frustration, and for a moment a fist of water rose around the Northern ship, grabbing at it like it would pull the longship down. But the *Wafiya* foundered, lurching deeper, and Desimi let vengeance go in favor of helping to keep their ship from sinking, as all the witches aboard were trying to do. Without discussing it, the crew brought up water from the deep. It was cold, but it broke up the slush surrounding the ship.

Too late, though. The upper deck was collapsing beneath their feet, ice particles melting but their job already done. The *Wafiya*'s bones creaked and screamed as they fell apart. Sesin burst up from below, dragging a half-dressed Hassin with Endat's assistance. Amidst the chaos of the hopeless task of trying to keep the ship in one piece, Nasira noticed them and her face contorted with fear. "Somebody help them."

Rasim ran for the struggling trio, but someone else was there before him, so he turned back to Nasira.

She stood frozen, incalculable loss etched on her features as the *Wafiya* broke into pieces around her. It was sinking slowly, given the damage it had taken—burst and broken planks everywhere, the masts shattered, water sluicing into the rowboats. Desimi was in one of those, inspecting it for soundness. Everyone besides the captain was in motion, less trying to sustain the dying ship than salvage what they would need to survive.

Then Nasira put away her mourning and she, too, threw herself into action, quick quiet orders cutting through the panic and helping to settle the crew into their duties. Seamaster ships didn't often sink, but it would be a very stupid sailor indeed who didn't train and prepare for the possibility. Desimi shouted that the shoreboat was safe, and jumped into another one to inspect it.

Lorens's voice sounded unexpectedly in Rasim's ear, oddly gentle in the chaos. "I *am* sorry, Rasim. I liked you. But gods above, you are an *endless* source of trouble, and we cannot afford your clever, disruptive mind in the middle of all this. I hope your goddess is kind to you when you sleep."

Rasim's gaze whipped toward the retreating Northern ship, finding Lorens standing at the prow. A smaller cloaked figure stood at his side, semi-familiar witchery dancing around her. A sky witch, but not Ilyaran, Rasim thought. Maybe Shenryalan, or maybe it was just that any witchery that wasn't Ilyaran had that same slightly foreign feeling to it, to him. He shaped sky magic himself, his voice hoarse as he asked, "Did you kill Missio?"

Even at the distance, he saw surprise filter across the prince's face before he shrugged. "I gave her the delzjha. I couldn't let her tell you that. It's a war, Rasim. People die in wars."

Blind fury rose in Rasim and turned into a surge of witchery that felt like it would empty the ocean. He thought that would be fine, as long as it took Lorens down with it. The sea around them turned violent, knocking the *Wafiya* about as hard as it did the Northern ship, and almost instantly, somebody closed their hands on his arms, yanking him around. "*Enough!*"

Rasim's vision swam back to focus to find the captain right in his face. "If you don't use that power to help keep us alive, I will forgo Siliaria's embrace and dedicate the rest of eternity to making *your* eternity miserable," Nasira snarled.

"But he—"

"I don't care, Journeyman!" the captain roared. "I! Don't! Care! Not now! Now, help us live!" She released him, almost with a shove, and as he staggered back, Rasim thought of the stonemaster Cindu.

Emotion, not exactly guilt, spread through Rasim.

He didn't want to understand the hurt and rage and power that had allowed Cindu to pull down Moran's sea walls, but the truth was, he did. It was easy to give in to grief and anger when he had the strength to make his enemies pay for their actions.

The difference, Rasim hoped, was that he was mostly glad Nasira had stopped him, but Cindu had finished the job in Moran when given the chance. Stomach clenched, Rasim turned away from memories of the stone witch and shaped a little skymastery to say, "Can you keep the Northern sky witch from hearing us?" to Arrat.

Arrat shot him a look, but nodded, and Rasim felt the air around them change a little. He said, "Don't put the shoreboats down yet," to Nasira, who gave him as sharp a look as the Skymaster had. "I don't think Lorens will stick around to watch us drown, but it'd be better if he didn't know we had seaworthy boats."

Nasira set her teeth together and closed her eyes, just for a moment. "How you can go from enraged to tactical in three heartbeats…"

"I haven't stopped being angry," Rasim assured her very quietly. He wasn't sure he would ever stop being angry, just then. The captain nodded and called out to Desimi and others inspecting the shoreboats to hold off, then, after a glance at Rasim, suggested they pretend the remaining boats weren't sound.

The handful in the shoreboats exchanged baffled looks and somebody muttered, "One of them *isn't,*" before Desimi yelled, "It's probably Sunburn's idea," and brief grins flashed among them. A moment later one of them came on board, shaking her head, and Nasira allowed herself a weary slump. They were all good performers, Rasim thought. Really good, given that they were acting in a life or death situation.

Wind caught in the longship's sail and it gave the *Wafiya* a wide berth as it sped to catch up with its remaining fleet. Somebody muttered, "At least they're still afraid of us," and a hard laugh ran through the crew.

"They don't want to risk getting caught in the vortex when she goes down," Nasira said softly. "And they don't know how far our witchery extends, probably."

A stillness washed over the crew, everyone looking after the fleeing warship. Rasim knew *he* was gauging whether they could take it down, at the ever-increasing distance, and supposed the rest of them were, too.

They could. Without question, they could. But it would be a self-sacrificing last stand, and none of them quite believed they wouldn't make it out of this, if they conserved their witchery and worked together. "It's hard to drown a sea witch," Rasim said aloud, and this time a growl rolled through the crew.

"Spite is a great motivator." Kisia crawled through an ice-dripping pile of wreckage, dragging a canvas of hard tack and dried meat. "I don't *think* it was spite that made me join the guild, but I'm not sure it wasn't."

"We'll spit in their eye," Nasira promised. "Lower the port side shoreboats, Desimi. Get the food into them, Kisia. We don't have much time left." The *Wafiya* was shuddering, huge wracking trembles like it, too, suffered from the mortal chill. It shouldn't have been too difficult to keep it afloat, even still, but everyone was *tired*. Submerging it, 'sailing' it beneath the water, losing heat to the immersion…any one of those things might have been enough to work through, but even Desimi was spluttering at the edges of his power. The *Wafiya* was lost. Saving the crew mattered now.

Sesin took Hassin and Endat into the first shoreboat. Pynda went next, with Arrat following somewhat reluctantly. "Don't be stupid," Nasira said as the Skymaster hesitated. "Even tired, most of us can keep ourselves alive in the water for a while. You," she said with a sharp look down at Hassin, who simultaneously looked less awful than he had, and also terrible, "are among the most vulnerable right now. You go in the shoreboats first. Everyone who's not a sea witch goes in first."

The last unbroken shoreboat hit the water minutes later, more because the *Wafiya* lurched deeper than because the crew intentionally lowered it. By then nearly everyone was in the boats, with Nasira still on deck watching her crew get to safety. The smaller boats were full, and riding too low in the water. The loss of even one shoreboat might mean the loss of a quarter of the crew. The people remaining on the *Wafiya* exchanged brief glances, then cast the last, broken-bottomed shoreboat into the water, too. Someone grabbed floating planks and tucked them into the bottom of the boat, obviously with the plan to repair the holes as soon as they were safely away from the *Wafiya*, and the last of the crew climbed into the boat, using witchery to keep it afloat.

"Loose ropes between you," Nasira commanded from above. "Make a web so we don't lose each other to drifting even if we all fall asleep at once."

Dressin called, "We wouldn't dare, Captain. You'd keelhaul us all," and got a low chuckle from the escaping crew. But they did toss ropes from one boat to another, tying them loosely together, before Nasira nodded.

"Cast off. I'll watch from above until I can't anymore, then join you."

Panic shot through Rasim's heart. He believed the captain, but the downward draft of a huge sinking ship was a lot to fight against, even for a master sea witch. Especially for a tired one. He drew breath, but it was Hassin who said, "Don't leave it too long, Nasira."

The captain's gaze softened a bit as she glanced toward the weary first mate. "I won't. You're ready enough for a captaincy, my friend, but it wouldn't be kind to leave you with this one, like this, now. Cast off," she repeated, and with a surge of quiet witchery, the entangled shoreboats did.

Not one of the crew looked to where they were going, though. They all kept their gazes to the aft, watching the *Wafiya* as she foundered farther into the deep. Then, without warning, a huge column of water slammed upward, smashing through her already-weakened keel and rendering one deck after another into a rain of splinters. Water fell back down in thunderous rain, bringing the *Wafiya* lower yet as Nasira scuttled her rather than let her die slowly on her own.

A soprano sprang up on one of the shoreboats, wavering as it began the tune that the guild sang to send its members into Siliaria's arms. Within a breath, others joined in, first the highest tones, then, with each new line, deeper voices, and deeper still, until even Sunmaster Endat's bass could be heard, rumbling low across the water as they said goodbye to the flagship.

Nasira walked, *walked*, away from the wreckage, walked across the shifting surface of the sea with such finely controlled witchery that that, too, made Rasim's throat tighten and tears spill down his cheeks. It cost her: he could see it in the cords in her throat and the ashen color of her skin. She would pay for the power she used, but in the moment it was a gift, a kind of final defiance for her ship, a promise that they would do the impossible to survive as the *Wafiya* disappeared in a foaming rush of bubbles behind her.

She joined the emptiest of the shoreboats, and of all of the witches on the sea, Nasira al Ilialio did not look back.

CHAPTER TWENTY-SIX

For a long time, no one spoke. There were tears and bouts of sobbing, and some people, utterly shattered, simply fell asleep, unable to fight exhaustion that had taken both a physical and emotional toll any longer. When they'd drifted far enough away from the wreckage, someone went into the water, repairing the bottom of Nasira's boat. When that work was done, the boats were drawn close together so people could move from the over-loaded ones into the emptier one. No one said anything as they moved, and no one used witchery to make it easier. Rasim wasn't sure they could.

Once the weight was better distributed among the four shoreboats, people huddled together for warmth and went to sleep. Rasim couldn't blame them, but his own exhaustion buzzed with a line of stress that wouldn't let him rest. They still had to survive an empty sea, and find their way home again. A crew of displaced sea witches had a far better chance of surviving than almost anyone else. They could purify water, and fish for food effortlessly once some of the exhaustion had faded. But they were still a hundred miles or more from the nearest Island shores, and this early in spring, the weather could turn at any time.

Captain Nasira looked dreadful, like she'd gotten twenty years older in the hours since the *Wafiya* had sunk. She sat painfully straight, shoulders squared, jaw tight and lifted. Her gaze was fixed forward, like she didn't dare think about what lay behind them. Like she could will them all to safety, which, after resting, she might be able to do. Rasim, mindful of the mostly-sleeping crew, murmured, "Captain."

He didn't use sky witchery, so he was a little surprised when she turned her head just enough to indicate she'd heard him. But then he didn't know what to say, and embarrassed guilt flooded him. He thought she would be angry if he said he was sorry, even if it was his own stupid idea that had brought them within range of Lorens's lightning witches.

He thought she would be even angrier if he said it wasn't her fault. So he sat in confused silence, glad he'd spoken but wishing he knew what to say next. After a while, Nasira turned her head toward him just that much more, and said, "Sleep, Rasim," in an unexpectedly gentle voice. "Let me…"

There were a lot of words he thought she might use next. Mourn, lead, save, help, *something* that he couldn't choose for her. She finished with, "think," though. "Let me think."

He managed a fragile smile. "That's supposed to be my job."

Nasira actually looked at him. She didn't quite laugh, but her eyes brightened and her mouth twisted in wry amusement. "Let me know if you come up with a good idea while you sleep, then, Journeyman."

Rasim whispered, "My ideas are usually awful," but, because his captain told him to, he closed his eyes and tried to rest, at least.

He didn't think he would, but time jumped forward: the sky had been bright with afternoon when he closed his eyes, and the cold woke him as the sun fell beneath the horizon and the air grew chillier. A glance at the stars told him they were off course for reaching the Islands, but they could correct for it, since they certainly weren't going home to Ilyara in a handful of rowboats.

A lot of other people were awake now, too, their voices quiet murmurs over the ocean's surface. There wasn't much wind, and the water was smooth, which Rasim was grateful for. Someone in his hearing said, "Red sky at night," clearly enough to be understood, and a murmur of faintly amused relief ran through the crew at the sailor's adage. Red sky at night, sailor's delight: it meant the calm weather was likely to continue.

The boats had drifted apart, bouncing lightly at the ends of the ropes that bound them. Captain Nasira was on her feet in her own little boat, looking west like she might be able to see the distant Islands. "Rasim."

Her voice cut across the water, followed by her

gaze, which, even in the increasing dark, was expectant. Rasim tested his witchery, seeing if napping had helped at all, and thought he could at least get to the captain's little boat without dumping himself in the ocean. He called up a spigot of water and joined her, both curious about and somewhat dreading what she might say.

"How did you call that stone snake?" was the last thing he expected. Rasim stared at her through the dusk a moment, not really able to even understand the question.

"I just called for help, Captain. It wasn't on purpose, any more than getting a dragon's attention was. W...why?"

"Because," Nasira said very softly. "We are in an extraordinary need of help, and you tend to be the source of extraordinary things. We're in the middle of an ocean, Journeyman. Do you think you can call for help from here? Not a stone snake, perhaps, but maybe a dragon?"

"What? No! I don't know! Why? What good would that do?"

Nasira took a deep breath. "It would give you a way out of here. A way home. Perhaps even a fast way home. I'm sure word has reached Ilyara about what happened in Moran, but King Taishm needs to know that the North has turned against us, and that we've made allies in Shenyral. And you, Rasim, are the only possible messenger I have."

"But we're in the *ocean*," Rasim protested. "Dragons are fiery. I think. Sea serpents, maybe, out here, and that might work but I'd be afraid they'd crush our boats if they surfaced near us. And there's nothing else out he...oh." He lifted his gaze again, looking through the clear air at the glittering stars. "No, I'm wrong. There is something else out here."

Nasira glanced skyward, too. "Don't tell me you can call the stars from the sky, Journeyman."

Rasim breathed laughter. "No. No, Captain, what are the two things that are constant when we're under sail?"

"The sea and the sky," Nasira said without hesitation, then inhaled softly as she understood his meaning. "Ah. The sky. Sky witchery."

"I can't do it by myself, I don't think. Skymaster Arrat could help, but it'd..." Rasim swallowed. "I think it would be better if it was me and Desimi. You'll need Arrat if a storm comes up out here, when you're in these little boats."

The captain's eyebrows twitched upward. "Then you'll be taking Kisia with you, or I'll have to drown her myself to stop the complaints."

"Are you sure, Captain?"

"I'm absolutely sure she'll complain endlessly if she's left behind."

Rasim couldn't stop a laugh. "That wasn't what I meant."

"I know, son." Nasira put a hand on his shoulder and sighed. "I'd say you wouldn't be remiss to ask Siliaria's blessing, Rasim. I think you'll need all the help you can get."

Rasim's throat tightened and tears burned in his eyes. "That's a good idea. I'll do that."

"We all might," the captain said dryly, then sighed again, this time melodramatically. "And I suppose you'll need something to stand on while you do all this witchery. Try not to wreck the shoreboat, Rasim. We'll need it when you're done." She lifted her voice, calling orders, and baffled sea witches began to move from her boat to the others. Nasira beckoned Desimi and Kisia to her side, and when they were safely aboard, witched a waterspout into existence. "Be careful, all of you. Safe home."

"You too, Captain." Rasim turned to his bewildered friends as the captain left. "Come on. We need to push off and get quite a bit of distance between us and the rest of them."

"Why?" Kisia's voice broke on the single syllable. "What are we doing?"

Rasim smiled, partly out of excitement and partly trying to hide sudden nervousness. "Desimi and I are going to find a glasswing in the wind, and it's going to take us home."

DESIMI SPENT most of the next half hour squeaking, "We're doing *what*?" as they put distance between themselves and the other shoreboats. By the time Rasim thought they were far enough away, he also thought he might kill Desimi before they could work up enough of a windstorm to get one of the delicate, dragonfly-like creatures' attention.

"Glasswings are *there*," he said for what felt like the fortieth time. "They're in the wind all the time, in the air. They're made of air, Desi, and mostly they're..." He squashed his hands together, trying to indicate that they were soft, somehow. Air-like.

"You mean they're like spirits. They're there but you can't see or touch them?" Kisia sounded fascinated.

"Yeah, kind of, I guess? But enough sky witchery draws their attention and they can become solid. Like, oh, you know what it feels like when a hard sudden wind comes up. Like it's punching you in the face. Air can feel solid. It just doesn't have *form*, exactly. Glasswings are what happens when air takes shape that we can hold on to."

"And you called one in the arena," Desimi said like he was barely clinging to sanity. Rasim thought that might be possible. They were on a smooth ocean, a long way from anybody else, and he intended to start a windstorm to convince a magical beast to appear literally out of thin air. That seemed a little insane.

"It was an accident then, but yes. We were fighting and there was so much air witchery and it was..." Hurt sliced through Rasim's heart. "I think we drove it crazy," he said unhappily. "It got shaped wrong because the witchery we were using was so violent. I had to kill it because it would have killed me otherwise, but it wasn't fair. It never had a chance."

"And this one will?" Desimi's voice rose again, and again, Rasim couldn't exactly blame him.

On the other hand, he was pretty sure of himself. "We won't be fighting, Desi. We're going to be cooperating. We're going to use all this magic, enough to make one of them solidify, and then we're going to ride it to shore."

"Which shore?" Desimi demanded. "The Islands? The continent? Ilyara itself?"

A bright grin flashed over Rasim's face. "I guess that depends on how cooperative it is, and how lucky we are."

A grin started to crawl over Kisia's face, too. "Well, if we're going to die, this is the most interesting way to do it that I can think of."

Desimi, horrified, said, "*Kisia!*" She and Rasim both laughed as his voice rose even further. "I don't want to die at all!"

"Well, neither do the rest of us." Rasim knelt in the bottom of the boat, reaching over the side to trail his fingers in the ocean's quiet surface. "The captain said I should ask Siliaria's blessing."

The other two sobered up fast and knelt with him, dipping their hands in the water, too. "That's a good idea," Kisia whispered.

Desimi only nodded, and for a few minutes the three of them were quiet. Rasim didn't know exactly what they were thinking, but even just touching the water for a minute or two helped settle his too-busy thoughts. Eventually, aloud, he said, "I know we've been all over the place, Siliaria, and a lot of it hasn't been on the water, but we're still your children, and we could use your blessing right now. Not just us." He lifted his gaze toward the other shoreboats, hardly more than dark shadows on the quiet sea. "For the rest of the crew, too, please. Maybe them more than us, even. Quiet seas for their journey, and safety at the end of it, if you would, goddess. As for us, if this would just work, we would really appreciate that."

Then he cast a crooked smile upward, adding, "And if Tilarea wants to look out for us, too, we wouldn't say no," to the sky itself.

They sat together for another long few moments, until Kisia, audibly disappointed, said, "I don't think she's actually coming this time," and Rasim laughed, realizing he'd been wondering if the goddess would appear, too.

"I guess not. Well, we've survived this long. I think we can assume that means we've got her blessings, right? So that'll be enough for today, too." Rasim started gathering sky witchery, feeling the still air stir under his command as Desimi *hnf*ed.

"Too bad. I wanted to meet her. Maybe someday."

"Next time," Kisia promised him. "But go on, call a glasswing. I want to see this."

"Yeah, yeah, all right, we'll try." Desimi's witchery joined Rasim's, grudgingly at first, but then with greater enthusiasm. "Do you think we can make Kisia fly?"

Kisia shrieked and Rasim couldn't tell if it was delight or terror. Maybe both, because she said, "Yes! Try!" and bounced on her toes. The boat rocked and both boys yelled incoherently. Kisia grimaced and held still, mumbling, "Sorry," but then brightening again. "But if I bounce it'll be easier to lift me up!"

"Let us get enough wind going first!" Rasim said. She puffed her cheeks at him and he grinned at Desimi. "Come on, let's try."

Standing in a rowboat was not at all the safest place to bring a windstorm to life. Kisia did help, steadying the boat as the boys, both grinning now, tried to out-do one another with gusts and twists of witchery. The sea around them danced with their efforts, then surged with it, whitecaps forming as wind raced across the surface. Sometimes their magic crashed into each other's, whipping upward in a spiral of gleeful speed that made them both laugh. Desimi staggered with it, then braced himself and leaned in, arms spread wide at first, then slowly closing like he was trying to capture something enormous between them. Rasim howled with laughter, his own power rushing around Desimi's until his hair stood on end, tangling hopelessly in the wind.

Kisia stood up cautiously, putting a hand toward the torrent of rushing air between them and gasping as its speed knocked her arm aside. "I think I *could* fly in that!"

"It has to be bigger to hold you," Desimi said breathlessly. He threw his arms open again, like he was letting the witchery expand, and suddenly they were in the heart of a roaring, bewitched windstorm. Kisia couldn't keep her feet, but she wasn't flying, either, just struggling to stay up and giggling helplessly with every buffet. Rasim felt like the whole ocean sky had paused to watch them, and in the heart of all that, felt the same brush of life that he'd felt when the glasswing began to take form in Moran. He threw his arms open wide, too, and Kisia shrieked as her feet actually did leave the boat's floor.

Desimi's power was unbelievable, much stronger than Rasim's own. All he'd needed was to find a way into it, Rasim thought. Unlike Rasim, Desimi wasn't unbalanced. All of the witchery he could ever want was right there, ready to be shaped, like it was just waiting for him to need it. The stars above them wobbled with the speed of their storm, and Rasim felt that touch of life again, as if a glasswing's presence was growing stronger.

Kisia said, "I'm gonna jump," and without further warning, did. Up, not out, but the wind was enough to push her a little. Desimi bellowed and the strength of the windstorm redoubled, catching Kisia and lifting her just a little more. Rasim, giggling with both effort and the sheer delight of pushing witchery to its limits to see where they were, tried to send wind beneath Kisia to boost her, and for a few thrilling seconds, she rose higher into the air.

Rasim wasn't sure he would call it *flying*, the way she flailed and laughed and screamed with nerves and excitement, but she definitely wasn't earthbound anymore. Another gust swept beneath her, and she shot skyward, squealing with terrified joy until the gust changed directions. Her squeal lost the joy, turning to terror alone.

A glasswing, gorgeous and black with stars and

water, formed beneath her, and Kisia landed on its back, just in front of the rapidly-beating fragile wings. She screamed again, this time in surprise and relief. The beautiful, delicate thing spun wildly in the air, reminding Rasim of a dolphin playing in the ship's wake. Kisia clung to its back, almost visible through its thin glassy body. Her laughter was tossed through the wind, bouncing back to Rasim and Desimi in little bursts.

Desimi's witchery died as he gazed up at the playful creature, its wings visible mostly from the way they blurred the stars. Under the quiet night sky it had none of the soft rainbow color the one that had come from the arena had had. Its scales glittered the same way, but only with darkness and stars, and its huge bug-like eyes were filled with night. It spun down toward them as if curious what had happened to the storm, and Desimi put a hand up to its nose.

Its long thin tongue darted out, tasting him, and he laughed sharply. Kisia yelled, "Desi!" and thrust a hand down. He grabbed hold and she grunted, hauling him upward. The glasswing cried out in surprise, a sound like crystal bells, and raced skyward again, spinning wildly. Both the journeymen aboard it screamed and held on for dear life. Rasim heard snatches of Desimi yelling, "Go back, go back!"

The glasswing did, mostly, Rasim thought, because he was still working his sky witchery, and it was curious. It didn't stop to investigate him, though, only rushed by in a blur of beauty and speed. Desimi reached for Rasim, barely managed to grab his hand,

and pulled him on the slender beast's back. It cried out again, but their weight didn't seem to affect its ability to fly, as it climbed back into the sky with ease.

Within seconds they were higher than any ship's mast, higher than Rasim had ever been except on the dragon's back, and its quick wingbeats drove them across the ocean. Rasim, still working witchery, tried to build an air current for it to follow. Desimi joined in, both of them weaving a braid of air and sending it east. Kisia shouted, "Where are we going?"

Rasim grinned into the wind, and told himself it was the speed and cold air that made tears slide from his eyes. "Home, Kees. We're going home."

TO BE CONCLUDED IN

WITCHMASTER, BOOK V OF THE GUILDMASTER
SAGA

ACKNOWLEDGMENTS

I owe editor KB Spangler my *life* for this book. Words are not enough to thank her with.

They are enough to thank Aleksandar Sotirovski for the utterly gorgeous cover art on this series so far, though, and Tara O'Shea, whose cover design elevates it.

Thanks, too, to Sharon Corbet, Rachel Gollub, Chelsea Jones, and Joe Fernandez, my Patreons whose sharp eyes have helped keep many errors from the pages of this book. My husband Ted also deserve a special shout-out for not saying "I told you so" when my editor confirmed what he'd been trying to tell me all along, which was I was right when I was afraid I had two books left in this series instead of one.

And most especially, thanks to Fiadh, who has been waiting patiently for the conclusion of this series for eleven years and is going to have to wait another year, because it ain't done yet.

ABOUT THE AUTHOR

CE Murphy began writing around age six, when she submitted three poems to a school publication. The teacher producing the magazine selected (inevitably) the one she thought was by far the worst, but also told her–a six year old kid–to keep writing, which she has.

She has also held the usual grab-bag of jobs usually seen in an authorial biography, including public library volunteer (at ages 9 and 10; it's clear she was doomed to a career involving books), archival assistant, cannery worker, and web designer. Writing books is better.

She was born and raised in Alaska, and now lives with her family in her ancestral homeland of Ireland.

You can find her online at CatieMurphy.com.

www.ingramcontent.com/pod-product-compliance
Lightning Source LLC
Chambersburg PA
CBHW061647190726
48289CB00006B/1772